STEALING MEXICO

MATTI MARTINEZ

Stealing Mexico

Copyright © 2025 by Matti Martinez

All rights reserved.

No part of this book may be reproduced, stored in a retrieval system, or transmitted in any form or by any means—electronic, mechanical, photocopying, recording, or other-wise—without prior written permission of the publisher, except for brief quotations used in reviews or articles.

This is a work of fiction. Names, characters, places, and incidents are the product of the author's imagination or are used fictitiously. Any resemblance to actual persons, living or dead, events, or locales is purely coincidental.

Printed in the United States of America

Paperback ISBN: 979-8-9921-1990-9

Hardback ISBN: 979-89921-1991-6

Ebook ISBN: 979-89921-1992-0

Published by Queer Ink Publishing

Cover Design: Markee Book Covers

Formatter: Vanessa Mena, Inkspark Digital

First Edition: 2025

10 9 8 7 6 5 4 3 2 1

To the victims whose voices have been silenced,
To those whose stories remain untold,
And to the countless lives stolen by injustice—
This is for you.
May we never stop seeking truth,
May we never stop fighting for justice,
And may your memory inspire the courage
To stand against the darkness.

PROLOGUE

DIEGO

Diego Cortez leaned against the cool stucco wall outside the house, allowing the faint hum of music from the party to drift around him. The warm October night was unusually quiet, even for Phoenix, and he could feel the faint prickle of sweat on his skin. He'd been standing here for a while, taking deep breaths of the dry desert air, trying to think—trying to relax. In his jacket pocket, his fingers brushed the flash drive's edges, a weight he'd been carrying around for a week but couldn't bring himself to hand over to anyone.

The truth was terrifying. The more he thought about it, the more his gut twisted with dread. But the fact itself—what he'd found, what it meant—was undeniable.

He closed his eyes, exhaling a long, shaky breath. Maybe it was better this way, away from Ethan, who was still inside, probably stewing after their argument earlier in the evening. Ethan had pulled Diego aside, wanting him to cover for him with his parents so he could spend the night with a friend.

STEALING MEXICO

But Diego couldn't lie to his host parents; he didn't want to keep weaving a web of deceit. His refusal had caused a small but tense argument, words exchanged in the heat of the moment, leaving an uncomfortable silence hanging between them.

With a sigh, Diego pushed away from the wall, glancing around at the quiet, sleepy neighborhood just off campus. Low-lying desert shrubs cast long shadows across the dry gravel lawns, and the distant city lights gave the sky a faint, pale glow. He turned toward campus, deciding to clear his mind on the walk home. The night was warm, with just enough of a breeze to bring the smell of creosote and dry earth to the surface. Familiar, comforting scents. He'd grown to love the way Phoenix felt in autumn, like a gentle reminder that cooler days were on their way.

As he made his way along the pathway, he noticed how empty the campus felt, the silence broken only by the soft shuffle of shoes and the distant hum of cars. Streetlights cast pockets of amber light across the courtyard, and he passed a group of students gathered on a bench, their laughter rising briefly before fading as he continued down the narrow pathway between two buildings.

The flash drive weighed heavily in his pocket, a constant reminder of what he'd found and the questions that haunted him. His fingers itched to hold it again, but he kept them shoved deep in his pockets, as if touching it might bring more trouble than he was already in.

The sound of footsteps shattered the quiet behind him. Diego tried to ignore it, telling himself it was just another student on their way across campus. Still, the footsteps grew louder, quickening to match his pace, and Diego felt a chill skitter up his spine. He glanced over his shoulder, catching sight of a figure emerging from the shadows—someone he recognized, someone he'd seen before.

He stopped, his pulse drumming in his ears, as the man

approached with slow, deliberate steps. Diego's mouth went dry, and he managed a weak, forced smile, hoping to dispel the sudden tension.

"Hey," he said, his voice unsteady. "What brings you here?"

The man didn't respond, his face shadowed and unreadable. Diego's fingers clenched inside his pockets, and he took a step back, his mind racing as he tried to think of something to say, something that would make sense of this strange, silent encounter.

Then, breaking the silence, the man spoke, his voice low and dangerous. "You're poking around in things you shouldn't be," he said, taking another step forward.

Diego's heart raced, fear flooding his veins. He wanted to deny it, to insist that he was just a student minding his own business, but the man's presence loomed large, making it impossible to speak.

Before he could react, the man lunged, and Diego's eyes caught a flash of silver—a movement so quick and fluid he barely registered it until a sudden, searing pain bloomed in his chest. He gasped, stumbling backward as his hand flew to the wound, warm and wet beneath his fingers.

He barely managed a weak, breathless cry, his legs giving out as he crumpled against the wall. His vision blurred, his breaths coming shallow and fast, and he struggled to focus as the man knelt beside him, reaching into his pockets with swift, practiced hands.

Diego wanted to fight, to push him away, but his strength was draining fast. He felt his phone slip from his pocket, followed by his wallet, and finally—the flash drive. The object that had started it all.

The man stood, slipping the items into his pocket before casting one last impassive look at Diego. Then he turned and disappeared into the shadows, leaving Diego alone in the empty, quiet courtyard.

STEALING MEXICO

As he lay there, his body slumped against the cool stucco wall, Diego's mind drifted to the secret he'd uncovered, the truth he had tried so desperately to hold on to. And as the last traces of his strength faded, he wondered if anyone would ever know.

The world grew dim. The surrounding sounds slipping away, and Diego's last breath left him in a shallow, trembling sigh.

PART ONE

CHAPTER 1

CARLOS

Carlos Santos stood at the edge of the crime scene, as the early morning sun crept over Phoenix, harshly illuminating the area where they found the victim. At twenty-six, he carried an imposing presence—tall and broad-shouldered, with dark hair that curled slightly at the ends. His face betrayed a detached calm, but his dark brown eyes hinted at something deeper: a steel resolve tempered by years of loss and careful emotional walls.

The yellow tape flapped in the breeze, slicing through the stillness. Carlos took a slow breath, the scent of the desert mingling with the faint, metallic tang of blood still lingering in the air. He was used to this—death in its various forms—but the young ones always hit different, though he wouldn't show it.

Steeling himself, Carlos stepped closer to the body slumped against a concrete wall, now covered by a sheet. The medical examiner glanced up at him, her pen scratching against her clipboard.

"What's the rundown?" Carlos asked, his tone calm and direct.

"Male, late teens or early twenties," she replied, brushing

STEALING MEXICO

her gloved hand over the edge of the sheet. "Single stab wound to the chest. No obvious signs of a struggle. Time of death looks like just after midnight."

Carlos absorbed the details, his sharp gaze sweeping the scene. His instincts gnawed at him—this wasn't just a robbery. The missing wallet and phone felt too convenient, like someone wanted Diego Cortez's story erased.

The scrape of boots on gravel drew Carlos's attention. Captain Marissa Davis approached, her sharp eyes scanning the scene. With her short-cropped hair and commanding presence, she was someone who expected results. Carlos had always respected that about her.

"Any leads yet?" Marissa asked, folding her arms.

"Nothing solid," Carlos replied, gesturing to the empty surroundings. "But something about this one feels... off. Like it's bigger than we're seeing."

Marissa studied him, then nodded. "Stay on it. We'll start canvassing students and neighbors. This one's going to attract media attention fast, so keep a tight lid on it."

Carlos gave a curt nod, already turning his focus back to the scene. His gut told him this case would not be straightforward. Cases like this never were.

"Diego!"

The anguished cry pierced through the quiet, drawing every head toward the voice. Carlos turned just in time to see a young woman sprinting toward the crime scene, her face twisted in panic.

"Diego!" she screamed again, tears streaming as she tried to push past the tape.

Carlos intercepted her, his hands gentle but firm. "Miss, I need you to stay back," he said, his voice calm but commanding.

"You don't understand!" she sobbed, trying to wriggle free. "He's my friend! Diego... he didn't deserve this!"

Carlos softened his grip but didn't let her move past him.

"I know it's hard," he said, his tone quieter. "But I need you to breathe. Were you close to him?"

She nodded, her entire body trembling. "Yes. We were in a study group together. His name is Diego Cortez. He's an exchange student... from Mexico."

Carlos's jaw tightened, though his expression didn't shift. The name hit like a weight, solidifying the young man into a real person—a life interrupted.

"Thank you for telling me," Carlos said, keeping his voice even. "What's your name?"

"Sophia Alvarez," she choked out, clutching her arms.

"Okay, Sophia," Carlos said, nodding. "Do you know who he was staying with? Family, friends?"

She sniffled, swiping at her tears. "He's staying with the Coles. They're his host family. Their son, Ethan, is in our year. They were close... but..."

Carlos frowned. "But what?"

Sophia hesitated, her voice faltering. "They had an argument last night. Diego didn't tell me everything, but I think... I think Ethan wanted him to cover for him about something, and Diego said no. He was frustrated. He just... he didn't want to lie anymore."

Carlos caught the hesitation in her voice, but let it go for now. "Did he say anything else? Anything about feeling unsafe or someone threatening him?"

She shook her head, looking away. "No. Just that he needed space. He was tired of it all."

Carlos gave her a reassuring nod, though inside, the weight of her words pressed down. "You've been helpful, Sophia. We'll take it from here."

Sophia nodded, fresh tears streaking her face as an officer led her away. Carlos turned back to Marissa, his expression unreadable.

"We're talking to the Coles first," he said. "I want their

STEALING MEXICO

version on record, and I want to know what their kid knows about this argument."

Marissa's eyes narrowed thoughtfully. "Think there's more to it?"

"Always is," Carlos muttered, his gaze falling back to the empty corner of the campus where Diego's life had ended.

Something told him this wouldn't just haunt him—it would unravel everything in its path.

CHAPTER 2

ASHER

Asher Rhodes stood just beyond the yellow tape, notebook in hand, his blue eyes darting from the faint footprints in the dirt to the students lingering on the edge of the scene. The afternoon sun beat down on the empty campus lawn, but the space beyond the tape felt anything but still. Tousled blond hair fell into his line of sight, but he didn't bother brushing it away. His mind was already chasing the angles—the pieces that would bring Diego's story to life.

The murder of a student on campus wasn't something that would fade from the headlines anytime soon, and Asher wasn't about to let the Phoenix Ledger be second to the story. Pulling his notebook from his bag, he jotted down details almost automatically. A smudge on the concrete wall. Faint footprints near the bushes. Likely nothing the police hadn't noticed, but these tiny fragments often shaped a story's edge.

A figure broke his focus—a security guard approaching, his posture equal parts suspicion and resignation. Asher raised his hand in a casual greeting, a smile playing on his lips as if standing this close to an active crime scene was entirely natural.

"Can I help you, son?" the guard asked, crossing his arms.

STEALING MEXICO

"Asher Rhodes," he said, holding up his press badge. "Phoenix Ledger. Just trying to get a little background for a piece on what happened."

The guard frowned, his eyes narrowing slightly, though he didn't immediately shut Asher down. "The press has no clearance for anything inside the perimeter yet. You'll have to wait for the official release."

Asher nodded, keeping his voice calm and unassuming. "Of course. I'm just here for some broader context. People are going to be anxious about this, you know?"

The guard hesitated, glancing back toward the scene. Finally, his posture softened. "It's a tragedy. A kid like that, barely in his twenties. You hate to see it."

"Exchange student, huh?" Asher asked, voice low enough to make it seem like a passing observation.

The guard shifted, his gaze flicking toward the students milling around in the distance. "Yeah. From Mexico. Poor kid. That's all I can say."

"Thanks." Asher offered a polite nod as the guard stepped away, still glancing back toward the taped-off area.

Watching him go, Asher felt the quiet buzz of excitement he always got at the start of a good story. He wasn't just here for the headline—this was a chance to tell the truth about someone who couldn't speak for himself anymore.

But scraps from a security guard wouldn't be enough. Flipping through his phone, he scrolled for anything useful. He paused at a name: Carlos Santos. The lead detective on the case. They'd crossed paths before, and Carlos had made it clear he had little patience for journalists like Asher, with what he'd once called a "knack for prying."

No matter. Carlos could wait. Right now, Asher needed context in Diego's last moments.

He headed toward a campus cafe, where clusters of students huddled over coffee and phones. Many looked oblivious to the tragedy that had unfolded just hours earlier. But not all of them.

Leaning against the counter, Asher ordered a coffee, his ears tuned to snippets of conversation. A group of students at a nearby table caught his attention. Two of them spoke in low, animated voices about a party last night, while a third—a girl with dark hair and wide-rimmed glasses—sat in silence, biting her nails.

"So, you don't think Diego was even going to stay?" one student asked.

"Hell no," the other replied. "He looked ready to leave as soon as he got there. Did you see him with Ethan? Those two were obviously arguing."

The girl flinched at the mention of Diego's name, her hands tightening around her coffee cup.

"Excuse me," Asher said, stepping toward their table. "Sorry to interrupt, but did I hear you mention Diego? Are you all friends of his?"

The trio stared up at him, their suspicion palpable. The girl's eyes flicked over him, her expression uncertain.

"Yeah, we knew him," she said hesitantly. "He's... gone."

"I'm so sorry," Asher said, his voice softening. "I can't imagine how hard this must be for you. I'm with the Phoenix Ledger—Asher Rhodes. I'm just trying to understand what happened."

They exchanged uneasy glances before the girl gave a slow nod. "I'm Sophia. Diego and I were in the same study group."

"Nice to meet you, Sophia." Asher kept his tone gentle, though his eyes remained sharp and attentive. "I heard he left the party early last night?"

Sophia nodded, her voice quiet. "Yeah. He and Ethan had some sort of argument, I think, but... I don't know what it was about. Diego just seemed like he needed space."

"Who's Ethan?"

STEALING MEXICO

"His host brother," the other said quickly.

Interesting. A host brother, a fight, and now Diego was dead. Asher scribbled the details in his notebook, the pen tapping against his fingers as he thought.

"Thank you for sharing that," he said, meeting Sophia's gaze. "It helps a lot."

She managed a strained smile. "Just... if you write about him, don't make him sound like some troubled kid. He was kind and smart. I don't want people to get the wrong idea."

"I'll do him justice. Promise," Asher said, his voice firm.

As he stepped out of the cafe, his mind raced. A fight with Ethan, something hidden between them, and now Diego was gone. Whatever secret Diego had been keeping, it was big enough to get him killed.

And Asher would uncover every last piece of it.

CHAPTER 3

CARLOS

The mesquite trees shaded the yard of the Cole house, tucking it neatly into a quiet Phoenix suburb and dappling the ground with October sunlight. It looked like any other family home—well-kept lawn, an SUV parked in the driveway—but something felt off. A curtain shifted in an upstairs window, and for a moment, Carlos thought he glimpsed someone watching. The house seemed to carry the weight of the tragedy inside, its cheerful exterior at odds with the grief it now sheltered.

Carlos stepped out of his car, adjusted his tie, and took a moment to steel himself. He wanted to approach this like any other case, but this one felt heavier. A young man had died, far from his home and family, and now Carlos would have to ask the people who had taken him in to relive their worst day.

When he rang the doorbell, a woman with red-rimmed eyes and a tight smile answered it. Her face was drawn, and her hastily tied ponytail hinted at a sleepless night.

"Mrs. Cole?" Carlos asked gently.

She nodded, glancing down at his badge before stepping aside to let him in. "Yes. Please... come in. I'm Allison."

The living room was immaculate, but small signs of strain

STEALING MEXICO

lingered—half-empty coffee mugs on the table, tissues balled up near the couch. A man with a graying beard stood by the window, his shoulders rigid as he stared out into the yard. Next to him, a teenage boy sat hunched forward, his hands wringing restlessly in his lap.

Carlos took in the details with practiced ease. Mr. Cole looked like a man used to being in control, but now completely unarmored, his gaze distant. The boy, Ethan, looked younger than his years, his sandy brown hair unkempt, his posture screaming guilt and unease.

"Thank you for seeing me," Carlos said as he took a seat in a chair opposite the family. "I know this is difficult, but I need to ask a few questions about Diego."

Mr. Cole nodded stiffly, still not meeting Carlos's gaze. Allison sat down next to Ethan, placing a hand on his shoulder. Carlos's attention lingered on the boy. He'd seen that look before—the way grief mixed with guilt, like a storm brewing beneath the surface.

"Ethan," Carlos said gently, "I understand you were with Diego last night?"

Ethan nodded without looking up. His voice came out soft, barely audible. "Yeah. We went to a party. Off campus. Just... to hang out."

Carlos watched him closely, noting the tension in his posture. "Did anything happen at the party? Did Diego seem upset about anything?"

Ethan's hands stilled, and he glanced quickly at his parents before looking down again. "We... we got into an argument. It was stupid. He left, and I stayed." His voice cracked slightly. "I should have walked with him. He... he'd still be here if I'd just gone with him."

Carlos's voice remained steady. "Ethan, can you tell me a little more about the argument?"

Allison's hand tightened on her son's shoulder as though

willing him to speak. Ethan shook his head, his jaw tight. "I don't know. It doesn't matter now, does it?"

Carlos leaned back slightly, letting the silence settle. "I understand this is hard. I just need to get a sense of what might have been on Diego's mind that night."

Ethan stayed quiet, but Allison cleared her throat, her voice trembling. "Detective... Ethan did nothing wrong. I know how this might look, but he wouldn't hurt Diego. They were close, like brothers."

Carlos nodded, his tone even. "I'm not here to make any assumptions, Mrs. Cole. I'm just trying to gather the facts."

She relaxed slightly, her hand falling to her lap. "Diego was... a good kid. So serious about everything. He was working on this project for school, and it seemed really important to him. Unlike most kids his age, he was different. He was... focused. Determined." Her voice broke. "We trusted him completely."

Carlos noted her words. "Do you know if anything had been bothering him recently? Anything out of the ordinary?"

Mr. Cole finally spoke, his voice heavy with exhaustion. "He had been preoccupied for the past few days. Not himself. He didn't talk about it, though."

Carlos nodded, the pieces beginning to form a faint outline. A focused, driven young man, distracted in his last days. An argument at a party. And now, a grieving family grappling with questions they couldn't answer.

He turned back to Ethan, keeping his tone soft. "Ethan, I don't mean to press, but anything you can tell me about that argument—anything at all—could help us understand what happened."

Ethan hesitated, his blue eyes flicking toward the window before meeting Carlos's gaze. "I... I don't really know, okay? He'd been acting weird lately, and I got frustrated. That's all it was."

Carlos nodded, recognizing the defensive edge in Ethan's

STEALING MEXICO

voice. A shield to protect the truth. "Thank you, Ethan. I appreciate you sharing that with me."

Allison's face softened, her hand brushing against Ethan's arm. Carlos stood, preparing to leave. "For now, we'll continue investigating. I promise you, we'll do everything we can to find answers."

As Carlos stepped outside, the weight of their grief pressed down on him. He was halfway to his car when hurried footsteps crunched on the gravel behind him. He turned to see Ethan running toward him, his face pale and strained.

"I—there's more," Ethan stammered, glancing back at the house as if checking to make sure no one had followed.

Carlos stayed still, giving Ethan space.

"The argument," Ethan said, his voice barely above a whisper. "It wasn't really about anything important. I just... I wanted him to cover for me, with my parents."

Carlos tilted his head, watching Ethan closely. "Cover for what?"

Ethan hesitated, his hands buried deep in his jacket pockets. "They don't know who I really am," he said, his voice trembling. "And if they did... I don't know if they'd even want me here."

The fear in Ethan's voice struck something in Carlos, a thread of recognition.

"So you asked Diego to cover for you?" Carlos asked gently.

Ethan nodded, his shoulders slumping. "I asked him to tell my parents I'd stayed at the party. But he wouldn't. Said he didn't want to keep lying. He thought it'd just make things worse." Ethan's voice cracked. "I got mad. Said things I shouldn't have. He stormed off, and I let him go."

Carlos placed a hand on Ethan's shoulder, his tone steady. "Ethan, you're carrying a lot right now, but what happened to Diego isn't your fault. Do you understand?"

Ethan nodded, though the guilt in his eyes lingered. "Yeah... thanks, Detective."

Carlos watched as Ethan walked back inside, his shoulders hunched under the weight of grief and unspoken truths. Whatever secrets Diego had carried, whatever choices Ethan regretted, they were all fragments of a much larger story. And Carlos knew he had to keep pulling at those threads until the full picture came into focus.

CHAPTER 4

ASHER

The October morning sun beat down on Asher as he sat cross-legged on a bench near the campus quad, his laptop balanced precariously on his knees. He barely noticed the sweat prickling at his temples; his mind was elsewhere, replaying yesterday's scene. Diego Cortez's death wasn't just another tragedy on campus. Something about the way Detective Carlos Santos carried himself—his somber expression, the weight in his voice—left Asher feeling there was more to the story than the police were letting on.

He closed his laptop, leaning back against the bench, and scanned the quad. Students milled about, laughter and conversation drifting through the air, but the atmosphere felt muted, as though the campus itself was mourning. His gaze landed on a girl standing nearby, her arms wrapped tightly around herself, her eyes cast downward. She looked familiar.

He straightened. "Hey," he called softly.

The girl flinched, her head snapping up. For a moment, her eyes were wide with surprise before recognition softened her features. Asher remembered her face from last night—one of the shaken students gathered near the scene.

STEALING MEXICO

"You're Sophia, right?" he asked, his tone gentle. "I'm Asher. I'm a reporter with the Phoenix Ledger."

She hesitated, her arms tightening around herself before nodding slowly.

He gestured to the space on the bench beside him. "Want to sit?"

After a moment's pause, she shuffled over, her movements tentative. She perched on the edge of the bench, her posture stiff, and glanced around as though wary of being overheard.

"I just..." Her voice cracked, and she took a shaky breath before continuing. "I thought maybe I could talk to someone about Diego. It feels like no one's really listening."

"I'm listening," Asher assured her. "Whatever you want to say, I'm here."

Her shoulders relaxed slightly, though she kept her gaze fixed on the ground. "Diego was... different. He didn't know a lot of people here, but he tried so hard to fit in. I think he wanted to impress his host family or make them proud. But... these last few weeks, he wasn't himself."

Asher tilted his head, his journalistic instincts sparking. "What do you mean?"

She hesitated, biting her lip. "He was working on this project for school. At first, it seemed normal—just another assignment. But then... he started keeping things to himself. He got jumpy, like he was always looking over his shoulder."

A chill ran down Asher's spine. "Did he tell you what the project was about?"

"No," she said, shaking her head. "I asked, but he said it was safer if I didn't know. He told me he was on to something big, but I didn't think..." Her voice broke, and she covered her mouth with her hand.

Asher leaned forward, his voice steady but urgent. "Do you think he found something dangerous? Something that could've put him in harm's way?"

22

Her eyes glistened with unshed tears as she nodded. "I don't know for sure. But I think... I think he found something he wasn't supposed to."

Asher handed her one of his cards. "If you remember anything else—anything at all—call me, okay?"

She clutched the card tightly, nodding again before getting up and walking away. Asher watched her retreating figure, the weight of her words sinking in. Diego hadn't just been another student. He'd been chasing something, and it might've cost him his life.

An hour later, Asher stood leaning against a wall at the precinct, his arms crossed as he scanned the hallway. He'd spent the walk over debating whether confronting Detective Santos was a good idea, but Sophia's words had tipped the scales. If anyone had answers about Diego's death, it was Carlos.

Finally, the detective stepped out of a room, his sharp gaze locking onto Asher almost instantly. His expression darkened.

"You again," Carlos muttered, irritation clear in his tone.

"Detective Santos," Asher said, pushing off the wall and flashing a disarming smile.

Carlos didn't return it. Instead, he folded his arms, blocking the hallway. "This is a police precinct, not a newsroom. What are you doing here?"

"Just hoping for a moment of your time," Asher replied, keeping his tone light. "We're both after the same thing here: the truth."

Carlos raised an eyebrow, his skepticism palpable. "Somehow, I doubt that."

Asher leaned in slightly, lowering his voice. "Come on, Detective. We don't have to be at odds. Maybe I can even help you."

Carlos's expression didn't budge. "Help me?" he repeated, his tone laced with disbelief. "Rhodes, the last thing I need is a reporter playing detective."

STEALING MEXICO

"I'm not playing," Asher shot back, though his grin remained. "I spoke to someone who knew Diego. She thinks he was working on something big before he died. Something that made him nervous."

Carlos's jaw tightened, but his face betrayed nothing else. "Even if that's true, it's not your business."

"Maybe not," Asher conceded, "but it is yours. And if he found something dangerous, don't you think it's worth knowing all the angles?"

Carlos stared at him for a long moment, his dark eyes unreadable. Finally, he let out a sharp exhale. "Let me make this clear. You're not part of this investigation. Stay out of it, or I'll make sure you do."

Asher raised his hands in mock surrender. "Alright, message received. But just so we're clear, I'm not going anywhere. This case is too important."

Carlos didn't reply. He turned on his heel and walked away, his back radiating a clear warning.

But as Asher watched him go, he felt a thrill stir in his chest. Carlos Santos wasn't an easy man to crack, but Asher wasn't the type to back down. Diego's story needed to be told, and if Carlos held the key, Asher was determined to unlock it—one way or another.

CHAPTER 5

CARLOS

The sun hung low in the sky as Carlos Santos sat in his car, parked a few blocks away from the Cole household. Rubbing his temples, trying to shake off the weight of the day as the late afternoon light stretched long shadows across the pavement. The investigation into Diego's murder had become a labyrinth of dead ends and false leads, and every new twist seemed to wind back on itself like a cruel joke. He took a deep breath, steeling himself for what lay ahead.

Carlos had left the precinct with a sense of urgency, driven by a mix of empathy for Diego and an instinct to protect Ethan. Clearly harboring something, the scared kid worried Carlos, but he couldn't shake the nagging feeling that Ethan wasn't guilty—just a young man drowning in circumstances he didn't fully understand.

As he approached the Cole home, the tension in the air was unmistakable. It clung to the house like a heavy mist, seeping into every crack and crevice. From the window, Carlos could see Ethan pacing back and forth, his eyes occasionally flicking toward the street as if expecting someone. Carlos's heart ached for him—he was a kid drowning in grief, confusion, and fear.

STEALING MEXICO

When the door opened, Ethan's mother greeted him, her expression a careful mask of controlled panic. "Detective Santos," she said, her voice trembling slightly. "Please, come in."

The interior of the house felt strangely sterile—tidy, and full of family photos that once spoke of happy moments now tainted with the shadows of tragedy. Carlos followed Ethan's mother into the living room, where Ethan was waiting. His posture was stiff, his expression clouded, as if every thought weighed down on him.

"Detective," Ethan murmured, his voice low but steady, though Carlos could hear the tremor beneath it.

"Ethan," Carlos replied, settling into a chair across from him. "I know this is hard, but I need to ask you a few questions. Can you tell me more about Diego?"

Ethan's eyes flickered briefly, then he glanced toward his mother, who stood just outside the room, her gaze filled with silent worry. "I don't know what else to say. He was smart. He just... he was trying to fit in."

Carlos leaned forward, sensing the layers of unspoken thoughts. "What about the project he was working on? I spoke to a reporter who mentioned Diego had been researching something. Do you know anything about it?"

Ethan shook his head quickly, a flash of frustration crossing his face. "No. He kept it to himself. But... he was acting strange, like he was worried about something."

"Worried about what?" Carlos asked gently, pushing for more without sounding confrontational.

"I don't know!" Ethan's voice cracked, his frustration bubbling over. "He wouldn't tell me. He just kept saying he needed to figure things out. I thought he was just stressed about school, but... it was more than that."

Carlos stayed quiet for a beat, watching Ethan, who shifted uncomfortably in his seat. There was something raw in his eyes—fear, regret, and a need for someone to hear him.

Carlos softened his tone, speaking more gently. "Look, I'm trying to understand what might have led to this. If Diego was involved in something serious, it could help us figure out what happened to him."

Ethan hesitated, rubbing the back of his neck, and his voice faltered. "I wish I knew. He was just... different lately. Like something was weighing on him, but I didn't press him about it."

Carlos met his eyes with a steady gaze. "Ethan, if there's something you're not telling me, now's the time. It could make all the difference."

Ethan's eyes flickered with uncertainty, and he let out a sigh. "I didn't want to push him. He didn't trust anyone with his stuff. He kept everything close. I... I didn't even know what was going on in his head."

Carlos could sense the boy's inner turmoil, the desperate need to help, but also the fear of making things worse. "Can you take me to his room? Maybe there's something there that can help us understand more."

Ethan hesitated, his eyes searching the floor for a moment, before he nodded. "Okay. I'll show you."

They ascended the stairs together, the air thick with unspoken words. Ethan led the way, his shoulders hunched, his hands trembling slightly. When they reached Diego's room, Carlos took in the scene at once—the organized chaos of books piled high, papers scattered across the desk, a laptop sitting closed, almost expectantly.

Ethan stepped inside, his gaze darting nervously around the room. "I haven't gone through his stuff. I didn't know what to do. It just didn't feel right."

Carlos gave a reassuring nod, scanning the papers on the desk. "It's okay. Let's see if we can find something useful." He picked up a few sheets of paper filled with Diego's neat handwriting, but nothing pointed to a specific project. His eyes then fell on the laptop.

STEALING MEXICO

"Do you know if Diego had a password for this?" Carlos asked, stepping closer to the desk.

Ethan bit his lip, looking at the laptop. "I... I don't know. He never shared it with me."

Carlos's brow furrowed as he examined the closed device. "Can you think of anything he might've used? A nickname, a favorite band, something like that?"

Ethan shook his head, his voice thick with frustration. "He was private about everything. Never let anyone in. I just thought... I thought he was just being careful."

Carlos sighed, still eyeing the laptop. "We need to get into this. There could be something important in here that could help us figure out what was going on."

He started gathering a few notebooks filled with Diego's notes, along with the laptop. "I'll take these with me. If we can't crack the password, I'll find someone who can."

As they searched the room, Carlos couldn't shake the feeling of unease that clung to the space. The room felt heavy, the walls closing in as they sifted through the fragments of Diego's life. Whatever Diego had uncovered, it had put him in danger—and now, it felt like it was pulling Ethan into that same dangerous spiral.

Amidst the investigation, Carlos's thoughts wandered briefly to Asher. The journalist's face lingered in his mind, sharp, challenging, and oddly... appealing. He'd become more than just an irritant in Carlos's mind—more than someone he'd tried to dismiss. There was something about Asher's presence that stirred a response in Carlos, something that made him uncomfortable but also curious.

Shaking off the thought, Carlos refocused on Ethan. "We'll figure this out, Ethan," he said softly, locking eyes with the boy. "But I need you to be honest with me. If there's anything you remember, no matter how small, it could make a difference."

Ethan nodded, a mixture of determination and fear in his eyes. "I'll try. I just want to know what happened to Diego."

Carlos's heart ached for him. "We will. We'll sort this out, I promise."

As they continued to search the room, the shadows outside seemed to stretch longer, and the weight of their task grew heavier. Whatever Diego had uncovered had made him a target, and now Ethan was being pulled into that same dangerous web. Time was running out.

CHAPTER 6

ASHER

Asher Rhodes stood in the middle of his apartment, surrounded by the chaos only a journalist could thrive in. Papers scattered across the coffee table, empty takeout containers piled high in the corner, and half-unpacked boxes littered the floor. The chaos was organized, perfectly reflecting his mind—constantly in motion, scattered yet somehow always making sense of it all.

He pushed aside a stack of magazines, frustration rising as he tried to make sense of the scattered information he'd gathered on Diego Cortez and his host family, the Coles. His laptop screen glowed with a series of tabs open to Diego's social media accounts. Asher scrolled through the posts with a laser focus, as though every image held the key to unraveling the mystery of the young man's death. But as he flicked through photo after photo—selfies, campus events, group shots—nothing stood out. No clues, no hidden messages, just ordinary, everyday moments.

Asher leaned back against the couch, running a hand through his tousled blond hair. "Come on, Diego," he muttered, voice tight with the pressure of the moment. "Where's the real story?" His eyes flicked to his coffee cup,

STEALING MEXICO

now lukewarm and forgotten. He grabbed it anyway, taking a sip for the rush.

Just as he was about to give up, something on the screen caught his eye. A single photo was among the sea of smiles and mundane college life. It was from a few weeks ago, Diego standing front and center at an immigration rights event. He was holding a sign that read, "Justice for All." The image was striking, not just because of the passion in Diego's eyes, but because of the implications it carried.

This was no ordinary college kid, Asher thought, leaning in closer to the screen. The image was brimming with potential, the kind of passionate activism that could stir controversy, the kind of thing that could make someone a target.

His pulse quickened. This was the lead he'd been waiting for.

Asher snapped a screenshot of the photo, his mind racing as possibilities exploded in every direction. There was a connection here, something bigger than Diego's surface-level life. A connection to the murder, to the hidden life Diego had been living, one that might have gotten him killed.

An excited, almost mischievous grin spread across Asher's face. "Oh, Carlos," he whispered to himself, picturing the detective's response. The furrowed brow, the skeptical silence, the arms crossed tightly—those walls that had been so hard to crack. But now... now Asher had something he could use. This wasn't just a journalist's hunch anymore. This was the kind of information that would get him into Carlos's orbit, into his case.

Asher stood up, his heart thudding with the excitement only a good lead could bring. He gathered his laptop and shoved it into his messenger bag, grabbed his keys, and made his way to the door. There was no time to waste. This find was too important.

He gave himself one last glance in the mirror, making sure

his grin was sharp, his posture confident. "Charm mode: activated," he said with a smirk.

The drive to Carlos's neighborhood was a blur. The streets of Phoenix flickered by under the low, warm light of the setting sun. Asher felt the familiar thrill of the chase wash over him, but this time, it was different. It wasn't just about a story anymore. It was about getting closer to the detective. He imagined Carlos's reaction: skeptical, of course, but intrigued enough to listen. Asher had the perfect angle—flirtation, charm, and the promise of something bigger. It was what could crack through Carlos's professional demeanor and get him to take a closer look at Asher, at what he had to offer.

He could almost hear Carlos's voice in his head: "This better not be another one of your stunts, Rhodes."

Asher's smile widened. Oh, it wasn't.

CHAPTER 7

CARLOS

Carlos sat at the small dining room table in his modest home, surrounded by the scattered notebooks, papers, and Diego's laptop. The faint aroma of his Abuela's cooking drifted in from the kitchen, filling the room with the comfort of home. He could hear her humming softly as she stirred something simmering on the stove. It was one of those rare evenings when the weight of the world felt just a little lighter, if only for a moment.

He flipped through the first notebook, his eyes scanning Diego's neat handwriting, the sketches, and ideas that seemed to pour out of a mind driven by passion and purpose. Each page offered a glimpse of the young man's determination—his desire to make a difference. A pang of regret settled in Carlos's chest as he realized Diego would never see his work come to fruition.

"Carlos! ¿Quieres frijoles o arroz?" his Abuela's voice called from the kitchen, warm and melodic.

"Frijoles, Abuela!" he replied, his tone distracted but grateful for the brief break from his thoughts.

A moment later, she appeared in the doorway, silver hair pulled back into a bun, a flour-smudged apron over her

STEALING MEXICO

simple dress. "You need to eat, mijo. You work too much. When will you bring a novio or novia to meet me?" she asked, a playful glint in her eyes.

Carlos looked up from the pages, managing a soft smile despite himself. "Abuela, you know I don't have time for that right now."

"You make time, Carlos. Life is not just work," she chided gently, setting a steaming plate of frijoles in front of him. The earthy aroma mixed with the spices of her cooking, filling the air with warmth. "You should meet someone nice. Someone who can make you happy."

He chuckled, the familiar weight settling on his shoulders. "Maybe when this case is over," he said, trying to steer the conversation away. "I've been looking into Diego's project. I just wish I knew more about what he was working on."

"Still on that, eh?" she replied, her tone shifting to one of understanding. "What do you think happened?"

Carlos sighed, running a hand through his hair. "I don't know, Abuela. All I know is that Diego had something important—something that got him killed. And I can't shake the feeling it's connected to his host family, especially Ethan."

"Ethan?" she echoed, a concerned crease forming between her brows. "Isn't that the boy who was with him?"

"Yeah. They had an argument at a party just before it happened. I spoke to a girl from Diego's class who said they fought over something," Carlos explained, the frustration clear in his voice. "But Ethan won't talk about it. I just... I'm worried about him. He's stressed, and I can see it."

She nodded, a knowing look in her eyes. "You care about him. You should talk to him more. He needs someone he can trust."

Carlos felt a wave of appreciation for her insight. "I know, but I can't let my feelings get in the way of the investigation. I have to find out what Diego was working on, and that laptop..." He gestured toward the table, where Diego's belongings lay scattered. "It's locked. Ethan doesn't know the password."

"Maybe he will tell you in time," she suggested softly, resting a comforting hand on his shoulder. "Just remember, mijo, sometimes people are more open when they feel safe."

Carlos opened his mouth to respond, but before he could, a sharp knock on the door startled him. The sound echoed through the quiet evening, making his heart race. He glanced at the clock—already past nine. Who could it be at this hour?

"Abuela?" he called, a surge of anxiety rising in his chest. "Did you invite anyone over?"

"No, mijo," she answered, concern threading her voice. "Go see who it is."

Carlos stood, pushing his chair back as he moved cautiously toward the door, unease coiling in his stomach. With everything that had happened recently, he had a feeling this wouldn't be a casual visit.

As he reached for the doorknob, he took a deep breath, bracing himself for whatever lay beyond.

CHAPTER 8

Asher shifted nervously on Carlos's doorstep, the cool evening air wrapping around him like a cloak. He stared at the modest home, waiting for Carlos to answer the door. The street was still, save for the faint hum of distant traffic, and Asher's thoughts churned with anticipation. Tonight could be a turning point in the investigation—if Carlos would just cooperate.

When the door finally opened, Asher faced Carlos, his dark hair mussed and his shirt hugging his frame in a way that made Asher's heart race. The detective's gaze flicked up in surprise, though his expression remained stoic.

"Rhodes," Carlos greeted him, his voice flat, though the slightest edge of curiosity lingered.

"As I live and breathe, Santos," Asher replied with a smirk, flashing his most disarming grin. "I've got something you might want to see."

Before Carlos could respond, an elderly woman appeared behind him, her face lighting up with recognition. "¡Hola! You're not Carlos's friend from work, are you?" she asked, beaming.

STEALING MEXICO

"Um, yes," Asher said, stepping forward with a polite nod. "I'm Asher. Nice to meet you!"

"Oh, Asher! What a lovely name!" she exclaimed. "Come in, come in!"

Asher stepped into the warmth of the house, immediately feeling the contrast between the cool evening air and the coziness of Carlos's home. The smell of something delicious wafted from the kitchen, and he could hear the clink of utensils and the rhythmic hum of someone moving about with purpose.

Carlos's grandmother, a small woman with silver hair pulled back in a neat bun, moved energetically around the kitchen, her warm presence immediately making Asher feel at ease.

"Have you eaten?" she asked, her voice full of concern, as if she had already decided that he was far too thin.

"I'm good, thank you," Asher said, but he could see the glint in her eyes, and he knew he wouldn't escape without at least a little something.

"Nonsense! You look too thin. I'll make you something quick!" she insisted, already bustling about with impressive speed.

Carlos stepped in, looking exasperated. "Abuela, we're kind of busy right now," he said, rubbing a hand over his face in mild frustration.

"Busy? You should eat first!" she called back, not missing a beat. "Mijo, you're working too hard. You need to take care of yourself."

Asher couldn't help but chuckle, enjoying the playful exchange. "She's right, you know," he said, leaning casually against the wall. "I could use a good meal before we dive into all this."

Carlos shot him a look, half-irritated, half-resigned. "Really? You're just going to play along with this?"

"Hey," Asher shrugged, never missing a beat, "I'm willing

to do whatever it takes to get on the case. Besides, your Abuela seems to know how to take care of business."

Before Carlos could protest further, his grandmother reappeared with a plate of food, steaming and overflowing with generous portions. She set it in front of Asher with a pleased smile. "Here you go, mi joven. Eat up!"

"Thank you, Abuela," Asher said, accepting the plate with genuine appreciation. As he sat at the table, the warmth of the food and the home made him feel momentarily grounded in a way he hadn't felt in a long time. Carlos lingered nearby, arms crossed, exuding the sort of impatience only someone used to constant work could manage.

As Asher dug in, savoring the comforting flavors of the meal, he knew the time to bring up business had arrived.

"So, I found something interesting while I was going through Diego's social media," he said between bites. "There's a photo of him at an immigration rights event. Could be significant."

Carlos raised an eyebrow, clearly uninterested. "We're not working together on this."

Asher leaned forward, not deterred by Carlos's immediate resistance. "Come on, Carlos. You can't just ignore this. It could give us insight into who Diego was. Maybe it ties into his murder. You need to see the photo."

Carlos sighed, clearly frustrated. "I'm not working with you, Rhodes. I'm here to investigate, not to collaborate with a reporter."

Asher's eyes narrowed slightly, but his resolve only strengthened. "I get that. But just look. I promise it's worth your time. If you really want to understand what happened, this photo could lead to answers."

The tension in the room thickened, and Carlos's eyes flicked to the side, clearly weighing the situation. Asher could tell that part of Carlos was reluctant to involve him in the

STEALING MEXICO

case, but another part was curious—curious enough to at least entertain the idea.

Finally, with a resigned grunt, Carlos gave in. "Fine. Show me the photo."

Asher couldn't suppress his satisfaction as he pulled out his phone. He quickly navigated to the image of Diego at the event and turned the screen toward Carlos.

Carlos leaned in, studying the photo for a long moment, the quiet hum of the house filling the space between them. "What exactly do you think this means?" he asked, his voice skeptical.

"I don't know yet," Asher replied, a flicker of determination sparking in his chest. "But we have to dig deeper. If Diego was involved in this kind of activism, he might've made some dangerous connections. He could've been a target. We need to identify his connections.

Carlos didn't immediately respond, his gaze fixed on the photo, his jaw tense. Asher could almost see the wheels turning in his head, his professional instincts at war with his desire to shut down the intrusion.

Asher pushed just a little further. "Look, I understand you don't want my help, but I want to know the truth as much as you do. If this photo can lead us somewhere, we need to pursue it together."

Carlos sighed, his frustration palpable. He shook his head, but Asher noticed the flicker of amusement in his eyes. "You're insufferable, you know that?"

"Only when it matters," Asher replied with a wink. "But really, what's the plan? We need to dig into Diego's connections. That event... there might be something there."

Carlos put his fork down, his expression unreadable now. As he stood up, Asher could feel the shift in the air. Despite Carlos's earlier resistance, something was changing between them. The tension, the reluctance, was giving way to something more... tentative. They were still on opposite sides of this, but they were both chasing the same answers.

Carlos glanced at him once more, his gaze sharp. "I'll consider it. But don't expect me to take you along for the ride."

Asher grinned, his voice light. "That's all I ask for right now."

Carlos nodded, his focus returning to the case. The conversation shifted back to Diego and the investigation, but there was an unspoken understanding now. Despite the friction and their differences, they shared the same goal.

As they finished eating, the warmth of the home and the food created a momentary sense of camaraderie. The distance between them was closing, slowly but surely. Asher wasn't sure where this partnership was heading, but he knew one thing for sure—it wasn't over. Not yet.

CHAPTER 9

CARLOS

The morning light filtered through the blinds of the precinct, casting a soft glow on the stack of unsolved cases littering Carlos' desk. His coffee sat lukewarm beside him, neglected in favor of the case files he'd been poring over since the early hours. Diego Cortez's murder had consumed his every thought, gnawing at him with an intensity he couldn't shake. But it wasn't just the case. It was the feeling of helplessness—the image of a young man, alone and terrified, in his last moments.

He rubbed his temples, trying to focus. He couldn't afford to get distracted. Not now. Not when there were so many unanswered questions. His phone buzzed, pulling him from his thoughts. He glanced at the screen and saw the name he'd been dreading.

Asher Rhodes.

Carlos gritted his teeth, answering it before it could ring a second time. "What?" His voice was flat, but there was a slight edge to it.

"Carlos!" Asher's voice was its usual cheerful, unbothered self. "We've got to go. I made an appointment with Diego's professor. We can't waste time on this one."

Carlos's jaw clenched. "We?" He bit back the urge to say something sharp, pushing down his irritation. He couldn't shake the image of Asher walking into the precinct the day before, like he was some kind of celebrity. He should've expected this. "I didn't agree to work with you, Rhodes."

"Oh, come on, Santos," Asher's tone was playful, confident, and irritatingly charming. "It's just a professor. He could have information we need, and you've got nothing else going on. Besides, you can't blame me for taking the initiative."

Carlos stood, pacing as he fought the rising frustration in his chest. The last thing he wanted was to be stuck with Asher —who had a way of making everything feel like a joke—but he couldn't deny it: the lead on Diego's project was important. Still, the idea of Asher tagging along…

He sighed, pinching the bridge of his nose. "Fine. I'll meet you in ten minutes."

Carlos hung up, feeling the anger simmer beneath his skin. His phone buzzed again, and he checked the message— Asher was at the station. As if that's what he needed right now.

He needed to get his head on straight. This was about the case. Not about some pushy reporter who kept getting under his skin.

The office door swung open with a soft creak, and Carlos stepped inside, his eyes immediately locking onto Marissa's. She looked up from the files on her desk, her sharp gaze quickly assessing him.

"Morning, Carlos," she greeted, but her eyes were knowing. She'd seen the exhaustion in him for days. "How's it going with the case?"

Carlos opened his mouth to speak, but before he could respond, Asher strode in, his smile too wide and too eager.

"Carlos! Captain!" he called out, as if he'd just walked into a party. "We've got work to do!"

Carlos froze, his stomach lurching with the familiar surge of annoyance. He felt a vein in his neck twitch as he glared at the reporter. Asher wore that damned grin, the one that made Carlos's blood boil for reasons he couldn't quite figure out.

"What now?" Carlos snapped, trying to rein in his frustration.

Asher didn't even flinch at Carlos's tone, leaning casually against the doorframe. "I made an appointment with one of Diego's professors. We're going to meet him and talk about the project he was working on. It could lead to something."

Marissa raised an eyebrow, clearly skeptical. She looked between Asher and Carlos, the tension between them palpable. "Carlos, did you agree to this?" she asked, her voice betraying a hint of amusement.

"No!" Carlos blurted out too quickly, his hand balling into a fist. "I was just trying to get him to stop talking. I didn't agree to—"

"I thought it'd be helpful for us to work together, since you're so busy, Captain," Asher interjected, flashing a grin at Marissa. "It's not like Carlos has any better leads at the moment."

Carlos shot him a glare. "This is not a partnership." His voice was tight, a warning hidden in the words.

"Oh, come on, Santos," Asher teased, undeterred. "It'll be fun. We'll crack this case wide open. Plus, I'm sure you'd love the chance to pick my brain." His eyes sparkled with mischief.

Carlos was about to snap back, to tell Asher exactly where he could stick his 'fun,' but something in the back of his mind

STEALING MEXICO

stopped him. The thought of Asher, grinning and so damn confident in front of him—he felt it again. The strange, tight knot in his stomach that had no place here.

"No," Carlos growled, trying to ignore it. "This is my case. You're a reporter. You don't belong here."

Asher's grin only widened, an obvious challenge in his eyes. "You sure about that?" he said, stepping forward, his presence suddenly overwhelming. "If I'm right, we're going to need each other. You can't do this alone."

Marissa was watching them both with a bemused expression, arms crossed. "Alright," she said after a long beat. "If you two are done with the staring contest, go. Just—please—keep me updated."

Carlos clenched his jaw but gave a stiff nod. He wasn't about to admit how much he wanted to be done with this conversation, to get away from Asher's constant buzz of energy that made him want to punch something—or maybe kiss something, and that terrified him even more.

Asher slapped him on the back, his touch far too casual, sending a jolt through Carlos's spine. "Great! Let's go, partner!" Asher said, practically bouncing out the door.

Carlos froze. Partner. That word.

"We are not partners," he muttered under his breath, following him out of the office, his chest tightening with a confusing mix of frustration and something else he didn't want to acknowledge.

As they walked toward the exit, Carlos's fists clenched at his sides, the only thing stopping him from grabbing Asher by the collar and shaking the stupid smirk off his face. He couldn't stand the way Asher looked at him, like they were two sides of the same coin, destined to fall into the same mess. He couldn't stand the way his heart beat faster when Asher smiled at him.

But that wasn't what this was. This wasn't about attraction. It wasn't.

Carlos forced the thoughts away. They were here to investigate, not get caught up in whatever insane draw he felt toward Asher.

But the feeling lingered. And as much as Carlos hated to admit it, he knew that working with Asher was going to be far more complicated than he'd ever wanted it to be.

CHAPTER 10

ASHER

"Do you ever shut up?" Carlos growled, his fingers tightening around the steering wheel as they pulled into the university parking lot.

The midday sun blazed overhead, the asphalt shimmering with heat, but Asher barely noticed. His focus was entirely on the man sitting beside him, whose perpetually grumpy demeanor had become something of a personal challenge.

"Only when I'm asleep," Asher quipped, grinning. He leaned back, arms casually draped over his messenger bag. "Although even then, I hear I'm a very charming sleep-talker."

Carlos let out a long, exasperated sigh. "Do you ever think before you speak?"

"Not if I can help it." Asher winked as he hopped out of the car, leaving Carlos to mutter curses under his breath as he slammed the driver's door shut.

They walked side by side toward the Political Science building, Asher struggling to suppress the smirk tugging at his lips. Carlos looked as tense as ever, his jaw clenched, and his brows furrowed into a permanent scowl. Yet, there was

STEALING MEXICO

something magnetic about that intensity—a pull Asher couldn't quite resist.

"You know, Santos," Asher began, glancing sideways at him, "for someone who spends so much time glaring at me, you'd think you'd have run out of steam by now."

Carlos glared harder, his dark eyes narrowing into a look sharp enough to cut steel. "I have plenty of steam, Rhodes. Don't tempt me."

"Ooh, scary," Asher teased, nudging him lightly with his shoulder. "Lighten up, partner. We're here to find answers, not brood like we're in a noir film."

Carlos stopped walking, turning to face Asher with a scowl that could've melted stone. "Stop calling me 'partner.' We are not partners. I'm a detective, and you're—" He gestured vaguely, the disdain clear in his voice. "You're you."

Asher grinned wider. "Aw, I think that's the nicest thing you've ever said to me."

Carlos groaned and resumed walking, muttering something in Spanish under his breath that Asher was pretty sure wasn't complimentary.

They reached Dr. Shannon's office, a cluttered space filled with bookshelves threatening to topple under the weight of countless volumes. The faint aroma of coffee and old paper hung in the air as the professor looked up from her desk, adjusting her glasses.

"Detective Santos. Mr. Rhodes," she greeted, standing to shake their hands. "What can I do for you?"

Carlos, ever the professional, stepped forward. "We're here to ask you about Diego Cortez and his research."

Dr. Shannon's smile faded, replaced by a somber expression. "Diego was a brilliant student. His death is a terrible loss."

Asher laid the photo they'd found on her desk. "This was on Diego's social media. Do you recognize the event?"

Dr. Shannon studied the picture, her brows knitting

together in thought. "Yes, that was an immigration rights rally a few weeks ago. Diego was passionate about these issues. He believed in giving a voice to those who are often silenced."

Carlos leaned forward, his hands resting on the edge of the desk. "What exactly was he working on?"

The professor folded her hands, her gaze distant. "Diego was researching immigration policies, but not just academically. He wanted to understand how these policies affect people on a personal level. Attending rallies, spoke to activists, and even connected with individuals on both sides of the debate. He was fearless in his pursuit of the truth."

Asher glanced at Carlos, noting the flicker of admiration in the detective's eyes. Carlos said nothing, but Asher could see the gears turning in his head, piecing together the implications of Diego's work.

"Did he mention anyone specific he was working with?" Carlos asked.

Dr. Shannon hesitated. "He didn't share names. Diego was very protective of his sources, especially those who were vulnerable. But I know he was meeting with several groups— activists, legal professionals, and even individuals who were critical of immigration reforms. He wanted a balanced perspective."

Carlos nodded, his expression grim. "Do you think his work could've put him in danger?"

Dr. Shannon's lips pressed into a thin line. "It's possible. Diego was determined to uncover the truth, no matter the risk."

Asher felt the weight of her words settle over them like a heavy cloud. "If you think of anything else, no matter how small, please let us know," he said, offering her a reassuring smile.

As they left the office, the tension between them was almost palpable. Asher, ever the optimist, couldn't resist

STEALING MEXICO

breaking the silence. "You know, Santos, for someone so grumpy, you're surprisingly good at getting people to talk."

Carlos shot him a sideways glare. "Is there a point to this, or are you just determined to be annoying?"

Asher grinned. "Both, probably."

They reached the car, and Carlos leaned against it, rubbing a hand over his face. "We need to get into Diego's laptop," he muttered, almost to himself.

Asher's grin widened. "Did you just say we?"

Carlos straightened, fixing Asher with a sharp look. "Shut up before I change my mind."

"Too late. I'm already your favorite sidekick," Asher quipped, earning an eye roll from Carlos.

Asher leaned closer, lowering his voice conspiratorially. "So, how do you plan to crack the laptop? Got a super-secret detective trick up your sleeve?"

Carlos crossed his arms, his expression unimpressed. "There are legal ways of getting into a locked computer."

"When in Rome…" Asher began, but Carlos cut him off with a disgusted look.

"Don't make this weird."

"Aye aye, partner," Asher teased, stepping back with a mock salute.

Carlos's glare softened ever so slightly, and for a moment, Asher thought he saw a hint of amusement flicker in the detective's eyes. But then it was gone, replaced by the familiar scowl that Asher was finding oddly endearing.

"I'm not your partner," Carlos grumbled, sliding into the car.

"Whatever you say," Asher replied, climbing in beside him. As they drove off, he couldn't help but feel that, despite Carlos's protests, they were making a pretty good team.

CHAPTER 11

CARLOS

The bright morning sun bathed the campus in a warm glow as Carlos and Asher made their way toward the library. Despite the cheerful atmosphere, the weight of Diego's case pressed heavily on Carlos's shoulders. They had spent the previous night combing through what little they had uncovered so far, barely sleeping.

Asher, however, seemed energized, his voice lively as he animatedly described a recent article he'd written for the Phoenix Ledger.

"And get this," Asher said, gesturing wildly, "my editor wanted me to cut the best part! You know, the section where I tied the whole story together? Absolute madness."

Carlos smirked despite himself. Asher's knack for turning even the smallest grievances into entertaining stories was infuriatingly endearing. His voice carried an infectious energy, his blue eyes sparkling with mischief as if the gravity of their task wasn't weighing on him at all.

"Maybe your editor has a point," Carlos teased, hoping to steer the conversation back to something relevant.

"You wound me, Detective," Asher replied dramatically,

STEALING MEXICO

clutching his chest. "But fear not, I'll win you over, eventually. Everyone loves my stories."

Carlos rolled his eyes, forcing his focus back on the library looming ahead. Asher's charm might work on others, but he wasn't about to let it distract him—not with so much at stake.

Inside, the scent of old books and coffee hit them immediately. Students filled every available space, hunched over laptops or thumbing through textbooks, the quiet hum of conversation and clicking keyboards blending into a steady background noise.

"We should split up," Carlos said, scanning the room. "I'll check the IT desk. You try to find someone who looks tech-savvy—someone who knows their way around a laptop."

"Tech-savvy?" Asher repeated, feigning a scandalized look. "What if I find someone with a degree in interpretive dance instead?"

Carlos gave him a flat stare. "Just find someone useful, Asher."

With a playful salute, Asher turned and headed toward a group of students at a table in the corner, his confidence drawing their attention almost immediately. Carlos shook his head and made his way to the IT desk, though his gaze flicked back toward Asher more often than he'd like.

For someone so obnoxious, he sure knows how to talk to people.

The IT desk proved unhelpful—mostly students working on their own projects or unwilling to break any rules. Carlos was about to head back to Asher when his name rang out from across the room.

"Carlos!"

He turned to see Asher waving him over, standing beside a young woman with short, choppy hair and an armful of computer science textbooks. Her sharp gaze flicked between them, her stance conveying an air of impatience.

"This is Jenna," Asher said, grinning. "Jenna here is a tech genius with a double major in computer science and criminal justice. Can you believe our luck?"

Jenna snorted. "Don't oversell it. What do you need?"

Carlos stepped forward, holding Diego's laptop. "We're trying to access this laptop. It belonged to a... friend who passed recently. We don't have the password."

Jenna narrowed her eyes, clearly skeptical. "If it's just a user login, I can probably get around it. If it's encrypted, though, that's a whole other beast."

Carlos nodded. "We just need to know what's on it. Anything might help us figure out what happened to him."

She hesitated for a moment, then jerked her head toward a quieter corner. "Come on. Let's keep this discreet."

They followed her to a secluded study table, and she set the laptop down, pulling a small toolkit from her bag. She worked quickly, her fingers darting across the keyboard with practiced ease.

Asher, for once, stayed quiet, watching Jenna work with an almost reverent fascination. Carlos used the rare silence to gather his thoughts, though his gaze occasionally drifted toward Asher. There was something about the way he stood —leaning casually against the table, his blond hair catching the light—that made Carlos's stomach twist. He glanced away, frustrated with himself.

"Okay, we're in," Jenna said, leaning back.

Carlos stepped forward, his pulse quickening. Folders and files cluttered the desktop, many labeled with words like "Research" and "Immigration".

"Can you see if anything's hidden? Encrypted folders, unusual files?" he asked.

Jenna nodded, clicking through the contents. "There's a lot here—articles, documents, PDFs. Looks like he was working on something big related to immigration law and policy." She frowned, her eyes narrowing. "But this folder—'Research'—is password-protected. This might be the jackpot."

STEALING MEXICO

"Can you crack it?"

"Not without risking corruption," she said, shaking her head. "If it's safe-locked, even trying could erase everything inside."

Carlos ran a hand through his hair, frustration bubbling beneath the surface. "Thanks for your help, Jenna. This gives us something to work with."

She shrugged, already packing up her tools. "Good luck, I guess. Just...be careful."

As Jenna walked away, Carlos stared at the locked folder, a sinking feeling settling in his chest. They were so close to answers, yet still a step behind.

"We've got more digging to do," he muttered.

Asher leaned in, his grin annoyingly smug. "We? I like the sound of that."

Carlos shot him a glare, though he felt the faintest tug of a smile. "Don't get used to it."

Asher chuckled, throwing him a playful wink. "Whatever you say, partner."

Carlos turned back toward the laptop, ignoring the warmth spreading through his chest. There was no room for distractions—not when the truth was so close, yet just out of reach.

CHAPTER 12

ASHER

Asher leaned back against the wall of the campus library, watching Carlos pace as they debated their next steps. The detective's dark brows furrowed in concentration, his hand rubbing the back of his neck—a habit Asher had quickly noticed whenever Carlos was deep in thought.

"So, what's the plan, Detective?" Asher asked, arms crossed, his voice teasing but laced with genuine curiosity. "We can't exactly take the laptop to a 'hackers for hire' hotline."

Carlos shot him a sharp look, his jaw tightening. "I'll figure it out. We don't need any more risks."

Asher rolled his eyes. "You mean you don't want me taking any more risks? Which, by the way, is ironic, considering you're dragging me through this investigation."

"I didn't drag you into anything," Carlos snapped. "You inserted yourself."

"Semantics," Asher said with a smirk, pushing off the wall. "Look, I get that this whole 'letting people help' thing isn't your strong suit, but we're on the same side here. You want answers. I want a story. It works out."

Carlos sighed, his frustration clear, but he didn't argue. Asher took that as progress.

The walk back to the parking lot was quiet, the library fading behind them as they stepped into the sunlight. Students milled about, their laughter and chatter a stark contrast to the tension hanging between them.

"You've been quiet," Asher finally said, breaking the silence. "What's on your mind?"

Carlos glanced at him, his expression guarded. "Diego's folder. Whatever's in it, he protected it for a reason. If we can figure out what he was working on, it might explain everything—why he was killed, who was after him."

Asher nodded thoughtfully, his usual humor giving way to a rare seriousness. "It's a good lead. We just have to be careful."

Carlos stopped abruptly, turning to face him. "Exactly. That's why you can't publish anything about this—not yet."

"Relax," Asher said, holding up his hands in mock surrender. "I gave you my word, didn't I?"

Carlos searched his face for a moment, as if weighing whether to trust him. Then, with a curt nod, he started walking again.

They reached Carlos's car, the black sedan gleaming under the morning sun. Asher hesitated before getting in, his fingers tapping against the roof.

"What?" Carlos asked, already settling into the driver's seat.

"Nothing," Asher said, shaking his head. "Just thinking."

Carlos raised an eyebrow but didn't push further. Asher climbed in, the tension between them shifting into something quieter, more contemplative.

Asher punctuated the mostly uneventful drive, only occasionally glancing at the focused Carlos. There was something about the way Carlos's hands gripped the wheel—firm—steady, like he was always braced for impact.

"Have you always been this... serious?" Asher asked, breaking the silence.

Carlos didn't respond immediately. "I take my job seriously."

"Yeah, I've noticed." Asher grinned. "But what about you? Outside of the badge, outside of all this?"

Carlos's lips twitched, almost like he wanted to smile but refused to let himself. "Not much of a separation these days."

Asher frowned, the answer hitting harder than he'd expected. "That sounds... lonely."

Carlos's hands tightened on the wheel. "It's not."

"Uh-huh." Asher let the conversation drop, sensing he'd pushed far enough.

The precinct was buzzing with activity when they arrived, officers bustling between desks, phones ringing incessantly. Carlos barely acknowledged anyone as they made their way to his desk, his focus already on Diego's laptop.

"You going to try guessing the password?" Asher asked, leaning against a nearby filing cabinet.

Carlos ignored him, instead pulling out a notebook where he'd jotted down details from Diego's room. Asher watched as the detective's brows knit together in concentration.

"You know," Asher said, breaking the silence, "if you'd let me do things my way, we might've already had this cracked."

Carlos shot him a warning look. "And if I let happen, the case could fall apart."

"Not everyone's out to ruin your day, Santos," Asher quipped, though he softened his tone. "I get it. Trust doesn't come easy for you. But we will get nowhere if you keep shutting me out."

Carlos didn't respond, but Asher could tell his words had landed.

Hours passed, the hum of the precinct growing quieter as the day wore on. Asher found himself restless, flipping through old case files out of sheer boredom. Carlos remained engrossed in his work, his determination almost hypnotic.

Finally, Asher couldn't take the silence any longer. "Okay, Detective, what's the next move?"

Carlos leaned back in his chair, exhaustion etched into his features. "The next move is finding someone who can help us with that folder—without compromising the case."

Asher grinned, his energy reigniting. "You mean you're going to let me find someone?"

"Don't push your luck," Carlos muttered, but there was a hint of amusement in his voice.

Asher smirked, feeling the tension between them ease ever so slightly. For all his gruffness, Carlos wasn't as impenetrable as he liked to pretend. And Asher? He wasn't about to let him forget it.

CHAPTER 13

CARLOS

Carlos sat at the dining table, Diego's notes, files, and laptop spread out before him like fragments of a shattered mirror. The air smelled of fresh tortillas and cinnamon, a comforting backdrop to his relentless search for answers.

Abuela hummed softly in the kitchen, her presence grounding Carlos even as his thoughts spiraled. He flipped through one of Diego's notebooks, his eyes scanning for connections. The kid's handwriting was tight and meticulous, filling every inch of each page.

Halfway through a section on local immigration advocacy groups, a name caught his eye.

Charles Holbrook.

Carlos leaned closer, the name underlined twice in bold strokes. Below it, Diego had written: "Part of the machine. Need proof. Check donations?"

Carlos's heart sank. Governor Charles Holbrook. The man wasn't just a politician—he was practically a kingpin of Arizona's political scene, celebrated for his leadership and his tough stance on crime and border control. If Diego had uncovered something involving Holbrook, it could explain why he'd been silenced.

STEALING MEXICO

"Mijo," Abuela called, snapping him out of his thoughts. She appeared in the doorway, wiping her hands on her apron. "You've been sitting there too long. Come, eat something."

"Not now, Abuela," Carlos said, his gaze still fixed on the notebook.

"You say that every day," she replied, shaking her head. "You can't solve anything on an empty stomach."

Carlos sighed, but offered her a small smile. "I'll eat later. I promise."

Abuela lingered for a moment before retreating, muttering something about stubbornness. Carlos barely registered it. He was already pulling out his phone, his mind racing.

If anyone might have dirt on Holbrook, it was Asher. The journalist's tenacity had already proved helpful—annoying, but helpful. Carlos scrolled through his contacts, found Asher's number, and pressed the call button.

The phone rang twice before Asher picked up, his voice bright and teasing as usual. "Carlos Santos! To what do I owe the honor of your voice before noon?"

"This isn't a social call," Carlos said curtly.

"Shame," Asher quipped. "I was about to invite you to brunch."

Carlos pinched the bridge of his nose. "Do you know anything about Governor Charles Holbrook?"

There was a pause on the other end. When Asher spoke again, his tone was more serious. "Holbrook? No, not really. Why?"

"I found his name in Diego's notes," Carlos explained. "Something about campaign donations and being 'part of the machine.' Does that mean anything to you?"

"Not off the top of my head," Asher admitted. "Holbrook's pretty polished—he keeps his public image squeaky clean. But..." His voice brightened slightly. "I might know someone who can dig into it."

Carlos sat up straighter. "Who?"

"A friend of mine," Asher said. "He's good at connecting dots—financials, political webs, that kind of thing. If there's dirt on Holbrook, he'll find it."

Carlos hesitated, weighing his options. Involving more people, particularly strangers, didn't thrill him. But if Diego's notes pointed to Holbrook, they were dealing with something much bigger than a lone investigation.

"Fine," Carlos said. "Call him. See what he can find out."

"Anything for you," Asher replied, the playful edge returning to his voice.

Carlos ignored it, focusing on the notebook in front of him. "Let me know the second you hear anything."

"Will do," Asher said. "And Carlos?"

"What?"

"I knew you'd come around," Asher said, his tone unusually soft.

Carlos ended the call without responding, setting the phone down on the table. He stared at the name Charles Holbrook underlined on the page, the weight of Diego's work pressing heavily on his chest.

Abuela reappeared with a cup of coffee, setting it beside him. She said nothing, just gave him a knowing look before returning to the kitchen. Carlos took a sip, letting the warmth spread through him.

He wasn't sure where this trail would lead, but one thing was clear: Diego had uncovered something dangerous. And now Carlos was stepping into the same storm, determined to see it through.

CHAPTER 14

ASHER

Asher sprawled across his couch, one leg draped over the side, his laptop balanced precariously on his stomach. The screen glowed in the dim light of his living room as he scrolled through articles, interviews, and every puff piece he could find about Governor Charles Holbrook. Most of it was standard fare: charity appearances, campaign trail highlights, and a polished biography that practically screamed "American dream."

He let out a theatrical groan, closing one tab and moving to the next. "Squeaky clean. Of course he is. Why wouldn't he be?" he muttered, tossing a potato chip into his mouth and missing entirely.

The crumbs scattered over his already cluttered coffee table, joining an empty soda can, three notebooks, and the remnants of last night's Chinese takeout.

Out of ideas, Asher reached for his phone and scrolled through his contacts until he found a name that promised better results: Nathan Shane. A fellow journalist with a knack for sniffing out secrets, Nathan had sources Asher could only dream of—and a track record of delivering the goods.

He hit call, and after two rings, Nathan's voice came

STEALING MEXICO

through, sharp and familiar. "Asher Rhodes. Finally, need someone to write your obit?"

Asher smirked, sitting up and balancing the laptop on his knees. "Not yet, gorgeous, but you'll be the first to know when I do."

"Oh, good. Saves me the trouble of pretending to care."

"Harsh," Asher replied, grinning. "Straight to the heart."

"Cut the charm, Rhodes. What do you want?"

"Why do you assume I want something? Maybe I'm calling just to hear your lovely voice."

"Because the last time you called me out of the blue, I ended up waist-deep in a state legislature scandal. You only call when you're desperate. Now spit it out."

"Alright, alright," Asher laughed. "I need intel. Governor Charles Holbrook. What've you got?"

There was a sigh, followed by the unmistakable sound of typing. "Holbrook, huh? He's clean—on paper, at least. You're not the first to sniff around him, though. He's got a lot of friends in high places who make sure nothing sticks. Why are you interested?"

"Call it a hunch," Asher said, leaning back against the couch. "What've you heard?"

"Not much," Nathan admitted, though the clicking of keys continued. "There's been some chatter about his campaign finances. A few inconsistencies here and there, but nothing anyone has managed to pin down. He's got a good cleanup crew—outsources the dirty work."

"Now you're talking my language," Asher said, his grin widening. "Who's doing the scrubbing?"

Nathan hesitated. "That's the interesting part. Rumor has it Holbrook's got someone on the inside—a personal assistant or something. They say this kid's sharp, ruthless, and handles all the unsavory stuff so Holbrook can keep playing Mr. Clean."

Asher sat up straighter, his curiosity piqued. "A kid? No name?"

"Not that I've heard," Nathan said. "But if the stories are true, you don't want to cross paths with him. The guy's a ghost, and ghosts don't leave witnesses."

"Spooky," Asher teased. "But come on, Nathan, you know me. I live for this kind of thing."

Nathan groaned. "I'm going to regret helping you, aren't I?"

"Probably," Asher said brightly. "But hey, that's what makes me charming."

Nathan muttered something under his breath, then added, "Listen, Rhodes, if you're really going to dig into this, be careful. Holbrook's untouchable for a reason, and whoever's protecting him won't hesitate to make you disappear if you get too close."

"When have I ever needed backup?"

Nathan snorted. "Famous last words. Just don't drag my name into whatever trouble you're about to stir up."

"Your secret's safe with me," Asher said, grinning. "Thanks, Gorgeous. You're the best."

"Don't make me regret this," Nathan muttered before the line went dead.

Asher tossed his phone onto the coffee table and stared at his laptop screen. A ruthless assistant, operating in the shadows to keep Holbrook's hands clean? Now that was a story worth chasing.

He pulled his laptop closer and opened a fresh document, his fingers flying across the keys. If Holbrook had a cleaner, Asher was going to find him—and he had a feeling this was going to be one hell of a ride.

CHAPTER 15

ASHER

Asher strode confidently through the front door of Carlos's house, boots clicking softly against the tiled floor. The familiar scent of spices and something roasting drifted from the kitchen, mingling with the faint sound of music playing in the background. The house felt warm and lived-in, a welcome contrast to his own chaotic apartment.

"Abuela?" he called out, knowing she'd be nearby. Sure enough, her voice came from the hallway before she even appeared.

"In here, mijo."

She rounded the corner with a warm smile, wiping her hands on a dish towel. "Carlos is in the bathroom. He's taking a shower."

"Perfect timing," Asher replied with a grin. "Thanks, Abuela."

Her eyes narrowed, but her smile didn't falter. "No seas travieso, Asher. Don't drive him crazy, por favor. He's had a long day."

"Who, me?" Asher asked innocently, the grin never leaving his face. "I'm a delight."

She gave him a look, one that spoke volumes with no need

STEALING MEXICO

for words, before stepping aside to let him pass. "Behave," she said, her tone a mixture of amusement and warning.

"Always," Asher quipped as he headed toward the bathroom.

Reaching the door, Asher didn't bother knocking. He pushed it open slightly, leaning against the frame with a smirk. Steam rolled out, blurring the edges of the room and creating a halo around the faint silhouette behind the fogged shower glass.

"Carlos, I hope you're not planning on taking forever in there," Asher called, loud enough to be heard over the spray of the water. "I've got important news."

There was a beat of silence, followed by a sharp reply. "Asher? What the hell are you doing? I'm in the shower!"

"Relax, Detective," Asher teased, the grin clear in his voice. "I'm not here to steal your soap. And trust me, I've seen enough guys in towels to last a lifetime. You're not breaking new ground."

Through the steam, Carlos muttered something in Spanish that Asher couldn't quite catch, but it didn't sound complimentary.

"Spit it out, and then get out!" Carlos barked, irritation dripping from every word.

"Fine, fine," Asher said, holding up his hands in mock surrender. "I talked to a friend—old journalist buddy of mine. Turns out your pal Holbrook has a helper. An assistant who handles all his dirty work. Bribes, shady deals, you name it."

Carlos paused, the sound of water shifting as he turned toward the door. "What are you talking about?"

"Rumor has it," Asher continued, "this assistant is a genuine piece of work. People call him a ghost—no one's got a name yet. But if Holbrook's involved in anything shady, this is your guy."

The water shut off with a hiss, and a moment later, Carlos's hand shot out from behind the shower door to grab a towel from the rack. Asher tried not to linger on the droplets trailing down the glass as Carlos wrapped himself up and stepped out.

Dripping and visibly annoyed, Carlos glared at him. "You couldn't wait five minutes?"

"I'm efficient," Asher quipped, arms crossed, the grin still plastered on his face.

Carlos scowled, his dark eyes narrowing. "Efficient at being a pain in my ass, maybe."

"Annoying, but useful," Asher countered smoothly. "Come on, admit it—without me, you'd be in the dark about this."

Carlos sighed, pinching the bridge of his nose. "Why do I put up with you?"

Asher shrugged, leaning against the doorframe. "Because you secretly like me. Now, are you going to thank me, or are you going to keep glaring until you melt the glass?"

Carlos didn't dignify that with a response. Instead, he muttered another curse in Spanish, pointed toward the door, and barked, "Out. Now."

"Sure thing, Detective," Asher said, turning to leave but pausing at the doorway. "By the way, nice abs. You should show them off more."

The door slammed shut behind him before Carlos could retort.

Asher chuckled as he headed back to the living room, the playful smirk still on his face.

Abuela was waiting, her hands on her hips and a bemused look in her eyes. "Did you make him mad?"

"Me? Never," Asher said, dropping onto the couch and kicking his feet up. "I'm a delight, remember?"

Abuela raised a skeptical eyebrow. "If you say so. But be careful, mijo. One day, he might actually throw you out."

Asher grinned. "Nah, he loves having me around. Keeps him on his toes."

STEALING MEXICO

Abuela shook her head, muttering something about troublemakers as she returned to the kitchen.

Asher leaned back against the couch cushions, tapping his fingers against his knee. Holbrook's assistant—this ghost—would not stay in the shadows for long. If anyone could uncover the truth, it was him.

CHAPTER 16

CARLOS

Carlos stepped out of the bathroom, towel wrapped tightly around his waist, hair still dripping from the shower. Steam clung to his skin, trailing behind him as he stepped into the living room—and froze.

Asher sprawled on the couch, looking entirely too comfortable, as if he belonged there.

"What the hell are you still doing here?" Carlos asked, his tone sharp. He tightened his grip on the towel, hoping to sound more annoyed than surprised.

Asher didn't even flinch. He glanced up with that same affable grin that made Carlos's teeth clench. "Making myself comfortable," he said, stretching like a damn cat. "You were in there forever. Thought I'd wait." He patted the empty cushion next to him. "Didn't think you'd mind."

Carlos glared at him, water dripping onto the floor. "You're not exactly big on boundaries, are you?"

"Not when they're unnecessary," Asher shot back, as though that was the most obvious thing in the world.

Before Carlos could respond, the clink of dishes came from the kitchen. His Abuela emerged, carrying two steaming

STEALING MEXICO

bowls of caldo de pollo, her warm smile softening the tension in the room. She set the bowls on the coffee table with care.

"Here you go, mijo," she said, her tone affectionate as she glanced between them. "Eat up. Both of you."

Carlos stared at her, dumbfounded. "What is this? You're feeding him now?"

Abuela shrugged, unbothered. "He's here, isn't he? Can't let him starve."

Asher leaned forward, the smell of the soup clearly winning him over. "Gracias, señora. Looks amazing."

Carlos sighed, running a hand over his damp hair as he sat on the arm of the couch. "You're like a stray dog," he muttered, watching Asher dive into the soup without hesitation. "Just show up uninvited and expect food."

Asher grinned mid-bite. "Maybe. But I'm house-trained. Mostly."

Abuela chuckled, wiping her hands on her apron. "He's funny, mijo. You could use more of that around here."

Carlos shot her a look, but she ignored him, retreating to the kitchen with a knowing smile.

For a moment, the only sound was the clink of spoons against bowls. Carlos watched Asher eat, the lines of irritation softening into something closer to curiosity. He hated how easily Asher had slipped into his space—how natural it felt, even when it shouldn't.

"You're too comfortable," Carlos said finally, his voice low. "What's the deal with you, anyway? You keep acting like you know something I don't."

Asher leaned back, spoon in hand, and gave him a lopsided grin. "Maybe I do."

Carlos arched a brow. "Try me."

Asher set his bowl down, his expression shifting to something more serious. "I think Holbrook's assistant is the one pulling the strings."

Carlos blinked, surprised by the abrupt shift. "Holbrook's assistant? What makes you think that?"

"Rumors, mostly," Asher admitted, his tone casual. "But it tracks. Holbrook's too much of a figurehead. Someone else has to be running things behind the scenes. And your guy? The assistant? He's got the perfect setup—close to the power, but far enough removed to stay out of the spotlight."

Carlos frowned, his mind turning over the information. It wasn't the first time he'd felt there was something off about the assistant, but Asher's certainty made it harder to dismiss.

"You have anything solid, or is this just another one of your hunches?" Carlos asked, his tone skeptical.

Asher shrugged, unbothered. "Not yet. But people like him? They always get sloppy. I'll find something."

Carlos stared at him, torn between irritation and a begrudging respect. As much as he hated to admit it, Asher had a point.

"Don't get ahead of yourself," Carlos muttered, picking up his spoon again. "We're not chasing ghosts."

"Who said anything about ghosts?" Asher's grin returned brighter than before. "This is just good investigative work, Santos. You should try it sometime."

Carlos rolled his eyes, focusing on his soup. Across from him, Asher's gaze lingered, and for once, he seemed to hesitate.

"You know," Asher said, his tone softening, "you don't have to do this alone."

Carlos froze, his spoon halfway to his mouth.

Asher continued, his voice quieter now. "I get it. You've probably been handling everything on your own for a long time. But sometimes, you need someone else to see things you can't."

Carlos felt a pang of discomfort—not because Asher was wrong, but because he was too close to the truth. He set the

STEALING MEXICO

spoon down, meeting Asher's gaze with a guarded expression.

"I'm not asking for help, Rhodes," Carlos said, his voice low and firm.

Asher didn't flinch. "I know. But maybe you should. And maybe you're starting to realize that."

For a moment, neither of them spoke. Carlos hated the way Asher's words settled in his chest, heavy and undeniable. He wanted to argue, to push him away, but the truth was harder to ignore than he'd like to admit.

Abuela's voice drifted in from the kitchen, light and teasing. "Mijo, don't be so stubborn. Pride solves nothing."

Carlos groaned, running a hand over his face. Asher smirked, clearly enjoying the moment.

"See? Even your Abuela agrees with me," Asher said.

"Don't push your luck," Carlos warned, but his tone lacked bite.

Asher leaned back, his grin impossibly smug. "Too late."

Carlos stared at his soup, stirring it absentmindedly. He hated how easily Asher had gotten under his skin—how natural it felt to have him there, even when it shouldn't.

And that, more than anything, was what scared him.

CHAPTER 17

CARLOS

Carlos lay sprawled across his bed, flipping through Diego's notes, half-absorbing the scrawled words while his thoughts wandered back to earlier that day—to Asher.

He'd never met anyone so exasperating. Brash, nosy, and relentless, Asher had a way of prying into every corner of Carlos's life without permission, as if he belonged there. And yet…

Carlos clenched his jaw, annoyed with himself. It wasn't just Asher's words that lingered in his mind. It was the way Asher leaned in when he challenged him, the spark in his blue eyes when Carlos snapped back, and that infuriating smirk. Damn it. This wasn't the time, and Asher wasn't the person. Yet the thoughts wouldn't go away, sneaking in even as he tried to focus on the case.

He flipped another page, forcing himself to concentrate. Diego's handwriting was meticulous in places, chaotic in others. Names, dates, scattered observations—all the marks of someone uncovering a thread of something larger. But just as Carlos was thinking he'd find nothing new, his gaze caught a scribble along the inner edge of a page:

Holbrook.

STEALING MEXICO

Carlos sat up, his body tensing. Governor Holbrook. The name, underlined twice, surrounded by hastily drawn arrows. What the hell was Diego digging into?

Adrenaline jolted him back into focus. He flipped to another page and then another, tracing Diego's increasingly frantic notes. If this was about Holbrook, it wasn't just some high school project. Diego was onto something serious—maybe too serious.

Carlos's heart thudded as he grabbed Diego's laptop and opened the encrypted folder. He stared at the password field, his fingers hovering over the keys. His mind replayed the notes he'd seen earlier, piecing together Diego's patterns.

Holbrook.

Carlos typed in the letters, holding his breath as he pressed Enter.

The screen flickered, and the file unlocked.

"Holy…" he muttered, his voice barely above a whisper. The flood of documents was overwhelming—charts, spreadsheets, photos, emails. Each file seemed more damning than the last.

He leaned forward, scanning the screen as his pulse raced. Diego hadn't just stumbled onto something. He'd uncovered a trail, and Carlos was following it straight into a minefield.

His thoughts raced as he grabbed his phone, dialing before he could second-guess himself.

It rang once.

"Carlos?" Asher's voice was groggy but instantly recognizable.

Carlos didn't waste time. "I got it," he said, his voice low and urgent.

There was a pause, then a rustling sound, like Asher was sitting up. "Got what?"

"The files. On Diego's laptop. They're about Holbrook." Carlos grabbed a shirt, tugging it over his head as he spoke. "I'm coming over."

Another pause, longer this time. Then Asher's voice came through, laced with surprise and a hint of something else Carlos couldn't quite name. "Guess I'll put on some coffee."

The line went dead.

Carlos exhaled, grounding himself at the moment. He didn't think twice about the hour, or what it meant to be heading to Asher's place in the middle of the night. Right now, none of that mattered.

But as he grabbed his keys and headed out the door, a small, unwelcome thought crept into the back of his mind.

He wasn't just letting Asher into the case. He was letting him in—period.

And that was a dangerous line to cross.

CHAPTER 18

Asher rubbed his eyes, blinking away the haze of drowsiness as he tugged on a pair of sweatpants. It was after midnight, and though the coffee machine hummed quietly in the kitchen, the buzz of anticipation did more to keep him awake than any caffeine ever could. He rifled through a chaotic pile of clothes for a shirt, deciding on a plain black one, when a knock echoed through the apartment.

Carlos.

Asher opened the door to find the detective standing there, Diego's laptop tucked securely under one arm. His gaze flicked over Carlos, taking in the casual gray sweatpants and a fitted shirt that hugged his chest and shoulders a little too well. This was a far cry from Carlos's usual crisp button-up professionalism—striking differently. Casual. Relaxed. Kind of... hot.

"I got into the file," Carlos said, his voice low and deliberate. His gaze swept over Asher in a brief, appraising glance, sparking an unfamiliar heat that settled somewhere between Asher's chest and his stomach.

"Well, come on in, Detective." Asher stepped aside, schooling his expression into something neutral despite the

STEALING MEXICO

way Carlos's presence seemed to fill the room. He motioned him inside, noting Carlos's momentary hesitation before he stepped over the threshold.

Carlos glanced around, his sharp eyes scanning the organized chaos of Asher's living room. Papers and notebooks precariously stacked on the coffee table supported an empty mug, while a heap of laundry had claimed the couch.

"Messy," Carlos observed, the faintest trace of amusement lacing his voice.

Asher shrugged, closing the door behind him. "I call it strategic clutter. I know exactly where everything is." He cleared a spot on the couch and gestured for Carlos to sit.

They settled in side by side, the laptop placed between them, their shoulders nearly brushing. Carlos opened the file, the glow of the screen reflecting in his dark eyes as the folder loaded. Their knees were so close they almost touched as they both leaned in.

The screen filled with documents—photos, email screenshots, spreadsheets. Asher's stomach tightened at the sheer volume of information.

"Damn," he murmured, his voice low, tinged with awe. He glanced sideways at Carlos, his words a near whisper. "You think he uncovered something? Something big?"

Carlos didn't look up, his gaze fixed on the screen with laser-sharp focus. "He was onto something. And whatever it was… it got him killed."

Asher reached for the laptop, their hands brushing. The warmth of Carlos's skin startled him, a jolt of electricity shooting up his arm. He masked the reaction by clicking on the first document in the folder. Carlos shifted closer, the quiet gravity of his presence both comforting and unnerving.

The document loaded, revealing a meticulous list of names, addresses, and financial transactions. Donations. Several of the aliases sparked recognition in Asher's mind, names he'd come across during his work at the Phoenix

Ledger. Politicians. CEOs. Entertainment figures. High-profile individuals funneling money under pseudonyms, their contributions tied to shadowy organizations with no public record.

Asher's heart thudded in his chest as his gaze darted to Carlos. The weight of the discovery hung heavy between them.

"What the hell?" Carlos muttered, his voice low but sharp with disbelief.

Asher swallowed, his throat dry. "Is this... real?" he asked, turning to Carlos, searching his face for some sign of certainty, something solid to hold on to in the storm of questions swirling in his head.

Carlos exhaled slowly, his brow furrowed as he leaned back slightly. His expression was grim, thoughtful. "It looks real enough," he said, his voice edged with quiet anger. "Diego stumbled onto this, and someone made sure he'd never talk about it."

The room fell into a tense silence, the only sound the hum of Asher's coffee maker in the background. Neither of them spoke, but the weight of what they'd just uncovered was palpable—an invisible thread linking them to something far larger and far more dangerous than either of them had imagined.

For the first time since they started working together, Asher saw the cracks in Carlos's armor. The quiet determination on his face wasn't just about justice—it was personal.

And Asher couldn't shake the feeling that they'd just stepped into something they weren't ready for.

PART TWO

CHAPTER 19

CARLOS

Morning sunlight spilled through the half-open blinds of Carlos's office, illuminating the cluttered desk where Diego's laptop sat surrounded by scattered notes and photos. Carlos leaned back in his chair, pinching the bridge of his nose, exhaustion sinking deep into his bones. Two days. He had been poring over Diego's files for two days straight, leaving his house only for the occasional caffeine run.

Diego had been meticulous. Carlos scrolled through a detailed flowchart the kid had created, his finger hovering over a web of connections—names, companies, shadowy organizations. Diego had carefully mapped out links between seemingly unrelated entities, exposing a network of political contributions funneled through dummy corporations, all circling back to the same handful of powerful individuals.

It wasn't just corruption. It was a well-oiled machine. A network pulling strings behind the scenes, shaping policies, and lining pockets.

"Damn, kid," Carlos muttered, running a hand over his face.

The password to Diego's locked folder had been "Holbrook." It didn't take a detective to connect that to Governor

STEALING MEXICO

Charles Holbrook. Yet, despite combing through every file, Carlos had found nothing directly linking the governor to the network. Why use Holbrook's name as a password, unless Diego suspected something?

The frustration gnawed at him as he stood and stretched, his back cracking from hours hunched over his desk. From the kitchen, his Abuela's voice carried down the hall.

"Carlos! Come eat something before you waste away, like a ghost in my house!"

He walked to the kitchen, drawn by the smell of her homemade chilaquiles. His Abuela glanced at him as he entered, her sharp eyes narrowing.

"How many nights has it been now, mijo?" she asked, sliding a plate toward him.

Carlos shrugged, avoiding her gaze. "A couple. It's not a big deal, Abuela."

She planted her hands on her hips, giving him a look that brooked no argument. "Whatever you're doing, it can wait. You work too much, and you forget to live. One day, you'll regret it."

Carlos smiled faintly, but her words stayed with him as he sat down, picking at his food. She was right—she always was. His mind drifted to Asher. Maybe she had a point.

When he returned to his office, he flipped through another notebook, more out of habit than hope, when a thought struck him. Asher had a knack for spotting patterns, for noticing the things that slipped past others. Carlos hesitated, his finger hovering over his phone.

Finally, he dialed.

After two rings, a groggy voice answered. "Carlos? Do you know what time it is?"

Carlos ignored the guilt and cut to the point. "I need to come over. There's something about this Holbrook connection that doesn't add up. Diego used his name for a reason, but I can't find it. I need a fresh set of eyes."

A pause. Then, the sound of rustling blankets. "I was beginning to think you forgot about me. Coffee's on me."

Carlos hung up, grabbed the laptop, and headed out.

The mid-morning Arizona sun was already blazing, the heat wrapping around him like a smothering blanket. But it wasn't the heat that made his stomach tighten as he knocked on Asher's door.

When the door swung open, the sight of Asher greeted Carlos—shirtless, sleep-mussed, and wearing nothing but a pair of sweatpants slung low on his hips. For a moment, Carlos forgot why he was there.

"Carlos," Asher said, his lips curving into a half-smile.

Carlos's gaze swept over him before he caught himself—clearing his throat. Focus. "Would you put on some clothes? We have work to do, and I need coffee."

Asher smirked, clearly amused. "Good morning to you, too." He stepped aside, letting Carlos in.

Carlos busied himself scanning Asher's living room—papers, empty mugs, and an inexplicably placed sock covered the coffee table and couch.

"Strategic clutter," Asher said, stretching as he disappeared into his bedroom to get dressed. "Don't touch anything—I know where everything is—mostly."

By the time Asher returned, now dressed in a snug t-shirt that didn't help Carlos's focus much, he looked more awake and no less smug.

"Alright, partner. Let's get to work," Asher said, brushing past Carlos as he grabbed his keys.

The word settled between them, heavy and strangely comforting. Carlos didn't protest this time.

STEALING MEXICO

As they walked out into the heat, Carlos glanced at Asher out of the corner of his eye. He wouldn't admit it out loud, but the guy's charm, irritating as it could be, was growing on him. Maybe, just maybe, Abuela was right. Life wasn't just about work.

Carlos shook his head, a faint smile tugging at his lips. This guy's going to drive me insane, he thought. And, to his surprise, he didn't mind the idea as much as he should.

CHAPTER 20

ASHER

Asher strolled up to the coffee shop counter, scanning the menu as though he didn't already have Carlos's coffee order committed to memory. It wasn't like Carlos had ever changed it—black coffee, no frills, as straightforward as the man himself.

The barista placed the drinks on the counter with a cheerful "Two coffees," and Asher snapped out of his thoughts. He thanked her with a smile before turning back toward the booth where Carlos had already settled in.

Carlos sat hunched forward, arms crossed on the table as he stared into the middle distance, clearly miles deep into his own mind. Even from across the room, Carlos exuded a quiet intensity, the kind that made people instinctively lower their voices when they walked past. Asher's gaze lingered on him longer than it probably should have.

He set the coffee in front of Carlos and slid into the seat opposite him.

Carlos barely glanced up, his fingers tapping an irregular rhythm on the side of his cup. "Holbrook?"

"Holbrook?" Asher echoed, leaning back with a casual shrug. "I know people tread carefully around him. His public

STEALING MEXICO

image is squeaky clean, but…" He let his voice trail off, gauging Carlos's reaction.

Carlos nodded, his sharp gaze locking onto Asher's. "Diego used his name as the password to that folder," he said. "Why would he do that? Unless he suspected that Holbrook was involved in all of this?"

"Maybe Diego wasn't just suspicious," Asher suggested. "Maybe he had something solid—or he was getting close to it."

Carlos didn't respond immediately, his jaw tightening as he stared out the window. "Diego didn't have anything concrete in the files. It's all breadcrumbs, nothing you could use to prove anything. But…" He exhaled slowly, rubbing the bridge of his nose. "He was onto something, no question about it. Holbrook's name isn't there for no reason."

Asher frowned, his mind racing as he sipped his coffee. "If Holbrook is really involved, maybe Diego was trying to play it safe, keeping things vague until he could make his move. That's a big target to take on."

Carlos's voice was quieter now, almost thoughtful. "He was just a kid trying to do the right thing. And he got killed for it."

The weight in Carlos's tone made Asher pause. Diego wasn't just another name in a file to him—this case was personal.

"Carlos," Asher said gently, leaning forward. "We're going to figure this out. Diego might not have gotten the chance to finish what he started, but we will. I'm with you on this."

Carlos's dark eyes met Asher's, and for a moment, the tension between them shifted, something unspoken passing through the air. Asher felt his heartbeat pick up, the intensity of Carlos's gaze almost overwhelming. But then, just as quickly, Carlos broke the connection, straightening in his seat.

"We need to go over everything again," Carlos said, his

voice back to business. "If Diego found anything concrete, it has to be buried in those connections he was mapping out."

"Agreed," Asher replied, stirring his coffee absently, though his thoughts were far from the case. He watched Carlos's hands as they moved, the firm lines of his jaw as he spoke, and his mind wandered to that night at his apartment. Seeing Carlos out of his perfectly pressed work clothes, relaxed and—dare he say—comfortable, had done something to him.

"Are you listening, or am I talking to myself?" Carlos's sharp tone cut through Asher's thoughts.

Asher blinked, snapping his gaze back to Carlos. "Sorry, yeah. Just thinking."

Carlos raised a brow but didn't press further. "If we're going to take this higher, we'll need more than speculation. Holbrook's the kind of guy who doesn't crack under pressure, so we have to be smart about this."

Asher nodded, forcing himself to focus, but it wasn't easy. The way Carlos commanded the room—even a coffee shop booth—was distracting. Infuriatingly so.

But as Carlos kept talking, Asher couldn't help but notice the faint softness in his voice now, the cracks in his armor that he tried so hard to keep hidden. And Asher realized he wasn't just drawn to Carlos because of his intensity. It was the way Carlos cared, the way he fought for people—even when it hurt him.

Carlos might have been guarded, but Asher could see the man behind the walls. And whether or not Carlos liked it, Asher was starting to think he wanted to stick around long enough to break through them.

CHAPTER 21

CARLOS

Carlos pushed open the door to Captain Marissa Davis's office, and the familiar weight of her gaze immediately landed on him. She hadn't expected him—he knew that much from the flicker of surprise in her eyes. She hadn't expected him to return after two days of silence, with the case growing colder by the minute, and with everything about to explode. But what really threw her off was the figure behind him—Asher.

"Well, look who it is," Marissa said, her voice dripping with sarcasm. Her eyes flicked from Carlos to Asher, narrowing with suspicion. "I wasn't aware we were hosting a press conference today. Got a new reporter in tow, Santos?"

Carlos could feel the heat rising in his neck, irritation biting at the back of his throat. "Asher's here to help with the investigation," he replied, his voice a little tighter than he meant it to be.

. "Right," Marissa scoffed, her arms folding across her chest as she leaned back in her chair. "You've been missing for two days, and now you waltz in with him. You're in over your head, Carlos, if you think bringing a journalist into this mess will help." Her gaze lingered on Asher, sharp and calculating.

STEALING MEXICO

"This isn't some cozy minor story for the paper. You're investigating a murder. A high-profile one."

Before Carlos could respond, Asher cut in, his voice steady and measured. "Captain, with all due respect, we've uncovered information that ties the investigation to Governor Holbrook. If there's even the smallest chance of corruption at that level, we have a responsibility to follow it."

Carlos could feel the air shift. Marissa's entire demeanor changed in an instant—her eyes narrowed, her shoulders tensed. She was suddenly all business, the stakes raising exponentially in her mind. The room, once filled with the low hum of the station, seemed to close in around them.

"Hold on." Marissa stood, her chair scraping against the floor as she leaned over her desk, locking eyes with Carlos. Her voice dropped, low and dangerously controlled. "You're suggesting that this investigation—this murder—could lead back to the Governor's office?" She repeated the words like she needed to hear them again, to make sure they weren't just some fever dream.

Carlos nodded, keeping his posture steady despite the rising tension. "It's circumstantial, but the connections are there."

"Circumstantial?" Marissa's voice rose, slicing through the air with a sharp edge. "You're talking about a sitting governor. Do you have any idea what you're getting into? You're telling me that we, the Phoenix PD, are going to open a case against Holbrook—on suspicion?" Her voice shook with a mixture of disbelief and a hint of fear.

Carlos felt the heat of her gaze. This was bigger than he had anticipated, bigger than any case he had worked before. But he couldn't back down now. "It's more than just suspicion," he said firmly, forcing himself to stand his ground. "We're looking at a complex web. Diego was on the trail of something serious. Holbrook's people are connected to it. We have to follow the lead."

98

Marissa's eyes flashed with something darker. She paced in a tight circle around her desk, her mind racing, the words tumbling from her mouth with barely controlled panic. "Carlos, you have to understand. This is dangerous. Really dangerous. Holbrook's got an army of lawyers, of connections everywhere. Whispering his name in connection with this case will crush you. The department won't survive it. Your career won't survive it."

Asher, standing at Carlos's side, spoke again, his voice cutting through the tension. "But if we let it slide, if we ignore even the hint of corruption at that level—don't we lose all integrity in this investigation? The people have a right to know the truth."

Marissa's gaze snapped to Asher with the force of a strike. "You," she spat, voice dripping with contempt. "As a journalist, your role is reporting, not law enforcement. You don't understand what this means. The potential impact of this is beyond your comprehension. You're playing with fire, and I'm telling you right now, it's not worth it."

Carlos felt the weight of her words pressing down on him, but he couldn't stop now. He couldn't back down. "It's not just about the case anymore, Captain. It's about more than just Diego's murder. There's a network of corruption that needs to be exposed."

Marissa took a step forward, her eyes blazing. "And I'm telling you that if you go down that road, you better be prepared for the fallout. It's not just your career that's at risk. This department? Everything we've worked for—everything you've worked for—it'll be gone in a heartbeat. You think this investigation is tough? Wait until the real fight comes. You don't want to cross Holbrook."

Carlos felt a chill seep into his bones. She was right. He had always known it would be dangerous, but hearing it from her—he realized just how much was at stake. The lines were blurring now, the investigation spiraling into something he hadn't expected. Something bigger.

Asher's voice broke through the tension, quieter this time, but insistent. "I get it, Captain. You're trying to protect him, but—"

Marissa cut him off, her tone venomous. "I'm trying to protect you." She turned back to Carlos, her eyes softer but still heavy with concern. "You're stepping into a battle you're not ready for. Do you really want to bring this down on yourself? On all of us?"

The weight of her words hung in the air, thick with threat. For a moment, Carlos didn't say anything. He just let the silence settle between them, feeling the pull of everything that was at stake.

Finally, he spoke, his voice quieter than before but still unwavering. "I'll be careful, Captain. But I'm not backing down. We're doing this. For Diego."

Marissa's eyes flickered, the concern still there, but she was no longer trying to stop him. Instead, her gaze softened with reluctant acceptance. "Fine," she muttered, the weight of resignation in her voice. "But you're on your own, Santos. I'm not getting tangled in this. And if you end up buried under a mountain of dirt, I don't know if I'll be able to pull you out."

Carlos nodded. He had expected as much. He knew the risks. But there was no turning back.

As Carlos left Marissa's office, the air felt heavier, like the walls of the station had closed in around him. He didn't know how to feel—conflicted, sure, but more than anything, he felt the pressure of the investigation mounting. Asher fell into step beside him, his presence a constant now, his silence somehow louder than any words.

"Do you get it now?" Carlos asked quietly, his voice low, still heavy with the weight of Marissa's warning. "This isn't just another case. We're in too deep."

Asher nodded, his expression serious. "I get it, Carlos. And I'm with you. No matter what."

Carlos turned to look at him, surprised by the sincerity in his voice, a sincerity he hadn't fully seen before. And for a split second, it hit him—the weight of everything they'd uncovered, and how far they were willing to go to see it through. He didn't know what it meant for them, for their partnership... but right then, he didn't care.

All that mattered was the truth.

CHAPTER 22

ASHER

The reception room was a sterile oasis of polished marble floors and campaign posters that shouted Governor Holbrook's promises for a brighter future. Colorful banners with smiling faces, all but begging for votes, lined the walls, and the hum of staffers buzzing through the space only added to the electric tension in the air. It was election season, and everyone was working overtime to make sure the Governor's re-election campaign went off without a hitch.

But none of that was in Asher's head. He wasn't concerned with elections or politics; his mind was consumed with Carlos.

Carlos sat a few feet away, his attention split between the notebook in his hands and the occasional flicker of his gaze that found its way to Asher. The intensity in those eyes was enough to make the air feel thick, like Carlos could see straight through him. The silence between them was never quite comfortable. It felt like there was so much more unsaid than spoken.

Asher had always read people—had made a career out of it, in fact—but Carlos was different. The man was an enigma. Dark, quiet, but never closed off in a way that made Asher

STEALING MEXICO

feel unwelcome. He was just... guarded. Asher couldn't figure out if it was a defense mechanism or if that was simply who Carlos was. And it drove him crazy. But it also sparked something in Asher—something he didn't fully understand.

It wasn't just the case anymore. It wasn't just the investigation they were tangled in. Asher was starting to feel like there was more to Carlos than just the hardened cop who had haunted his thoughts since that first night they met. He felt the pull—the magnetic force that was both thrilling and terrifying. Carlos had this quiet power about him, a raw intensity that made Asher's chest tighten when he looked at him for too long.

Carlos's jaw clenched slightly as he flipped through the pages of his notebook, the movement sharp, almost calculated. Asher wanted to ask him about it—whatever had him so closed off. But he knew better than to pry.

The silence stretched, thick and uncomfortable. Asher was trying to concentrate on the investigation, on the looming confrontation with Holbrook, but his thoughts kept circling back to Carlos. His instincts—the ones that had always served him so well—told him there was something more between them than the polite tension they were playing at.

But now wasn't the time. Not with the stakes this high.

"So..." Asher started, breaking the silence, his voice slightly rough. "What happened to your parents?"

Carlos stiffened immediately. His body went rigid, and Asher saw him draw in a deep breath before slowly looking up, his eyes unreadable. "I'd rather not talk about that," Carlos replied, his tone sharp and defensive.

The words cut through the air, and the brief flicker of vulnerability in Carlos's eyes was gone in an instant. Asher felt his heart sink a little, the question hanging between them like a phantom.

He opened his mouth to apologize, to backpedal, but the words caught in his throat. It wasn't his place to push. He respected Carlos's boundaries, even if he didn't fully understand them.

"Sorry," Asher muttered, looking away, trying to give him space. But the weight of the silence settled back between them, deeper than before.

Trying to shift the mood, Asher looked for something else to talk about, anything that wouldn't send them spiraling into that uncomfortable silence again. "Your Abuela seems nice. She seems... pretty supportive of you," he ventured, his voice softening in an attempt to keep things light.

Carlos's lips twitched into something like a smile, but it didn't quite reach his eyes. "She's old-fashioned. Always pushing me to find someone... a novio or novia," Carlos said, his voice softening just slightly. But even as he spoke, there was a shadow crossing his features, something Asher couldn't quite place.

"You don't seem too into it," Asher teased gently, hoping to draw out a more playful side of him.

Carlos's shrug was nonchalant, but the tightness in his expression gave him away. "I'm not exactly looking for a relationship right now."

"Yeah, I get it." Asher tried to keep the conversation casual, but his heart skipped at the thought of Carlos not being interested in anything more than the case. He wanted to push again, ask why, but he knew better than to ask something that personal. Carlos had never been one to open up easily. And after the brush-off, Asher wasn't sure he would get another chance to ask. "Focus on the case, right?"

"Right," Carlos replied, but there was something in his tone, something Asher couldn't quite read. His gaze flickered toward Asher, but the words that seemed to hang between them remained unspoken. The air was shifting, changing, and Asher could feel it. They were standing on the edge of something—whether it was the start of real understanding or something far more complicated, he couldn't tell.

STEALING MEXICO

Before he could linger on the thought, the door to the Governor's office swung open with a soft whoosh, and a neatly dressed aide stepped out. "Mr. Santos, Mr. Rhodes," the aide called, his tone crisp and professional. "The Governor will see you now."

Carlos stood up immediately, smoothing his jacket as he gave Asher a brief glance. It wasn't reassuring; it was the calm before the storm.

As they walked toward the door, Carlos leaned slightly toward him, voice low but firm. "Remember, we stick to the facts. No wild theories, okay?"

"Got it," Asher replied, forcing a smile. His insides churned with a mix of nerves and anticipation. He couldn't shake the feeling that the next few moments would change everything. It wasn't just about confronting the Governor anymore. It was about something else—something deeper, something between him and Carlos.

As they entered the office, the door closing softly behind them, Asher's mind raced. He was prepared to face Holbrook —to push for answers. But the more he thought about it, the more he wondered how much longer he could keep his feelings for Carlos buried.

For now, though, he'd focus on the case. Diego deserved justice. And maybe, just maybe, he'd uncover the mystery of Carlos, too.

CHAPTER 23

CARLOS

The air inside Governor Holbrook's office was thick with polished charm and unspoken tension. The room was every bit as curated as the man himself: sleek furniture, a massive mahogany desk, and walls adorned with framed accolades and photos with influential figures. Yet beneath the surface of this perfect image, Carlos could feel something twitching—like a string pulled too tight.

Governor Holbrook rose from behind his desk with a practiced smile that didn't quite reach his eyes. "Detective Santos, Mr. Rhodes," he said, his voice as smooth as the suit he wore. "What can I do for you today?"

Carlos ignored the pleasantries, stepping forward with deliberate calm. "We're here to ask a few questions, Governor. About Diego Cortez."

Holbrook's expression softened into a well-rehearsed mask of sorrow. "Ah, yes. Such a tragic loss. My heart goes out to his family. A bright young man taken far too soon." He paused, letting his words settle before adding, "But I'm not sure how I could assist. I've already spoken publicly about my condolences."

Carlos studied the man's reaction. The carefully measured

STEALING MEXICO

tone. The faint sheen of sweat beginning to glisten at his temple. "We believe Diego might have been looking into something important before his death," Carlos said. "Something big enough to put him in danger. Did he ever contact you or your office?"

Holbrook's smile faltered, just for a second. He recovered quickly, but the crack was there. "Detective, I don't... recall any direct contact. As you can imagine, my office receives hundreds of communications weekly, but I can assure you we take every concern seriously, especially when it involves the immigrant community."

"Diego wasn't just any concerned citizen," Carlos pressed, his voice low and even. "He was an activist. His research involved people connected to your office. Are you saying you never heard of him?"

"I—I'm not saying that," Holbrook stammered, his hands twitching slightly before clasping together on the desk. "It's possible he reached out in some capacity. But I don't personally handle every matter that crosses my desk, you understand. My staff—"

"Would have brought something this significant to your attention," Carlos finished, his sharp gaze pinning the governor in place. "Especially if it could impact your office. Or your reputation."

The room seemed to shrink as Holbrook's practiced demeanor cracked further. He shifted in his chair, glancing briefly at Asher, who was silently watching with a journalist's predatory focus. "Detective," Holbrook said, his tone turning defensive, "I don't appreciate the implication that I—"

"No one's implying anything, Governor," Carlos cut in smoothly, though his voice carried an edge. "But the more we dig, the clearer it becomes that Diego's work was striking a nerve. If there's anything you're not telling us—anything at all—it's going to come out. Better for you if it comes out now."

MATTI MARTINEZ

Holbrook's hand tightened around the armrest of his chair, the thin veneer of control slipping entirely. "I've already told you," he snapped, his voice rising slightly. "I didn't know the boy! Whatever he was involved in had nothing to do with me or my administration."

Carlos leaned in slightly, his tone sharp. "Interesting choice of words. You said, 'Whatever he was involved in.' How would you know what he was involved in if you didn't know him?"

Holbrook froze, the blood draining from his face. The silence stretched, heavy and damning.

"I—I only meant..." Holbrook trailed off, scrambling for a coherent response. "It was a poor choice of words, Detective. Don't twist this into something it's not."

Carlos straightened, his mind racing as red flags flared in every corner. "Of course, Governor," he said, his tone neutral but clipped. "If anything else comes to mind, you know how to reach me."

Holbrook didn't respond immediately, his jaw tight as he forced a strained smile. "I'll be sure to do that."

The moment they stepped out of Governor Holbrook's office, Carlos's instincts kicked into high gear. The exchange inside had left an unpleasant taste in his mouth. Holbrook's carefully constructed facade had cracked under pressure, and his slip of the tongue had sent Carlos's thoughts racing.

"You caught that, right?" Carlos muttered as they hurried toward the exit.

"Oh, I caught it," Asher said, his voice low but electric. "You think he knew Diego?"

"Without a doubt," Carlos muttered, his eyes scanning the lobby. "The way he panicked? He's hiding something. We just don't know what yet."

As they descended the grand marble staircase leading to the exit, Carlos felt it—a subtle prickle at the back of his neck. Someone was watching them. His gaze swept the

109

STEALING MEXICO

crowd, landing on a man leaning against a column near the entrance.

The man was sharp-dressed, blending seamlessly into the flow of suits and ties bustling through the government building. But something about the way he stood, too still, too focused, set off alarms in Carlos's mind. His dark eyes locked onto Carlos for a fraction of a second before sliding away, feigning disinterest.

"You okay?" Asher asked, glancing at him.

Carlos didn't answer immediately. "See the guy by the column near the door?" he asked under his breath.

Asher frowned, subtly shifting his head to look. "The one in the suit? What about him?"

"He's watching us," Carlos said. "Been standing there since we came down. Act natural and keep walking."

Asher's lips pressed into a thin line, but he obeyed, quickening his pace alongside Carlos. "Think he's with Holbrook?"

"Could be."

The warm Arizona sunlight hit them as they exited the building, but the weight of the stranger's gaze didn't fade. Carlos caught a faint reflection of the man in a nearby window, trailing at a careful distance.

"He's following us," Carlos whispered.

"What do we do?" Asher asked, his voice tight.

Carlos considered their options, his mind moving quickly. If this guy was connected to Holbrook—or worse, to whoever killed Diego—they needed to find out his intentions.

"You're going to the car," Carlos said firmly.

Asher scoffed. "You really think I'm going to just—"

"Yes, you are," Carlos snapped, his tone brooking no argument. "Take a different route and stay alert. I'll handle him."

"As much as I enjoy playing bait, this doesn't sound like a splendid plan," Asher muttered, but he started moving toward the parking lot.

Carlos slowed his steps, giving the man time to catch up. Sure enough, he saw the shadow of his follower closing the gap.

Good. Let's see what you want.

He turned a corner, stepping into an alley that opened onto a bustling street. It was quieter here, just the hum of traffic and the murmur of a few pedestrians. Carlos glanced behind him.

The man was still there, closer now.

Carlos quickened his pace, pretending to be unaware. At the last second, he slipped into another alley, breaking into a sprint as he tried to circle back around and catch his pursuer off guard.

But when he emerged back onto the street, the man was gone.

Carlos cursed under his breath, his chest heaving. The crowd surged around him, oblivious to the tension that crackled in the air. Whoever the man was, he was good—too good. Carlos had lost him, but the encounter left him with more questions than answers.

He turned back toward the parking lot, weaving through the flow of pedestrians until he reached his car. Sliding into the driver's seat, he scanned the crowd one last time, searching for any sign of the stranger.

Nothing.

Carlos exhaled sharply and gripped the steering wheel, his pulse still racing. A minute later, his phone buzzed with a text from Asher:

Almost there. You good?

Carlos quickly replied.

Yeah. Just get here.

STEALING MEXICO

As he waited, the unease lingered, curling in his chest like smoke. Whoever the man was, one thing was clear: they weren't just being watched. They were being hunted.

CHAPTER 24

ASHER

Asher glanced at his phone, Carlos's text glaring back at him like a lifeline.

> Yeah. Just get here.

His fingers gripped the edges of the phone as he let out a shaky breath, relief flooding him. Carlos was safe. For now.

Turning back the way he came, Asher weaved through the thinning crowd, his heart still hammering in his chest. Something was wrong, and Asher couldn't shake the feeling that the danger was closer than ever.

He glanced over his shoulder, his eyes darting to every shadow and unfamiliar face. A cold knot of dread twisted in his stomach as the city's buzz seemed to fade into the background.

Almost there. Just a few more blocks.

Then it happened.

A hand like a steel vice clamped down on his arm and yanked him with bone-jarring force into a narrow alley. His phone clattered to the ground as he stumbled, the rough shove slamming his back against a wall of cold brick. The

STEALING MEXICO

wind rushed out of his lungs with the impact, leaving him gasping for air.

"Hey! What the—"

The words barely escaped before he saw him—the man from earlier. Shadow shrouded his face, but his eyes glinted with predatory sharpness, chilling Asher.

"What are you doing here?" the man growled, his voice low and dripping with malice.

Asher struggled against the grip pinning him to the wall, but it was useless. The man was stronger, his body blocking any escape. "I don't know what you're talking about," Asher shot back, his voice cracking despite his best effort to sound defiant.

The man's lips curled into a cruel smirk. "Wrong answer."

Before Asher could react, the man's fist slammed into his stomach, knocking the breath out of him in a brutal rush. He doubled over, coughing, his ribs screaming in protest as pain radiated through his body.

"Let's try that again," the man said, his tone almost conversational now, as if they weren't in a filthy alley and Asher wasn't fighting to stay upright. "Why are you sniffing around places you don't belong?"

Asher forced himself to straighten, his hands braced against the wall for support. "I'm a journalist," he spat, his voice hoarse but steady. "It's my job to ask questions."

The man chuckled darkly, shaking his head. "Brave, huh? Or just stupid?"

Before Asher could respond, the man's hand shot to his waistband. The glint of metal under the dim streetlight made Asher's stomach drop. Though small, the knife was sufficient. The blade gleamed wickedly as the man pressed it against Asher's neck.

The cool steel bit into his skin. Not enough to draw blood, but enough to remind Asher how thin the line between life and death was.

"You think this is a game?" the man hissed, his face inches from Asher's. "I could slit your throat right now, and no one would even hear you scream over this city's noise."

Asher's chest heaved, his mind racing for something—anything—that might get him out of this alive. "If you kill me, you'll just draw attention," he choked out, forcing his voice not to tremble. "People will ask questions. Is that what you want?"

The man's grip on the knife tightened, the edge pressing harder against Asher's throat. "You've got some nerve," he said, his voice like a snarl. "But the nerve won't save you. Stay away from the Governor. Stay away from the kid. You keep digging, and you'll end up just like that Cortez boy."

Diego. Asher's eyes widened despite himself, his fear briefly overtaken by a surge of anger. "What did you do to Diego?"

The man sneered, his free hand grabbing a fistful of Asher's shirt. "I warned you once, journalist. Don't make me warn you again."

Asher gritted his teeth, trying to hide the way his body trembled. "You're scared," he said, his voice low but steady. "That's why you're doing this. You know we're close to something."

For a second, just a flicker of a second, the man's expression faltered. Then, with a furious growl, he slammed Asher against the wall again, the impact rattling through him.

"You talk too much," the man spat.

Asher gasped for air, his head spinning from the pain and lack of oxygen. He could feel the knife's edge scrape against his skin, a sharp—biting warning.

But then, just as quickly as it started, the pressure eased. The man pulled back, the knife disappearing back into his waistband with a flick of his wrist.

"Consider this your last warning," the man said, his voice

STEALING MEXICO

cold and final. "Stay out of it, or next time, I won't be so gentle."

Asher slumped against the wall as the man turned and melted into the shadows of the alley. For a moment, all he could do was breathe, his chest heaving as he tried to steady himself.

Then reality crashed back in. He scrambled for his phone, his hands trembling as he picked it up from the ground. Without thinking, he bolted out of the alley, his legs carrying him faster than they ever had before.

The sight of Carlos's car was like a beacon in the darkness. Asher practically threw himself into the passenger seat, slamming the door behind him.

"Carlos," he panted, clutching his side as he tried to catch his breath. "We need to go. Now."

Carlos turned to him, his sharp gaze scanning him for injuries. His jaw tightened as he saw Asher's disheveled state. "What the hell happened?"

Asher wiped at his neck, his hand coming away faintly red where the knife had grazed him. "That guy—he grabbed me. He knows. About us, about Diego. And he's serious, Carlos. He said—"

Carlos's knuckles whitened around the steering wheel. "He said what?"

Asher swallowed hard, the man's words still echoing in his head. "That if we keep digging, we're dead."

Carlos didn't respond immediately. He shifted the car into gear, his expression a mask of barely controlled fury. "Then we dig faster," he said, his voice sharp and resolute.

The car roared to life as they sped away, leaving the alley —and the threat it held—behind them. But Asher knew this wasn't over. Not by a long shot.

CHAPTER 25

CARLOS

Carlos yanked Asher through the front door, slamming it shut behind them. The sound rang through the house, harsh and final. For a moment, the world outside—the chaos, the danger—seemed to fade away, leaving only the two of them in the stillness of the quiet home.

Asher collapsed onto the dining room chair, his face pale, the color drained from his skin. Carlos flicked the light switch, his heart sinking when he saw the dark crimson line across Asher's neck. His blood ran cold.

The mark was jagged, stark against Asher's skin, and Carlos could feel his anger rising, burning hot. He closed the distance between them in a few long strides, kneeling in front of Asher. The sight of the wound, the sight of Asher looking so damn vulnerable, set something primal inside Carlos off.

"What the hell happened?" His voice was low, dangerous.

Asher flinched slightly, but didn't pull away. His eyes darted around the room, still processing the ordeal. "He grabbed me in the alley," he began, voice shaky, but his eyes met Carlos's. "He said he knew exactly what we were investigating. Told me to stay away from the kid."

Carlos's jaw tightened. "What kid?" His mind raced.

STEALING MEXICO

Asher swallowed hard. "He didn't say a name. Just 'the kid.' Then he pulled a knife—held it to my neck. Told me if I didn't back off, I'd be the next one to end up dead."

Carlos clenched his fists at his sides, trying to contain the fury that was bubbling up inside him. His heart pounded, his mind reeling. This was it—this was the first real threat they'd faced.

"Did you get a good look at him?" Carlos asked, his voice strained with urgency.

Asher nodded, his eyes flickering with the memory of the encounter. "Yeah, he was tall—around six feet, dark hair. He had this... look in his eyes, Carlos. Like he could kill me without a second thought... and the way he held that knife... it was like he knew exactly what he was doing."

The weight of Asher's words settled heavily between them. The room seemed to close in, the silence stretching long as Carlos's mind worked through the implications. He took a step back, his eyes narrowing. He did not need confirmation —didn't need to ask more questions. This was bigger than just Diego now. This was a warning—a personal one.

"We need to figure out who that guy is," Carlos said, his tone hard. "We can't let this go. Not after what he just did. He's working for someone—this threat didn't come out of nowhere."

Asher let out a shaky breath. "I know, Carlos. But we're not just dealing with some random thug. This... this guy's dangerous. I'm not sure I want to know what'll happen if we stop digging deeper."

Carlos's jaw clenched as he moved closer to Asher. His anger flared at the thought of someone threatening him—of what could have happened if Asher hadn't gotten away. The image of the knife against Asher's throat, so close to taking everything from him, made Carlos's stomach twist.

"We need to be careful," Carlos said, his voice softer now, though his worry was clear. He reached out, his fingers brushing lightly against Asher's skin where the mark from the knife had been. It was a gentle touch, but it carried a weight of meaning, of things unsaid between them. "I'm not going to anyone hurt you."

Asher met his gaze, his own fear masked by a layer of determination. "I'm fine. I'll live." His eyes flickered briefly to the towel Carlos had grabbed, and he let out a soft sigh. "It's just a cut, Carlos."

But Carlos wasn't so sure. He grabbed a towel and eased it over Asher's neck, wiping away the blood, his movements careful. The sight of the injury, even as minor as it seemed compared to the threat, still made his blood run cold.

"This wasn't supposed to happen," Carlos muttered, his voice tight. "You shouldn't have been put in that position. I should have protected you. I should have been there."

Asher shrugged, trying to shake it off. "I don't need anyone to protect me."

Carlos froze, his hand lingering against Asher's neck longer than necessary, his breath catching. Something in the air shifted—an unspoken understanding between them. They weren't just partners in this case. They were something else. And the realization made Carlos's heart race in a way he couldn't ignore.

"We're not stopping," Carlos said, his voice hoarse. He straightened, stepping back and shaking his head, trying to force the emotions aside. "We need to get to the bottom of this before anyone else gets hurt."

Asher nodded, but Carlos could see the same lingering fear in his eyes. It wasn't just the threat they had to worry about. It was the reality that whoever was behind this was willing to do whatever it took to stop them from finding the truth.

And Carlos wasn't sure they were prepared for just how far this would go.

CHAPTER 26

ASHER

Asher stepped into the bustling Phoenix Ledger office, his pulse quickening. The usual noise—the clicking keyboards, ringing phones, and hum of conversations—seemed louder today, sharper, more oppressive. Ever since the incident in the alley, he'd been hyper-aware of everything around him. The echo of the man's threat still lingered in his mind, like a dark shadow that refused to fade. The knife against his skin, the cold edge of it, the sense that his life could have ended in that instant—it kept replaying over and over in his thoughts.

As he made his way through the maze of desks toward his own, he cast a quick glance around him. He wanted to dive into the Diego case, to dig deeper into Holbrook's connections, but he was careful. Who could he trust? For all he knew, someone in this office was feeding information right back to those involved in the web of corruption. He couldn't afford to be careless—not now.

His eyes landed on Mara, leaning against the edge of her desk. Her gaze followed him with an intensity that made his skin prickle. They'd worked together for over a year, covering stories side by side, but today, a cautious suspicion seemed to

STEALING MEXICO

radiate from her. He couldn't quite shake the feeling that something was off. As he approached, he did his best to keep his expression neutral.

"Hey, Ash," Mara greeted, standing up a little straighter. "Heard you've been investigating that college kid's case. Diego, right?"

Asher tensed. He forced a casual smile, but inside, his mind raced. "Yeah, just doing some digging," he replied, keeping it vague. "Nothing concrete yet."

"Come on, you're never 'just digging,'" she said, her voice low and teasing, but her eyes were sharp, probing. "You've been on it for days. What have you actually found?"

Asher's heart pounded, and his instincts screamed at him to be careful. He considered brushing her off with a throwaway answer, but the memory of the man in the alley made him wary. "Still piecing things together," he drawled. "Not enough to say anything definitive."

Mara crossed her arms, her eyes narrowing as if she were trying to read him. "You're sure? You're practically glued to this story—kind of unusual, even for you."

She was pressing too hard, and Asher could feel the distrust seeping into his bones. He'd always liked Mara, but today, something about her demeanor felt different. Her gaze was too calculating, too focused. He could almost feel the wheels turning in her mind, and it made him feel cornered.

"Look, it's just a story, Mara," he said, trying to sound casual. "Nothing worth diving into yet."

Mara's expression didn't soften. Instead, she leaned in a little closer, lowering her voice. "Doesn't seem like 'just a story' if you're going to these lengths. And now you're working with a detective on it? That's... different. You sure there's nothing else you can share? Because if this is as big as it seems, maybe we could crack it together."

Asher's chest tightened. He was used to trading information with colleagues, bouncing ideas off each other—but this felt different. With Diego's case, there were too many unknowns, too many risks. He couldn't afford to let his guard down. Not now. Not after what had just happened.

"I'm good on my own," he replied, his voice tight.

Mara raised an eyebrow, her expression skeptical. "Really? You're not usually this tight-lipped. We could both get something big out of this if you'd let me in."

He looked away, avoiding her gaze. "If I find anything worth reporting, you'll know," he said, his tone sharper than he intended.

Mara held his gaze for a moment, then let out a quiet sigh. "Fine," she replied, her voice tinged with irritation. "Just don't get so wrapped up in it, you forget how to be a team player."

As she walked away, Asher exhaled slowly, his shoulders tense. He couldn't shake the feeling that something wasn't right. Every face in the newsroom seemed a little too watchful, every glance a little too curious. He wasn't paranoid—he was just more aware than he'd ever been before.

He sat at his desk, opening his laptop and typing in Governor Holbrook's name. The screen filled with articles, campaign data, anything that might offer a glimpse into his connections. As he scrolled through, one headline caught his eye—Holbrook's promises to protect immigrant communities and fight hate crimes. Asher felt a bitter twist in his gut. The public image Holbrook projected was pristine, almost too perfect. A carefully curated lie, one that stood in stark contrast to the corruption and danger that seemed to swirl beneath the surface.

Asher's gaze flicked up, and he caught Mara's eyes again from across the room. She glanced away, but not before he saw the faint flicker of suspicion in her expression. He knew she didn't believe him, and the feeling only solidified his resolve.

He couldn't trust anyone—not here, not now. Carlos was

the only person he could count on. And for Diego's sake—
and his own—he wouldn't let anyone, not even Mara, get in
the way of finding the truth.

CHAPTER 27

CARLOS

Carlos stepped into Captain Davis's office, his mind still reeling from the events of the previous day. He'd barely slept, the image of Asher's pale face and the tension in his voice after the attack replaying in his head. They had talked little about it—Asher hadn't wanted to dwell on what had happened in the alley, but Carlos could see it in his eyes. The fear, the uncertainty. It was hard to miss, especially after the threat he'd received.

He didn't waste time. "Asher was attacked last night. After our meeting with Holbrook. The guy who went after him—he wasn't just some random thug. He knew exactly who Asher was. He knew what we were investigating. And he threatened Asher, said we needed to stop looking into things, or... Asher would end up like Diego."

Davis didn't flinch, her gaze sharpening as she leaned back in her chair. "Did you get a look at the guy?"

Carlos's eyes narrowed. "Yeah. I saw him too. He's about six feet tall, broad-shouldered, dark hair, some stubble. He was wearing a black jacket. Asher and I both saw him clearly."

Davis's expression was unreadable, but her fingers

STEALING MEXICO

drummed against the desk, a sign she was thinking it through. "You're sure this man is connected to Diego's case?"

Carlos nodded slowly, frustration rising in his chest. "One hundred percent. It's too much of a coincidence that we're followed, and Asher gets attacked right after we talk to Holbrook, though."

Davis leaned forward slightly, her voice measured but firm. "I don't want to jump to conclusions. Just because this man showed up doesn't automatically link him to Holbrook. It's suspicious, yes, but we can't assume we know everything just yet."

Carlos's jaw clenched. "Look, I know it's hard to make a direct connection, but the timing... it doesn't sit right. Holbrook got uncomfortable when we questioned him. He tried to deflect, acted like he didn't know anything about Diego or the issues we brought up. He was trying to hide something and there's too much lining up." Pausing, frustration lacing his tone. "I can't say for sure that Holbrook's involved, but everything points to him."

Davis studied him for a moment, her expression softening slightly. "I understand your frustration, Santos. But jumping to conclusions now could blow everything we've got. We need to be discreet about this. We can't let Holbrook or anyone else know we're looking into him too closely. If there's a connection, we'll find it. But right now, we need to stay low."

Carlos exhaled sharply, his frustration still simmering, but he knew Davis was right. They couldn't expose themselves just yet—not when they were so close.

"Sure," Carlos said, his voice tight. "But we can't let this go. Not after everything that's happened."

Davis nodded in agreement. "I'll have someone put on the case to track down the man who attacked Asher. We need to know who he is and what his connection is. But be careful,

Carlos. If Holbrook is involved—and that's a big if—we need to be sure before we move forward."

Carlos gave her a curt nod. He was ready to do whatever it took to get to the truth. But he also knew she was right—this was a tightrope walk, and one wrong step could bring everything crashing down.

Davis gave a brief pause before standing up. "Right now, though, I need you to see Dr. Patel. She's got some information that could help with Diego's case. Go talk to her immediately."

Carlos turned toward the door, his mind already racing ahead. There was too much at stake now. Asher's attack had made it clear how dangerous this was, and the truth about Diego was getting closer—too close to stop.

But with every new piece of the puzzle, he couldn't shake the feeling that the danger wasn't just in the investigation. It was everywhere now.

CHAPTER 28

CARLOS

Carlos stepped into the sterile, fluorescent-lit hallway of the medical examiner's office, the cool air hitting him like a shock.

He hadn't wanted to split up. The thin red line across Asher's neck stuck vividly in his mind, but the work demanded it. Asher was at the Ledger, likely tracking down anything he could find on Holbrook's political dealings. He couldn't get the image of Asher's tense, hardened expression out of his mind. He missed the sharp wit, the offhanded comments, the disarming smirk—the things he'd started to look forward to. Things he hadn't let himself want for a long time.

Shaking off his thoughts, Carlos focused on the task ahead. He was here to see the medical examiner, Dr. Patel, and to find out what she had found out. But as he neared the office, he spotted a small group of people gathered at the door. A woman, about fifty, with graying hair pulled back in a simple braid, clutched the arm of a man who looked to be her husband. Beside them, a younger girl—no older than sixteen —clung tightly to her mother's side, her face hidden.

Diego's family.

STEALING MEXICO

Carlos's heart clenched. He hadn't known they were here, hadn't anticipated facing them. He took a breath, composed himself, and approached, though the woman spotted him before he even reached the door. Her dark, grief-ridden eyes met his, and for a second, Carlos faltered. The cold, methodical part of him, the one that compartmentalized and held back, slipped.

"Detective Santos?" she asked, her voice thick with emotion, every syllable a weight she could barely carry.

Carlos nodded, throat tight. "Yes, ma'am. I'm... I'm so sorry for your loss."

The woman's face crumpled, and she turned, pressing her face against her husband's shoulder. His own face worn and broken, the man held her tightly, barely able to meet Carlos's gaze. The young girl looked up at Carlos, her eyes wide with that desperate, searching look—like a person still waiting for something they knew would never come.

Carlos felt it then—something raw, jagged in his chest. He'd seen loss before, the hollowness that comes with it, but this—this was different. He saw Diego's parents and their daughter, broken in ways words could never explain, and the familiar ache settled deep within him. It was a pain he'd buried for so long, the kind of loss he hadn't let himself acknowledge, not even to himself.

The man took a steadying breath, eyes red, but there was a fire in his voice. He was holding on to his anger. "Señor Santos... Diego, he was a good boy. Smart. Always talking about making a difference." His voice cracked. "We... we don't understand. Why would anyone do this to him?"

Carlos's breath hitched. He hadn't expected this—to feel so exposed, so vulnerable in the face of their grief. He swallowed hard, trying to regain his composure. "I wish I had an answer for you," he said, the words thick in his throat. "Diego was... caught up in something dangerous. Something he might not have even fully understood." He paused, his eyes flitting to the girl, who was still clinging to her mother's side. The quiet stillness of her sorrow hit him like a weight. He could almost feel her pain, too. "But I promise you, we will find the truth. We'll find out who did this."

The mother looked up, her grief-stricken eyes searching his face for any sign of assurance. "¿Lo va a encontrar? ¿Quién hizo esto?"

Carlos nodded, though he knew no matter how many times he repeated it, no promise could ever ease their pain. "Sí, señora. I will find out." The words were a quiet vow, and this time, he meant them more than anything. For them. For Diego.

The father, though holding his wife tight, finally met Carlos's eyes. He reached out a trembling hand, placing it gently on Carlos's shoulder. "Gracias, Detective," he mumbled, his voice filled with a weight of thanks and surrender.

Carlos nodded, though the gratitude in the man's voice seemed to cut deeper than anything he'd heard in his career. He had always kept the weight of his work separate from his emotions—until now. His chest tightened, and for the first time in a long while, he let the walls crack just enough to feel it. To feel what these people had lost—and what he himself had buried for so long.

As Diego's family disappeared down the hall, their steps slow and heavy, Carlos remained frozen for a moment longer. The sting of his own emotions surprised him, like salt on a wound he'd been too afraid to touch for years. The loss, the grief, the anger—it was all too familiar.

But this time, it wasn't his own.

Taking a deep breath, he forced himself to focus. The mission. The case. But he couldn't shake the image of Diego's family, their pain etched into every inch of their being. And suddenly, he felt the deep pull of empathy—the one thing he hadn't allowed himself to feel in years.

STEALING MEXICO

Dr. Patel's door creaked open, and Carlos stepped in, trying to shut off the emotions swirling inside him. But as Dr. Patel spoke, all he could hear was the heavy silence left in the wake of that family's grief. The thought of finding out who had taken Diego from them made Carlos's hands tighten around the edge of the table.

His voice cracked a little as he spoke, a vulnerability slipping through the hardened exterior. "Tell me everything," he said, his tone low but firm. "I need to know what killed him."

Dr. Patel, always meticulous, adjusted her glasses and spoke, her voice calm and controlled. "Diego Cortez. Male, 19 years old. Cause of death: exsanguination from a single stab wound to the abdomen."

Carlos's chest tightened at the words.

"The weapon used was a hunting knife—large, with a serrated edge," Dr. Patel continued. "The wound was deep and caused significant internal bleeding. Diego likely died within minutes of the attack. The blood loss was rapid, and he wouldn't have survived long enough to defend himself."

Carlos's mind raced. One stab, but the damage it caused was enough to kill quickly. He could picture the scene— Diego, vulnerable, caught off guard. No struggle. Just a single, brutal strike.

"Was there any sign of drugs or sedatives in his system?" Carlos asked, trying to dig deeper.

"No," Dr. Patel replied, shaking her head. "He was alert and unimpeded at the time of the attack."

Carlos absorbed the information in silence, the weight of it pressing on him. This wasn't random. The attack had been quick, efficient, and brutal.

"Thank you, Dr. Patel," he said, his voice steady despite the turmoil in his mind. He turned to leave, his thoughts already working through what he had learned.

As he walked out of the morgue and into the sterile hall-way, Carlos couldn't shake the image of that single deadly wound. It had been too clean, too purposeful. Whoever had done this to Diego had known exactly what they were doing.

Carlos sat in his car, the keys still in the ignition, his hands clenched around the wheel as a storm of thoughts churned inside him. Diego's mother's hand had felt heavy in his own, her quiet plea for answers reverberating in his chest. He was no stranger to carrying burdens, to shouldering responsibilities alone. But this time, the weight felt different. It was as if something inside him had cracked, creating an unexpected urge to share and finally open up to someone. And the only person he wanted to turn to was Asher.

Without letting himself overthink it, Carlos pulled out his phone and dialed Asher. The line rang twice before Asher's voice filled his ear, a little surprised but with a familiarity that eased something in Carlos's chest.

"Carlos?"

Carlos took a deep breath, trying to steady the turmoil inside him. This was it—the moment he had been avoiding for too long. "Meet me at my house tonight," he said, his voice steady but laced with a quiet urgency. "I have some things I need to tell you."

There was a pause on the other end, and Carlos could almost hear Asher processing the words. "Alright," Asher finally responded, his tone softening, the weight of the conversation not lost on him.

Carlos ended the call and leaned back against his seat, letting his head fall back against the headrest. He hadn't expected this to be so hard. He'd spent years locking away parts of himself, burying the memories, and keeping everything at arm's length. His past. His parents. The reasons he never let anyone close enough to see the cracks.

But somehow, Asher had seen them. Little by little, he'd chipped away at the walls Carlos had so carefully built. And now, Carlos knew that if he didn't let go of the weight he was carrying, it would consume him. The case. The past. Emotions he'd pushed aside. All of it.

Maybe tonight, just for once, he'd let someone see the real Carlos Santos—the man behind the badge.

CHAPTER 29

ASHER

Asher shifted his weight from foot to foot, glancing down at his watch. He knew he was a little early, but he'd rather be early than risk losing his nerve. With a deep breath, he knocked—and to his surprise, the door swung open almost immediately. Standing in the doorway was Carlos's abuela, her eyes lighting up with recognition and a smile that felt like a warm hug.

"Ah, Asher!" she greeted, her voice full of cheer. "Carlos isn't home yet, but you come in." Without waiting for a reply, she ushered him inside, her presence both commanding and comforting.

The living room was alive with energy. A group of elderly Mexican women were gathered around a table, their laughter filling the air as they waved their Lotería cards in playful competition. Asher hesitated for a second, thinking of politely waiting outside, but before he could, Abuela had already introduced him. Within moments, the crowd swept him in, and their warm welcomes and playful teasing quickly erased his discomfort.

The women didn't give him a chance to shy away. They handed him a Lotería card, correcting his hesitant Spanish

STEALING MEXICO

with every draw, their laughter easy and infectious. Each correction was followed by more laughter, as if the very act of including him in their world was a celebration. They insisted he sample the churros and tamales laid out on the table—sweet, crunchy churros and tamales warm with the familiar, earthy flavor of home.

Though part of his mind remained focused on Carlos, the vibrant energy of the room captivated the rest of him. It was impossible not to smile, even as his thoughts wandered to the case, to Carlos... To everything that had happened. But then, something in the conversation cut through his distracted thoughts.

"Oh, I heard Governor Holbrook's fundraising event next week is invite-only," one woman said, fanning herself with a hand, a conspiratorial look in her eyes. "They say only the top supporters get to attend."

"He has enough money in that campaign already," another replied. "But I bet some of it isn't from the nicest people." She leaned closer, lowering her voice. "You hear things, you know?"

Asher's ears perked up, his attention snapping to the conversation. "Holbrook's campaign?" he asked casually, hoping to glean more.

Abuela noticed his interest and raised an eyebrow. "Ay, muchacho, don't you know? These women know everything. You think the papers have all the details? These señoras have ears everywhere."

The women exchanged sly smiles, and Asher's mind raced, piecing together bits of information. He'd been scouring official channels, following leads, but these unfiltered snippets—grounded in the everyday world—felt like the missing pieces to a puzzle.

"Did you hear about that assistant of his, the young one?" one woman whispered, as though sharing a secret. "Something about him doesn't sit right."

"Yes, yes!" another woman added, leaning forward. "He's always hanging around, but never says much. Like he's hiding something. People say he handles the things Holbrook doesn't want to deal with personally."

Abuela leaned in closer, her voice dropping as if sharing the juiciest gossip. "They say he arranges all those private meetings—ones no one's supposed to know about. No one even knows where he came from."

"And why is he even with Holbrook, hmm?" another woman mused. "Holbrook must have something on him, or maybe it's the other way around. Either way, that assistant's too quiet for his own good. El Niño, that's what they call him."

"El Niño?" Asher asked, eyebrows furrowing in confusion.

"The Kid," one woman explained with a knowing nod.

The Kid. Asher's heart skipped. Stay away from the kid, the man in the alley had said. He'd been talking about Governor Holbrook's assistant.

Before he could probe further, the conversation shifted again, the women turning their attention to him.

"So, Asher," one of them teased, "do you have someone special? A novia, maybe?"

Asher blinked, thrown off by the sudden change in topic. "Ah, well..." he stammered, cheeks warming as he tried to figure out a diplomatic answer.

Abuela raised an eyebrow, her playful smile widening. "What's this 'maybe' nonsense?" She gave him a pointed look. "He's Carlos's special friend."

The room erupted into gasps and giggles, leaving Asher scrambling for words. He raised a hand, about to correct the assumption, but before he could get a word out, the women bombarded him with questions.

"Oh, look at him, he's blushing!"

"How long have you two been together?"

STEALING MEXICO

Asher's face turned crimson, his mind racing as he tried to find a way out of the situation. Just as he was about to speak, he heard footsteps at the door.

Carlos walked in, pausing mid-step as he took in the scene before him. His gaze flicked between Asher, still red-faced, and the group of women who were now grinning at him with conspiratorial smiles. Amusement quickly replaced Carlos's confusion as his eyes softened, the corners of his mouth twitching upward in a smile.

Asher opened his mouth to explain, but his words faltered when he saw Carlos's amused expression. He couldn't help but laugh at the absurdity of the situation, but his attempt to clarify dissolved under the weight of the teasing smiles surrounding him.

CHAPTER 30

CARLOS

Carlos led Asher down the hallway, the sound of his Abuela's laughter from the living room faint but still carrying through the walls. The amused giggles and comments from her friends made Carlos grit his teeth in mild embarrassment, but he said nothing. His home was his sanctuary, but it wasn't immune to the invasion of well-meaning prying.

When they reached his bedroom, he shut the door behind them with a soft but deliberate click, trying to block out the noise of the evening. A quiet hum of tension lingered, but here, in this small room, with the muted light from the bedside lamp spilling across the floor, it felt like a different world. He motioned for Asher to sit beside him on the bed.

Asher hesitated, looking for a place to settle, clearly out of his element. The uncertainty in his posture—those half-second pauses before he made any move—made Carlos's lips twitch into a brief smile. He patted the space next to him, a silent invitation.

"You didn't have to sit through all that, you know," Carlos said, his voice low, though there was a touch of amusement in the words.

Asher let out a soft laugh, sitting next to him but still

STEALING MEXICO

keeping a little distance between them. "Your Abuela's friends are... quite the crowd," he said, his tone light but genuine. His eyes flickered toward Carlos, as though gauging him. Maybe trying to make sure Carlos was okay after the scene they had just escaped.

Carlos glanced sideways at him, unsure how to start. He hadn't planned on having this conversation tonight, but the day's events—Diego's family, the investigation, the constant pressure—had been building up, and now the weight of it all sat in his chest. He could feel it pressing against his ribs, constricting his breath.

There were too many things he hadn't said, and with Asher here, sitting so close, it felt like the time had come.

"There's... something I haven't told you," Carlos said, voice slower now. His gaze flicked briefly to the floor, focusing on a small mark in the hardwood. "It's not about the case. It's... personal."

Asher straightened, his easygoing demeanor softening into something quieter. He gave a small nod, his eyes trained on Carlos now, waiting for him to continue.

Carlos exhaled slowly, his mind racing to find the right words. "I met Diego's family today, at the medical examiner's office. Seeing them... well, it brought back some things. Made me think of... my parents."

Asher's expression softened, and Carlos could feel the shift, like the room had just grown quieter, more intimate. He felt the unspoken understanding in Asher's eyes, the way he listened, no judgment, just waiting for Carlos to share whatever he needed to.

Carlos took another breath. The words were harder now, the memories coming back, as painful as they'd ever been. "My dad was a detective," he continued, his voice low. "One of the best in Phoenix, they said. He was... everything I wanted to be when I grew up. Tough, smart, driven." A faint smile tugged at the corner of Carlos's lips. A fleeting thing.

He could almost see his father again in the dark recesses of his mind. "He taught me a lot about this job. A lot of what keeps me going is... him."

His throat tightened, and he swallowed. It hurt to say these things aloud, to let them out. He'd buried them for so long, kept them hidden under layers of time and distance. But there was something about Asher's quiet presence, the way he was just there without asking for anything more, that made Carlos feel like maybe it was okay to let the walls come down.

"He never came home one night," Carlos went on, the words tasting bitter. His gaze dropped to his hands, still clenched at his sides, as though holding on to something he wasn't quite ready to let go of. "Car accident. I was just a kid, but I remember the call, my mom's reaction... everything. And after he was gone, my mom..." He trailed off, the finality of it catching in his chest. "She just faded, you know? Like she couldn't find herself anymore without him. Eventually, she just..."

Carlos couldn't finish. He didn't need to. The hollow space in his chest—the one that had been there since they were both gone—spoke for itself. His heart felt heavy, but there was something about sharing it, about speaking the words aloud, that made the weight seem just a little lighter.

"I became a cop to feel close to him," he added, his voice quiet now, a bit of wonder in the way it trailed off. "Or maybe to understand what drove him. But after losing them both, I thought it was better, easier, to keep people at a distance. To avoid... attachment. Safer, you know?"

Asher didn't say anything at first, but Carlos felt the air between them shift. It wasn't just silence—it was understanding, gentle, but firm. The way Asher's gaze held him made Carlos feel like the words he had just spoken mattered, like he hadn't just confessed some weakness, but had shared a part of himself, a part that was worth hearing.

STEALING MEXICO

Asher reached out, his hand landing on Carlos's shoulder. A grounding touch. Carlos looked up, meeting his eyes. "Doesn't have to be that way," Asher said quietly, his voice low but steady. "People will take the risk, Carlos. Because... you're worth it."

Carlos's chest tightened again, but this time it wasn't from grief. It was from something else, something unfamiliar. Hope, maybe. The words sank deep into him, filling cracks he hadn't realized were there. For the first time in a long time, he let himself believe it.

"Maybe," Carlos murmured, his voice softer now. But there was no defensiveness, no immediate urge to push the moment away. He didn't pull away from Asher's hand, either. He let it stay, the warmth from Asher's touch soothing something inside him.

The room fell into quiet, but it wasn't uncomfortable. There was no pressure, no expectation. Just the two of them, side by side, with the weight of everything hanging in the air. Carlos felt something shift inside of him, a flicker of something he hadn't let himself feel in years.

Asher's thumb moved gently over Carlos's shoulder, tracing the outline of his shirt. It was a slight gesture, but it grounded him, helped him stay in the moment. He could feel the electric charge between them, the silent pull that had always been there but now felt undeniable.

"Do you ever think about... letting people in?" Asher's voice was quiet, vulnerable in its own right. "I mean, really letting them in."

Carlos hesitated, weighing his response carefully. It wasn't a question he had asked himself, at least not lately. But he had been asking it in other ways, just not out loud.

"It's complicated," he finally admitted, his words feeling like a confession. "I've spent so long pushing people away. It's easier that way. You don't have to worry about losing anyone if you don't let them close."

Asher's gaze softened, and there was something almost comforting in his silence, the way he just watched Carlos. No judgment, only acceptance.

"But that means you're also missing out on having people who care about you," Asher said, his voice still soft but firm. "You can't live in the shadows forever, Carlos."

Carlos felt the weight of those words, and for a moment, everything seemed to still. The last time he had let someone in, he had lost everything. But now, with Asher sitting next to him, the words felt less like a challenge and more like an invitation.

"Maybe I'm just not ready," Carlos said, his voice rougher than he intended. He didn't meet Asher's gaze.

Asher's face shifted slightly, concern flickering in his expression. "You don't have to be perfect, Carlos. You just have to be you. I get that you're scared. I am, too. But this—" he gestured between them, "this is worth the risk."

Carlos felt his breath hitch, the words crashing into him like waves. He had feared this. The vulnerability. The exposure. But Asher's sincerity—his steadfastness—made him want to reach out, to close the distance between them.

"I could have lost you last night," Carlos admitted, his voice barely above a whisper. "I just... don't want to lose you."

Asher's expression softened further, and then, without another word, he leaned in. Their faces were inches apart, the quiet space between them suddenly charged with a kind of raw energy. And then Carlos did what he had been trying to fight off for so long.

He kissed him.

They didn't rush it. It wasn't forceful. Tentative at first, a soft meeting of lips. But the moment their mouths touched, a spark lit inside Carlos, a warmth that flooded him from head to toe. He hadn't realized how much he'd been starving for this, for connection, for something real.

STEALING MEXICO

Asher responded, his hand moving to cup Carlos's cheek, his thumb brushing over the rough skin. The kiss deepened, slow and deliberate, each movement speaking volumes they hadn't said out loud. It wasn't just about the kiss—it was about everything that had led up to this moment: the trust, the shared pain, the quiet promises.

When they finally pulled apart, breathless and wide-eyed, Carlos searched Asher's face, his heart racing.

"I don't think I'm ready for this," Carlos admitted again, but this time, it didn't feel like a rejection.

Asher's lips quirked into a small smile, his eyes twinkling with something mischievous and understanding all at once. "I don't know if I am, either," he replied softly. "Just take it one step at a time."

Carlos's breath hitched as Asher's fingers traced the line of his jaw, the touch both tender and teasing. The world outside seemed to fall away, leaving only the heat building between them. Asher's gaze was intense, questioning, and when he leaned in slowly, his lips barely brushing Carlos's, Carlos didn't pull back. He let the kiss deepen, moving with the same urgency that thrummed through his veins.

Asher's hands slid to the back of Carlos's neck, pulling him closer, their bodies pressed together, the connection electric. Carlos's hands roamed, finding Asher's shirt, lifting it with a quiet growl of need. The moment was raw, unfiltered, every touch and kiss a silent declaration. Carlos was done hiding, done pushing away what he felt.

When Asher's chest met his, their hearts racing in tandem, Asher paused, his voice low. "Are you sure?"

Carlos didn't answer with words. He answered with a kiss, deep and slow, his fingers tracing the curve of Asher's spine as he felt him shiver under his touch. Asher responded, pulling him closer, his hands now working at the waistband of Carlos's jeans. In a rush, they discarded the fabric; the only sound between them was the soft rustle of sheets and their breathless murmurs.

The kiss was relentless, a dance of tongues and hands, each movement deliberate, savoring the moment but pushing for more. Carlos's mind was a blur of sensation, the feel of Asher's skin against his, the heat of their bodies together. Every inch of him was alive with wanting, and he knew, deep down, that this was something different. Something worth the risk.

Asher's breath was warm against his ear, his voice hushed but urgent. "I don't want to rush you, but I need you."

Carlos pulled Asher back to him, their lips meeting in a kiss that was raw and deep, the kind that spoke without words. Carlos guided them both with his hands until they were tangled in the sheets, the world outside a distant memory. The intensity between them built, slow but steady, until it shattered, a quiet release that left them breathless, holding onto each other in the stillness that followed.

Asher's fingers brushed gently across Carlos's chest, his lips brushing against his shoulder. "You're okay?"

Carlos's lips curved into a soft smile, his chest rising and falling with the steady rhythm of his breath. "Yeah. I'm more than okay."

And for the first time in a long time, Carlos felt something that had been missing for years—he felt whole.

CHAPTER 31

ASHER

The room was still thick with the quiet that came after something profound. Asher lay next to Carlos, both of them tangled in the sheets, naked and warm in the afterglow of what had just passed between them. He could feel Carlos's chest rise and fall with every breath, the steady rhythm comforting in its consistency. Asher's mind, though, raced. His heart, still beating a little faster than normal, couldn't shake the weight of everything they were uncovering.

It felt strange to be so close to Carlos, yet so unsure of what the next step was. The truth hung over him like an unanswered question, one that tugged at his mind even as he tried to stay present in the moment.

Carlos shifted slightly, his hand moving under the sheets to find Asher's. He didn't speak, but the touch was enough. Carlos was waiting for him to say something. Asher hesitated, his fingers brushing Carlos's as he gathered his thoughts.

"I learned something new," Asher said, his voice quiet, as though the words needed to be spoken carefully.

Carlos's thumb brushed lightly over his skin, urging him to continue.

STEALING MEXICO

"Earlier, Abuela's friends were talking," Asher explained, his gaze tracing the shadows on the wall. "About Holbrook's assistant."

Carlos's brow furrowed slightly, his eyes still closed. "What about him?"

Asher hesitated for a moment, then let out a breath. "He goes by 'The Kid.' That's what they were calling him."

Carlos's body stiffened just slightly at the mention of the name. Asher could feel the tension in him, even as his fingers tightened around Asher's, the weight of this new information sinking in. His eyes popped open.

"He's who the man was talking about," Carlos said, his voice laced with a quiet urgency. "The one we are supposed to stay away from."

Asher nodded. He'd connected the dots himself, but hearing Carlos say it out loud made it even more real. "Yeah, that's him. It's starting to make sense. Abuela's friends said he's been pulling a lot of strings behind the scenes with Holbrook. I don't know what exactly, but they seemed to think he had some kind of influence. Or the other way around."

Carlos's grip on his hand tightened, his expression darkening. "We still don't know who he is."

"No," Asher said, shaking his head slightly. "The more I hear, the more I feel like we're missing something big here."

Carlos remained silent for a moment, his eyes watching Asher with an intensity that made his heart race again, but differently this time. There was a quiet understanding between them, an unspoken agreement that they were both in deep now.

"I need to keep digging," Asher said, his voice steady, but the uncertainty in him was growing. "We still don't know what Holbrook's up to, but this guy—'The Kid'—he's connected. And if he's tied to Holbrook, then we're dealing with something bigger than we thought."

Carlos's fingers brushed against Asher's cheek, a silent gesture that conveyed more than words ever could. He seemed to know what Asher needed without him having to say it out loud. "We'll figure it out," Carlos whispered. "But we need to be careful. Holbrook's too high-profile to be messing around with someone like this without getting attention. We need to look into Holbrook without him knowing that we are, and find out who this assistant really is. I don't want you going off on your own. We do this together."

Asher's heart skipped a beat at the softness in Carlos's voice, the reassurance that wrapped around him like a protective shield. He didn't feel so lost, so unsure anymore. They were in this together.

"I know," Asher whispered. "I trust you."

Carlos's hand brushed through Asher's hair, his fingers smoothing it back gently as he pulled Asher a little closer, pressing him against his side. For a moment, the weight of their case, the danger they were facing, seemed distant, tucked away in the quiet space between them.

They both knew the road ahead was dangerous, but in that moment, as they lay together, everything else fell away.

PART THREE

CHAPTER 32

CARLOS

The soft light of morning filtered through the curtains, casting a gentle glow over the room. Carlos lay still, savoring the warmth beside him. Asher was asleep, his body pressed close to Carlos's, one arm draped across his chest. The intimacy of the moment felt both foreign and deeply comforting, as if everything in the world had shifted, become more tangible, more real. It was as though the heaviness that always hovered around him had been lightened, just for a moment, by the presence of the man beside him.

Carlos had never realized how much he craved this connection until it was right here. Asher's soft breath against his skin stirred something in him, a desire to protect, to shield him from the harsh realities outside their little bubble. It felt like a turning point, like a promise that something deeper was blossoming between them.

He replayed their kisses in his mind, the laughter that had filled the space between them, the way it had cut through the darkness he often found himself lost in. Just hours ago, he'd felt a fleeting flicker of hope. But now, like a storm on the horizon, reality reared its ugly head.

His phone buzzed, pulling him away from the warmth of

STEALING MEXICO

those thoughts. He glanced at the screen—Marissa. His heart sank.

"Detective Santos," he answered, trying to shake the grogginess from his voice.

"Carlos, we've got another body." Marissa's voice was steady but urgent. "A shopkeeper downtown. Another immigrant. Get there now."

The words hit him like a punch. Another murder. His stomach twisted as the weight of it settled in, pushing aside the lightness that had taken root in the quiet moments he'd shared with Asher.

He hung up, his pulse racing. "Hey, Asher," he whispered, gently shaking him awake.

Asher stirred, his blue eyes fluttering open, a mix of confusion and concern in his expression. "What's wrong?"

"We have to go," Carlos said, urgency creeping into his voice. "Another murder. A shopkeeper."

Asher pushed himself up, the sheets falling from his shoulders as he quickly gathered himself. Carlos tried not to notice the sight of his body—there was no time for that now.

"Another one?" Asher's voice was sharp with disbelief.

"Yeah," Carlos replied, trying to keep his voice steady. "An immigrant. A shopkeeper. I don't know anything else yet."

Asher nodded, and within minutes, they were both dressed, the earlier intimacy replaced by the cold reality of their jobs. Carlos could feel the shift between them, the moment of warmth replaced by the chill of a new case that would demand everything from them.

Once in the car, the drive to the crime scene felt agonizingly long. The hum of the engine was the only sound between them, the weight of the investigation pressing down on both of them. Carlos gripped the steering wheel, his knuckles turning white, his mind spinning with thoughts of what this murder could mean.

When they arrived, flashing lights greeted them, the scene already bustling with officers and investigators. The small shop, once a peaceful corner of the neighborhood, now stood as a grim reminder of how easily life could be taken.

Carlos's stomach churned as he took in the scene. The familiar scent of blood, antiseptic, and asphalt stung his nostrils. Another life snuffed out, another victim to add to a growing list. He pushed through the crowd of officers, feeling the weight of the investigation bear down on him again; this time, however, it felt heavier, as if the stakes had just been raised.

"Stay close," he murmured to Asher, who had fallen into step beside him, his eyes scanning the area with sharp focus.

Asher's voice was low, filled with quiet concern. "Do you think it's connected?"

Carlos paused, his gaze sweeping over the chaotic scene. "It feels too similar. Same kind of violence. Another immigrant." His gut twisted. "It's starting to look like a pattern."

They made their way past the yellow tape, and Carlos saw the body being wheeled away on a stretcher. His stomach lurched, the image of it cutting through him like a knife. Each death felt personal, each loss another crack in the world he was desperately trying to hold together.

A technician was taking photographs, moving with practiced precision as she documented the scene. Carlos approached a nearby officer, who was already briefing another detective.

"What do we have?" Carlos asked, keeping his voice steady despite the heaviness pressing on his chest.

The officer looked up, recognition flashing across his face. "Shopkeeper, early forties. Luis Morales. Found stabbed behind the counter. No witnesses yet."

Carlos's mind raced. "Stabbed? What kind of knife?"

"Unknown at this time," the officer said, his tone grim.

STEALING MEXICO

"The M.E. will know more after the autopsy, but we're guessing it's the same MO as before."

Asher's brow furrowed. "This is too close to Diego's case. Too much of a coincidence."

Carlos nodded, his insides twisting. "We need to find a connection. Diego was investigating something, and now this? It's too much."

Asher's voice dropped lower, a quiet urgency there. "What if they're tied together? We still don't have anything concrete on Diego's case."

Carlos felt the weight of that truth settle in his chest. They weren't just dealing with isolated incidents—they were facing something much larger, and if they didn't figure it out soon, more lives could be lost. The need to protect Asher, to make sure nothing happened to him, surged inside him, making his protective instincts flare.

"Let's talk to the M.E.," Carlos said, his voice firm. "We need answers, and we need them fast. If this is connected to Diego, we can't waste any more time."

Asher nodded, his gaze steady, determination blazing in his eyes.

CHAPTER 33

ASHER

Asher stood back, watching Carlos move with the focus that only years of experience could cultivate. He could feel the tension in the air—thick, charged with the weight of unspoken questions. The crime scene was alive with movement: officers scurrying, yellow tape flapping in the wind, and onlookers whispering just out of earshot. But Asher barely heard any of it. His attention remained solely on Carlos. The detective moved like he was one with the scene, methodical, measured. Every step he took had purpose.

Normally, Asher would have been all over this—pressing for answers, pulling on every thread until something snapped. But now? Now he was silent. Observing. Watching Carlos in a way that made something unfamiliar stir in him. He'd been a thorn in Carlos's side from the start, always pushing, always questioning. But tonight, something had shifted. He wasn't just here to get the story. No, this felt different. A connection existed between them he couldn't yet fully understand. But as he watched Carlos work, it was clear he wasn't just here as a reporter anymore.

Asher snapped a few pictures of the scene, the crowd,

STEALING MEXICO

trying to capture the emotions behind the chaos. The faces in the crowd told stories all their own—some hopeful, some desperate, most simply waiting. His phone buzzed with a message from his editor, but he ignored it, his eyes still scanning the area. That's when he saw him.

The man.

The one who had held a knife to his throat just days ago. The man standing just beyond the yellow tape, watching Asher with cold, calculating eyes. Asher's breath caught in his throat, his heart slamming in his chest. The man's gaze never left him, burning with an intensity that was almost suffocating. For a moment, everything else disappeared. The crowd, the noise, the flashing lights—they were all gone. It was just him and this man, locked in a silent standoff.

Instinct kicked in. Asher's fingers hovered over his phone, but he slowly lowered it, the buzz of anxiety in his veins growing sharper. His eyes locked on the man's face, and a chill ran down his spine. He couldn't move. Fear and an unnamed feeling paralyzed him, cementing him to the ground.

His phone buzzed again, and he glanced at it, barely registering the message. It didn't matter. The man was staring at him like he knew him—like he knew everything. Words, threats, and a blade pressed to his skin. The danger he'd felt just days ago was back, alive, and real.

He's here.

Asher didn't think twice. He sent the text to Carlos and slowly backed away, trying to seem casual, even though every nerve in his body was screaming. He didn't want to make a scene, but he couldn't ignore the instinct that urged him to get Carlos's attention.

Carlos didn't even hesitate. His gaze snapped up, his eyes narrowing as he scanned the crowd. The shift in his demeanor was immediate. The calm, composed detective disappeared in a heartbeat, replaced by a man who was all focus. Asher watched, breath catching, as Carlos's hand moved instinctively to his sidearm, his body tensing as he prepared for whatever was coming next.

"He's here," Asher said under his breath, just loud enough to be heard over the rising din of the scene.

Carlos didn't waste time. He barely glanced at Asher before he was already moving, his powerful stride cutting through the crowd. "Stay here, Asher," he ordered, voice low, but there was no mistaking the command. "Stay out of this."

But Asher didn't listen. He couldn't. Not when that man was still out there. Not when Carlos was going after him alone.

Before Carlos could take another step, Asher was on his heels, pushing through the crowd, fighting the knot of panic in his chest. "Carlos, wait!" His voice was barely heard, drowned out by the noise, but the urgency was clear. He couldn't let Carlos go after this man on his own. Not with the way things had escalated between them—not now.

Carlos's pace didn't falter. He didn't even acknowledge Asher's call. He was in full pursuit mode, eyes locked on the man now making a break for it. The chase was on.

Asher's heart pounded as he ran to keep up, pushing his legs harder, faster. His feet were a blur of motion as he followed Carlos down the street, trying to match his pace. The world around him seemed to slow, the sounds of the crime scene muffling as the chase took over everything. They were moving as one—Carlos leading, Asher trailing, both locked in the same relentless pursuit.

The man was fast, darting down side streets, weaving through gaps in the buildings. But Carlos was faster. Carlos calculated every move and made every step purposefully. Asher pushed himself harder, heart thumping in his chest as the gap between him and Carlos grew smaller.

"We can't lose him!" Asher yelled, desperation coloring

STEALING MEXICO

his voice. He wasn't sure if Carlos heard him, but he didn't care. The man was close now. He could feel it.

Carlos didn't break stride. He kept his eyes on the suspect, unrelenting. The man glanced back over his shoulder, his eyes catching Asher's for the briefest of seconds before he ducked around a corner, disappearing from view.

Asher's breath hitched in his throat. The alley was just ahead, and they were closing in on the man. He could hear his pulse in his ears, the rhythmic pounding of his heart now matching the rhythm of their chase.

Carlos didn't slow as they turned the corner. He was there in an instant, moving into the alley, eyes scanning the dark shadows between the buildings. The air was thick with tension, and Asher felt it settle deep in his bones. The scent of danger, of something primal, hung in the air like smoke.

The man was nowhere to be seen.

Carlos halted abruptly, his eyes flicking around the alley, his senses on high alert. Asher stepped up beside him, breathless but determined.

"He went this way," Asher said, pointing to the narrow gap between the two buildings. The shadows loomed long and heavy, and Asher could feel the weight of the moment pressing down on them.

Carlos's jaw tightened, his fingers inching toward his gun. "Stay close," he ordered, his voice low but firm. "If he's armed…"

"I know," Asher interrupted, his own nerves tight, but his voice steady. He could feel the adrenaline coursing through him, his mind sharp despite the fear clawing at the edges. They had to hurry. They couldn't let this man slip away.

Together, they moved into the darkness of the alley, side by side. Asher's heart raced, but it wasn't just fear. It was something else, something electric that coursed through him as he followed Carlos, trusting him—no, needing him to lead the way.

The shadows were their only companions now, and Asher didn't know what would come next. But he knew one thing: whatever happened, he wasn't leaving Carlos alone. Not again.

"Let's go," Carlos said, and Asher fell in step beside him, ready for whatever came next.

CHAPTER 34

CARLOS

"Damn it!" Carlos hissed, halting at the far end of the alley. He scanned the empty street stretching out in front of him. They'd lost him.

But before he could process his frustration, the clatter of metal rang out from further back in the alley. Carlos whipped around just in time to see the man scaling a fire escape, gripping the scaffolding as the loose ladder wobbled beneath him. He scrambled, almost slipping, but hauled himself onto the platform.

Carlos pulled out his phone, punching in a quick call to his captain. "Marissa, I need backup at the old Harrison building. Suspect's on foot."

"Already en route," Marissa replied, her voice all business.

Carlos barely had time to acknowledge her response before he heard the crunch of footsteps approaching. Two officers rounded the corner behind him, and another bolted toward him from the far end of the alley. Carlos pointed upward, directing their attention to the man struggling with the fire escape above them. "He's going inside! Cut him off around the front!"

STEALING MEXICO

One officer nodded and took off toward the building's main entrance, but Carlos reached out, stopping another officer before he could join in the pursuit. He turned, glancing briefly at Asher, who looked torn between concern and the urge to jump right into the chase.

"Keep him here! Do not let him get hurt!" Carlos commanded, his tone leaving no room for argument.

"Carlos—" Asher started, clearly ready to protest, but Carlos cut him off with a look, the intensity in his gaze enough to keep Asher rooted in place.

Without another word, Carlos launched himself toward the fire escape, grabbing hold of the ladder and pulling himself up. The rickety metal groaned under his weight, but he ignored it, focusing instead on the suspect, who was scrambling up onto the second level. Carlos moved fast, forcing himself to keep pace despite the narrow, slippery steps.

He climbed with determination, adrenaline flooding his veins as he chased the man up the fire escape. The dry wind whipped against his face, and the city noise below faded, replaced by the clang of metal and his own pounding heartbeat.

"Stop!" Carlos shouted, his voice cutting through the scorching air as he climbed higher.

Carlos reached the top of the fire escape, bursting through the unlocked window and into the dimly lit interior of the old Harrison building. Shadows played across the peeling wallpaper, and the smell of mold and dust hung thick in the air. He glimpsed movement in the far corner of the abandoned office space—a shadow darting between the crumbling cubicles.

He moved silently, the soles of his boots barely making a sound against the cracked linoleum as he slipped around a corner. Suddenly, the man was there, lurking just ahead, his back to Carlos as he seemed to assess an exit route.

"Stop!" Carlos shouted, leveling his gun at the man. "It's over. Put your hands up!"

The man whirled around, his eyes wide for a split second —then narrowed with a feral gleam. Before Carlos could react, he lunged, his arm swinging up. Carlos caught a flash of metal—the knife. The same knife he had held to Asher's throat.

Carlos stepped back, barely dodging the blade as it arced toward him, but the man didn't relent. He charged, aiming low this time, his arm swinging in a vicious arc. Carlos sidestepped, grabbing the man's wrist in a firm grip, but the man twisted, driving an elbow into Carlos's ribs with enough force to knock the wind from his lungs.

The gun slipped from his hand, clattering to the ground.

They were close now, struggling against each other as Carlos tried to regain control. The man was unrelenting, swinging the knife with a wildness that spoke of desperation, of someone willing to do whatever it took to escape. Carlos grunted as he grabbed the man's forearm, shoving him back into a cubicle wall. The thin plaster cracked under the impact, but the man rebounded, slamming Carlos backward into a desk that shattered under their combined weight.

Carlos's head spun from the impact, but he forced himself to stay focused. He blocked another slash from the knife, twisting his body to send a brutal knee into the man's stomach. His attacker staggered, his grip loosening on the knife just enough for Carlos to wrest it from him. But the man was fast; he recovered, grabbing Carlos by the collar and slamming him into the wall.

"You should have stayed out of this," the man hissed, his face inches from Carlos's, his hand tightening around Carlos's throat.

Carlos's vision blurred, his lungs burning as he struggled for air. Gathering his last reserves of strength, he shoved his knee upward, slamming it into the man's thigh. The man yelped in pain, loosening his grip just enough for Carlos to twist free. He lashed out with a fist, connecting squarely with the man's jaw, sending him reeling back into a cubicle.

Carlos lunged after him, driving the man to the ground with the full force of his weight, pinning him there. His fists moved on instinct, raining down a series of punishing blows as adrenaline and fury took over. He didn't stop until the man lay sprawled beneath him, gasping and bloodied, his fight extinguished.

Grabbing his cuffs, Carlos rolled the man onto his stomach, securing his wrists behind his back with a click. He finally allowed himself a breath, his chest heaving as he hauled the man to his feet, wiping blood from his split lip with the back of his hand.

"You picked a fight with the wrong guy," Carlos muttered, satisfaction hardening his voice as he picked up his gun and dragged the man toward the door.

CHAPTER 35

ASHER

The relentless Arizona sun baked the alley, the heat radiating off the pavement and sinking into Asher's skin. He paced anxiously, his heart racing, glancing repeatedly at the battered building Carlos had disappeared into. Every nerve in his body screamed at him to go inside, but he knew he'd only make things worse. His phone sat heavy in his hand, the screen blank as he debated calling someone—anyone—for an update.

The scene replayed in his mind: the knife too close to his neck for comfort, Diego... the shopkeeper. Then Carlos, walking into the fight like it was any other day at work. Except it wasn't. It was dangerous, reckless, and Carlos hadn't let him stop him.

Asher's foot tapped against the pavement, his frustration mounting. Waiting didn't suit him, especially not this kind of wait where every moment felt excruciatingly long.

A sharp bang jolted him from his thoughts—the door to the building swung open with a violent snap, crashing against the wall.

Carlos emerged, bruised and battered but upright, dragging the suspect in cuffs. The man stumbled forward, his face

STEALING MEXICO

bloodied, his glare as sharp as ever. A smear of blood streaked Carlos's torn shirt, but his grip on the suspect was like iron.

Asher sprinted toward him, relief and panic colliding in his chest. "Carlos!"

Carlos glanced at him, the faintest smirk playing on his lips despite the state he was in. "It's handled," he said, his voice rough but steady.

Asher's gaze darted between Carlos and the man he'd subdued. The man glared at him, his lip curled in a sneer that made Asher's stomach churn, but it was nothing compared to the fury brewing in his chest.

Carlos handed the suspect over to the officers that waited for him without ceremony, his exhaustion evident in the tightness of his shoulders.

"Get him to the precinct," Carlos instructed. His voice carried an edge of authority that brooked no argument, even as he wiped a streak of blood from the corner of his mouth.

The officers nodded, leading the man away toward a waiting cruiser. The suspect growled something under his breath, but Carlos didn't flinch, his dark eyes fixed on him until the car door slammed shut.

When the alley finally fell silent again, Asher took a cautious step closer. "You look like hell," he said, his tone softer than his words.

Carlos raised an eyebrow, brushing dust from his pants. "I've had worse."

Asher shook his head, exhaling sharply. "You could've been killed, Carlos. What were you thinking, going in there alone?"

Carlos's smirk faded, his expression hardening. "I was thinking that guy had already hurt you once, and I wasn't going to let him do it again."

Asher opened his mouth to reply, but stopped. The raw honesty in Carlos's voice, the quiet determination, left him momentarily speechless.

Carlos sighed, running a hand through his sweat-dampened hair. "Look, I know it was reckless. But we needed answers, and he wasn't going to give them willingly."

"What now?" Asher asked after a long pause, his voice subdued.

Carlos's jaw tightened as he glanced back at the building. "Now, we figure out what he was so desperate to hide. We've got the knife. If we can tie it to Diego's murder or the shopkeeper's, we've got leverage."

Asher crossed his arms, his frustration simmering beneath the surface. "And Holbrook? The Kid? They're still out there."

Carlos nodded grimly. "They are. But this is a step closer. We just have to be careful—" He glanced at Asher pointedly. "—and smart about our next move."

Asher's lips pressed into a thin line. "Careful isn't exactly what we're doing right now."

Carlos's faint smirk returned, though it didn't reach his eyes. "Then we'll do better."

Asher huffed a quiet laugh despite himself. "You say that like it's going to be easy."

"Nothing about this is easy," Carlos replied, his tone softening. "But we'll get there."

The weight of the moment hung between them, heavy with unspoken thoughts and shared resolve. Asher glanced at the blood drying on Carlos's cheek, the bruise blooming along his jaw, and felt the tension in his chest shift into something else.

He stepped back, his mind already racing with questions about the next move. They weren't out of the woods yet—not by a long shot. But for now, Carlos was alive, and the suspect was in custody.

And that was enough to keep going.

CHAPTER 36

CARLOS

Carlos paced the small interrogation room, the fluorescent lights buzzing overhead. The man sat slumped in the chair across the table, arms crossed defiantly. His bruised face bore a smirk that did little to conceal his fear.

"You think you can intimidate me?" the man challenged, trying to project confidence.

Carlos sat down, leaning forward, elbows resting on the table. "You're not as tough as you think. You held a knife to my partner's throat. Think that's going to get you anywhere?"

The man's smirk wavered, but quickly returned. "I was just doing my job, man. It's not personal."

Carlos narrowed his eyes. "Your job? Is that what you call killing people?"

"Look, I didn't kill anyone!" the man said, shrugging nonchalantly. "I was just doing a job."

Carlos clenched his jaw. "Then what were you doing with that knife? Why threaten my partner?"

The man shifted in his chair, clearly trying to deflect. "Like I said, just doing what I was paid for. People were getting too loud. Someone needed to make them back off."

Carlos leaned forward. "Who hired you?"

STEALING MEXICO

The man didn't flinch, staring straight ahead. "I don't ask questions. I get paid. That's all I know."

Carlos took a deep breath, trying to keep his cool. "So you're telling me you don't know who's behind this? You don't know who's pulling the strings?"

The man shrugged, unbothered. "Does it matter? I'm just a guy who does his job."

Carlos's fingers tightened into fists, his frustration mounting. "You're telling me you don't know anything about who's running this operation? About who's behind all the threats?"

"I'm not the one making the decisions, man," the man said with a careless shrug. "I just do the work. Someone tells me where to go, and I go."

Carlos's tone hardened, but he kept his voice steady. "What about Governor Holbrook? You ever work for him?"

The man didn't react. His face remained impassive. The silence between them stretched, but the man didn't flinch.

Carlos raised an eyebrow. "No reaction? You sure you haven't worked with him or anyone close to him? You're telling me you haven't been involved with Holbrook's people?"

Still no response. The man's expression was a mask, unreadable.

Carlos pushed further. "What about 'The Kid'? You ever heard of him?"

This time, the shift was unmistakable. The man's jaw tightened, his eyes narrowing for a split second before he regained control. A faint tremor ran through his hands, but he quickly clasped them together, trying to maintain composure.

Carlos caught the slight change and leaned in closer, his voice dropping to a sharp whisper. "Who is he? Where did he come from? There's no way you don't know anything."

The man's defiance evaporated for a moment, his eyes darting toward the door. But then he stiffened, his features hardening again. "I know nothing about that," he muttered, voice low, as though trying to shut down the conversation before it went any further.

Carlos wasn't backing off. "You've got something. I can see it. What's 'The Kid' to you?"

The man clenched his jaw, his body tensing. "I know nothing," he snapped, his voice final.

Carlos's jaw tightened. He wasn't getting anywhere. "What about the knife? You tell me that's just some random tool you happened to have? Just so happens that both Diego and Luis Morales were both stabbed."

The man shifted again, uncomfortable with the line of questioning but not ready to break. "I killed no one. Like I said, just doing my job. Nothing more to it."

Carlos leaned in closer, his patience running thin. "Who is it you work for? Who are you really scared of?"

The man sat back, still defiant but now visibly uncomfortable. "I don't know any names. I'm just following orders."

Carlos's blood boiled. "Just orders? You don't think you've got more responsibility than that? More to do than just follow someone's whim?"

The man didn't flinch. He was calm, too calm. "You think I care about your little game? I'm not the one you're looking for."

Carlos stood up suddenly, slamming his hand on the table. "You're damn right you're not. But I will find out who's pulling the strings."

The man didn't flinch. He just leaned back, crossing his arms with an almost bored expression. "Go ahead. You won't get anything out of me. I've told you all I know."

Carlos stood there, seething, his fists clenched at his sides. His mind was racing, frustration clouding his thoughts. The man's casual dismissal, his refusal to answer questions, was like a slap in the face. Carlos could feel his control slipping, and it pissed him off even more.

The man shifted in his chair, almost smug, as if he could

sense Carlos's frustration. Then, with a sudden, offhand comment, he broke the silence.

"You know," he said casually, "Diego didn't have to get involved. He should've just stayed quiet. But he kept poking around. He got what was coming to him."

The words hit Carlos like a punch to the gut. His hands trembled, but he bit back the rage rising in him. Diego—the name was like salt in a wound that hadn't fully healed. The man's nonchalant tone made it worse, like he was discussing nothing more than a passing inconvenience.

Carlos gritted his teeth. "You're done," he spat. "I don't need to hear any more of your excuses. You think you can get away with this? Think again."

Without waiting for a response, Carlos turned and stormed out of the interrogation room, his blood boiling. The man's defiant attitude, his refusal to answer any of Carlos's questions, had pushed him past his breaking point. He was no closer to the answers he needed, but now he had a new fire inside him.

The clock was ticking, and he would not stop until he found who was behind all of this.

Carlos stepped out of the interrogation room, the frustration boiling over. He swung his fist hard against the wall, the sharp crack of impact echoing in the otherwise quiet hallway. The pain radiated through his knuckles, a welcome distraction from the suffocating anger and helplessness he felt.

"Santos!" Captain Marissa Davis's voice cut through the tension like a knife. She rounded the corner, her expression a mixture of concern and reprimand. "What the hell was that about?"

Carlos clenched his jaw, refusing to meet her gaze at first. "That guy is a coward. He knows more than he's letting on, and I can't get anything out of him," he snapped, rubbing his sore knuckles.

Marissa crossed her arms, her stance authoritative. "Taking your anger out on the wall isn't going to help us solve this case. You need to keep your head clear."

"I'm fine," he shot back, though his voice betrayed the simmering frustration beneath. "We're not fine. There's a killer out there, and I can't get a damn thing from this guy. He just keeps deflecting."

"Maybe because he knows you're not in control right now," she said, stepping closer. "I get that you're emotionally invested in this case, but you can't let that cloud your judgment. You're risking your career—and your safety."

Carlos took a deep breath, trying to ground himself. "I can't help it. This is personal. He threatened Asher."

He clenched his fists at his sides, but Marissa's words hit harder than the punch he'd thrown against the wall. He could feel her eyes on him, sharp and assessing, as if she was trying to figure out just how deep his emotions ran this time.

"I'm going to pretend you didn't just say that," she said, her voice low but carrying the weight of warning. "You want to talk about personal? Fine. But you better make sure that doesn't cloud your judgment. I don't want to have to pull you from this case because you've got a personal agenda getting in the way of your work."

Carlos felt his blood run cold. The words stung more than he wanted to admit, the reality of what she was saying settling into his chest like a stone. He had always separated his emotions from his work—always. But lately, that line was blurring.

"I know," he muttered, not trusting himself to say more.

Marissa's gaze softened, but the steel was still there. "I know you care about Asher, Santos. But this—this isn't a case

STEALING MEXICO

where you get to play hero. Not when you're on the line for everyone else. Especially not when it's about getting justice for Diego."

Carlos swallowed hard, his jaw tight as he held her gaze. He didn't want to admit it, but there was truth in what she said. His proximity to it was dangerous; if he wasn't careful, it could lead him down an irreversible path. He needed to rein it in, for Asher's sake. For his own.

"Understood," Carlos said, his voice barely a whisper as he fought to keep his temper in check.

Marissa nodded, her face still set in that no-nonsense expression. "Good. Now let's get back to the case. We can't afford to lose time. You're not alone in this, Santos, but you've got to keep it professional. Don't forget that."

Carlos gave her a curt nod, knowing she was right. His emotions had been running wild, and it was only a matter of time before they caught up with him. He couldn't let that happen. Not now. Not when everything was on the line.

He let out a slow breath, trying to center himself as they walked. But as much as he tried to push his emotions aside, the words Marissa had said—personal agenda—kept echoing in his mind. Would it be enough to keep him on the case? Or would his feelings for Asher be the thing that finally unraveled him? Did he have feelings for Asher? Was that what this was?

He didn't know the answers. But he was damn sure he wouldn't stop until he figured it out. For Diego, Asher, and everyone else who depended on him to rectify the situation.

CHAPTER 37

ASHER

Asher stood by the entrance of the precinct, watching Carlos pace back and forth with a tension that seemed to hang in the air around him. There was something off about him today—more distant, more closed off. The usual warmth in his eyes was absent, replaced by a cool detachment that made Asher's stomach twist uncomfortably.

He cleared his throat, trying to get Carlos' attention. "How'd the interrogation go?" he asked, trying to sound casual, though his gaze flickered to Carlos' stiff posture.

Carlos glanced at him briefly, then looked away, his lips forming a tight line. "Didn't go," he muttered. His clipped, almost dismissive tone made Asher pause.

The silence stretched between them, and Asher could feel the weight of it pressing down. He wasn't used to this, to Carlos shutting him out. It was like a wall had gone up, and it bothered him more than he expected.

"Come on, man. You're not even going to tell me anything?" Asher prodded, the edge creeping into his voice without him meaning for it to.

Carlos didn't meet his eyes. "There's nothing to tell," he

STEALING MEXICO

spat, his words short, like he was deliberately keeping Asher at arm's length.

Asher's frustration flared. "Jesus, Carlos. What the hell's going on with you?" His words came out sharper than he intended, but it didn't matter. The quiet had gone on long enough.

Carlos stopped pacing and finally looked at him, his jaw clenched tight. "I'm not in the mood to talk about it, Asher," he said, his voice low.

Asher stared at him, taken aback. "Not in the mood? I'm trying to—" He cut himself off, taking a step toward Carlos. "You've been acting weird ever since I got here. What is this? Is it the case? Or is it something else?"

Carlos's eyes darkened, and for a moment, it seemed like he was about to snap. But instead, he took a breath, his frustration simmering beneath the surface. "You wouldn't understand."

Asher's heart pounded, a mixture of confusion and something deeper flaring up inside him. "Try me." He was too tired of being kept in the dark, too tired of feeling like an outsider in a situation that was supposed to be about them working together.

Carlos's lips pressed into a thin line, his hands curling into fists at his sides. He looked like he was holding back, like there was something he desperately wanted to say but couldn't.

"Is this because of the damn case, or is it something more?" Asher pressed, his voice quieter now, as though the question had weight, something unspoken hanging in the air between them.

The silence stretched out, thick and uncomfortable. Finally, Carlos shook his head, muttering something under his breath. "I don't know, alright? It's everything. It's this damn case, it's you, it's... I don't know how to do this. How to do any of this."

Asher blinked, thrown off by the rawness of Carlos's words. He hadn't expected that. The walls had come down, just like that, and now all the frustration, the tension, the things they'd never said to each other, were hanging in the air like a storm waiting to break.

"I'm not... I'm not trying to make this harder," Asher said quietly, his voice softer now. He stepped closer, his eyes locking with Carlos's. "I just want to know where we stand. We're in this together, right?."

Carlos's eyes flickered toward him, and for a moment, Asher thought he saw something break in his expression. But it was gone as quickly as it had appeared. Carlos sighed, his breath sharp. "It's nothing," he muttered, his voice low.

"No, it's not nothing. You're shutting me out," Asher said, the words coming out a little sharper than he meant. He crossed his arms, refusing to let the silence stretch any further. "What the hell is going on?"

Carlos finally stopped pacing and turned toward him, his eyes dark with a mix of frustration and something else—something that Asher couldn't quite place. "I'm just... struggling to separate everything," Carlos said, his voice rough. "This case, what's going on with you... it's all blending together. And it's screwing with my head."

Asher blinked, thrown off by the honesty in Carlos's words. He hadn't expected this. Not from Carlos. "Blending together? What does that mean?"

Carlos shook his head, his hands gripping the edge of the desk as if he were trying to steady himself. "I've never had this happen before," he admitted. "I've always been able to keep things separate—my work and my personal life. I knew where the lines were. But now... it's like I can't see them anymore. Everything's... bleeding into each other. And it's throwing me off. It's not just the case, it's..." His words faltered, like he was caught between saying too much or nothing at all.

STEALING MEXICO

Asher could feel the weight of his silence, the unspoken truth hanging in the air. It wasn't just about the case. It was about something deeper. About what had happened between them the night they spent together, about the things neither of them had said.

"You're saying this is about me?" Asher asked quietly, his voice steady despite the sudden vulnerability he felt.

Carlos looked at him, his expression a mix of frustration and regret. "No," he said, his voice thick with something unspoken. "It's everything. I don't know how to manage this... whatever this is." He gestured between them, the confusion and anger simmering beneath his words.

Asher took a step closer, the knot in his chest tightening. "Carlos," he said softly, his gaze steady. "You don't have to figure it all out right now. But we're in this together, okay? I'm not going anywhere. We're doing this—this case—together."

Carlos's eyes softened, but he still didn't fully let his guard down. "I don't know how to do this. How to do any of this," he murmured, his voice barely above a whisper.

Asher could hear the conflict in his tone, and it cut through him. This was more than just a case. More than just the job. This was something deeper, something that neither of them could ignore anymore.

Asher stayed quiet for a moment, letting the words sink in. He could feel the pull between them, the unspoken tension that had been building ever since they let themself cross the line of temptation. It was hard to ignore, even harder to pretend it didn't matter. But right now, this wasn't about what had happened between them. It wasn't about the emotions they hadn't voiced yet.

"We need to forget about everything for now," Asher said suddenly, his voice steady, though there was a flicker of something vulnerable in his eyes. "Forget about what happened between us, about everything. The case is bigger than this. Diego... Morales—those are the things that matter right now. Not us."

Carlos nodded slowly, his expression softening just a little, though his mind was clearly still on what he had just admitted. "You're right," he muttered. "I've got to focus. We've got a job to do."

Asher took a step back, relieved that Carlos seemed to be getting his head back in the game. But he wasn't done yet. There was still something that needed to be said. "So, what happened in the interrogation?" he asked, keeping his voice casual, though his curiosity burned.

Carlos's jaw tightened again, but he met Asher's gaze, the words spilling out with frustration. "I pushed him. I brought up the Governor's name—nothing. He didn't flinch. But then... when I mentioned 'The Kid,' Morales got defensive. He wouldn't say anything after that. It's like he's hiding something big. And I can't get anything more out of him."

Asher considered this, frowning. "So we know he's connected, but he's not talking."

"Exactly," Carlos said, his voice tight. "It's like he knows something, but he's playing it cool. And I don't like it."

"Then we need to find another way in," Asher said, his mind already moving. "We need something solid."

Carlos nodded slowly, his eyes sharpening with determination. "We'll go see Dr. Patel. She might have something that can connect Diego and Morales. Because that means that asshole is connected, which takes us right back to Holbrook and 'The Kid'."

Asher nodded, his resolve matching Carlos's. "Right. We need to tie him to the bigger picture. Maybe we can finally get the proof we need."

They both turned toward the exit, their minds focused back on the case. The tension between them hadn't disap-

STEALING MEXICO

peared, but they knew they had to put it aside. Diego's death —and now Morales—were the things that mattered. They couldn't afford to let anything else get in the way.

For now, they had a lead to follow. The rest could wait.

CHAPTER 38

CARLOS

The room was chilly, the sterile scent of the morgue hanging heavily in the air. Carlos walked in, his footsteps muted by the thick, white linoleum floor. Dr. Patel, the Medical Examiner, was bent over the table, examining the body of Morales, the shopkeeper. The stillness of the body, draped in a white sheet, felt unnervingly final. Carlos's eyes flickered to Asher, who stood beside him, shifting uncomfortably. Asher's face had gone pale, his eyes avoiding the body on the table as though it might suddenly spring to life.

"You don't have to stay," Carlos said softly, glancing sideways at Asher, noticing the way he was fidgeting with his fingers. "I know this isn't easy."

"I'm fine," Asher muttered, though the tightness in his voice told another story. His gaze remained fixed on the far wall, clearly doing his best to shut out the reality in front of him.

Carlos nodded, but didn't press the issue. Instead, he turned to Dr. Patel, the weight pressing heavily on him. "Was the knife we recovered from the man who attacked Asher the one that killed Morales?"

Dr. Patel's head shook slowly, her brow furrowing. "No,

STEALING MEXICO

the knife doesn't match. But the nature of the wounds tells me something important." She straightened up, running gloved fingers over the sheet, lifting it to reveal the damage to Morales's body. "A blade similar to the one used in Diego's murder inflicted the fatal, deep, slashing wound. However, this attack was more brutal." She motioned to the numerous lacerations across the chest and arms. "These wounds tell a different story. Morales fought back. Whoever killed him had to overpower him."

Asher shifted his weight, clearly uncomfortable, but his curiosity was aroused. He took a small step forward, despite himself. "So, you think whoever killed Morales also killed Diego?"

Dr. Patel's eyes met Asher's, and she nodded. "Yes. The shape of the wound, the depth, even the angle—this is the same person. Whoever killed Diego is likely the one who killed Morales. But Morales fought harder, which makes this attack seem... messier. More chaotic."

Carlos clenched his jaw, absorbing the details. His gut twisted. The connection between Diego and Morales was undeniable now. But it didn't bring them any closer to identifying their killer. Morales had fought back, which meant he had been awake, aware, and perhaps struggling to keep his life. Carlos's stomach churned at the thought.

"So he fought back?" Carlos asked, his voice sharper now, desperate for more information.

Dr. Patel's hands hovered over the defensive wounds on Morales's arms. "Yes," she said. "These wounds are consistent with someone trying to protect themselves—slashes to the arms, defensive positions. The attacker was likely trying to subdue him quickly. There's a lot of evidence to suggest this was a personal attack, though."

Carlos's mind raced as he processed everything. The violence was escalating. The attacks weren't random, and the more they learned, the more he understood that whoever was behind these murders was sending a message. But what was that message? And who was next?

"We're not sure yet of the murder weapon. We'll need to analyze it further," Dr. Patel continued. "But the wounds on both Diego and Morales indicate a single assailant. I have someone analyzing the wounds to see if we can pinpoint the exact murder weapon. It just takes time."

Asher's voice broke through Carlos's thoughts, softer than before. "We don't have time."

Dr. Patel's eyes lingered on Asher before returning to the body. "I understand, but I'm doing everything I can. I'll let you know as soon as I find out more."

Carlos nodded, swallowing hard against the lump in his throat. Asher was right beside him, still uncomfortable but not pulling away. The weight of their investigation was becoming heavier, and Carlos could feel it pressing in on both of them.

The drive away from the morgue was quiet, the tension between them palpable. Carlos glanced at Asher, who was staring out the window, his knee bouncing anxiously. His usual sharp wit was absent, replaced by a silence that unnerved Carlos more than he wanted to admit.

As they hit a red light, Carlos broke the silence. "You've been quiet."

Asher's head turned slightly, but he didn't meet Carlos's gaze. "I'm fine," he said, though his voice lacked conviction.

Carlos didn't press immediately, waiting until the car was in motion again. "You don't have to keep it together for me," he said, keeping his tone gentle. "God knows I haven't even been able to keep it together."

STEALING MEXICO

Asher let out a shaky breath, finally looking at him. "It's just... seeing Morales like that, on the table..." He trailed off, his voice catching. "It could've been me, Carlos. That guy had a knife to my throat, and—" He stopped, his hand running through his hair. "I can't stop thinking about it. What if next time we're too late? What if—"

"Hey." Carlos cut him off, his voice firm but warm. He pulled the car to the curb and put it in park, turning to face Asher fully. "That will not happen."

"You don't know that," Asher shot back, his voice rising slightly. "You can't promise that."

"I can promise that I'll do everything in my power to make sure it doesn't," Carlos said, his dark eyes steady. "I won't let anything happen to you, Asher."

Asher looked at him, his expression a mix of vulnerability and fear. "But what if it's not enough? What if—"

"It will be," Carlos interrupted, his voice softening. "I know the risks. And yeah, I'm worried too. But we're not alone in this, and we're not going to stop until we figure out who's behind all of this."

The words hung between them, heavy and yet comforting. Carlos could feel the sharp edge of his own fear, the thought of Asher in Morales's place gnawing at him. They'd agreed to put their feelings aside, to focus on the case, but moments like this made it impossible for Carlos to ignore the way his heart clenched at the thought of losing Asher.

He reached over and placed a hand briefly on Asher's, giving it a small squeeze before pulling away. "You're not alone in this. I'm not going anywhere."

Asher nodded, his expression softening, though the worry in his eyes didn't completely fade. "Thanks," he murmured, his voice quieter now.

Carlos let the moment linger for a beat before starting the car again. "We've got work to do," he said, his tone shifting back to business, though a hint of warmth lingered in his voice.

"Where to?" Asher asked, his voice steadier now.

"We're paying another visit to the Governor's building," Carlos said. "We need to find out who this assistant is."

Asher blinked, surprised. "You think that's safe?"

Carlos's jaw tightened as he merged back into traffic. "I don't know. But we don't really have a choice. It's worth looking into. Besides, if anyone knows what Morales and Diego were getting close to, it's someone in Holbrook's inner circle."

Asher nodded, his determination returning. "Then I guess it's our only option."

Carlos's grip on the steering wheel tightened slightly, his mind already turning over how to handle what was ahead. They were walking into dangerous territory, and he couldn't shake the feeling that they were being watched. But as he glanced at Asher again, catching the spark of resolve in his eyes, he reminded himself why he couldn't let fear win.

CHAPTER 39

ASHER

The towering office building loomed ahead, its sleek, glass facade reflecting the Phoenix skyline. Asher kept his focus forward, but the tight knot in his chest refused to loosen. He adjusted the strap of his messenger bag, the weight feeling heavier than usual.

Carlos shot him a sidelong glance. "You good?"

Asher nodded, though the nervous energy thrumming through his body betrayed him. "Yeah. Let's just do this."

Carlos didn't press further, leading the way through the revolving doors into the building's pristine lobby. The air inside was cool and sharp, with the faint scent of lemon cleaner. At the reception desk, a young woman in a sharp blazer focused on her computer screen, her fingers flying over the keyboard.

As they approached, her head lifted, and her composed expression flickered with surprise. "Can I help you?"

Carlos stepped forward, his badge flashing briefly. "Detective Carlos Santos. We need to speak with Governor Holbrook's assistant."

The receptionist's eyes widened, darting to Asher and back to Carlos. "Um, Mr. Grant isn't… available right now."

Carlos didn't waver. "It's important."

She hesitated, clearly caught between protocol and the authority standing in front of her. Her gaze lingered on Asher for a beat too long, her lips pressing into a thin line as if trying to puzzle out his role.

"And you are...?" she asked, her tone wary.

"Asher Rhodes," he said smoothly, giving her a polite smile. "I'm with the Phoenix Ledger."

Her eyebrows shot up, and the unease in her expression deepened. She picked up the phone, holding it between her ear and shoulder as her fingers hovered over the keypad. "I'll... see if he's available."

The line connected quickly, and while Asher couldn't hear the voice on the other end, her side of the conversation gave away more than she probably realized.

"Mr. Grant? A detective and a journalist are here to see you." She paused, her expression tightening. "Yes, sir." Another pause, this one heavier. "Okay, sir." She lowered her voice slightly. "I'm sorry, sir."

Asher exchanged a glance with Carlos, raising a brow. He couldn't hear the exact words, but the subtext clearly indicated Oliver's lack of enthusiasm for their visit.

Finally, the receptionist hung up the phone and stood. "Right this way."

She led them down a long, quiet hallway, the sound of their footsteps muffled by the plush carpet. Asher caught the faintest tremor in her voice as she gestured to a polished wooden door at the end. "Mr. Grant will see you now."

Carlos gave her a curt nod before opening the door, and Asher followed close behind, already bracing himself for whatever lay ahead.

The office they stepped into was cold and clinical, all glass and chrome, with little personality to speak of. Behind the sleek desk sat Oliver Grant, the governor's assistant, dressed sharply in a tailored suit that screamed authority. His perfectly styled hair and calm facade didn't quite hide the tension in his eyes as he looked up at them.

"Detective Santos," Oliver greeted coolly, his gaze sliding to Asher with thinly veiled disdain. "And Mr. Rhodes. To what do I owe this surprise visit?"

Carlos wasted no time. "We need to ask you some questions regarding the murders of Diego Cortez and Luis Morales."

Oliver's lips pressed into a thin line, his expression tightening. "I wasn't aware we were under investigation."

"You aren't," Carlos said flatly. "But two people are dead, and we have reason to believe there is a connection with Governor Holbrook's administration."

Oliver shifted in his seat, his polished demeanor slipping for a moment before he straightened, his expression hardening. "I'm not sure what you think I can tell you. Governor Holbrook supports immigration reform—everyone knows that. But we have no involvement in the personal dealings of individuals like Cortez and Morales."

"Is that so?" Asher interjected, leaning casually against the chair opposite Oliver's desk. His tone was light, but his words were deliberate. "What makes you think this is about immigration?"

Oliver's jaw tightened, but he didn't respond immediately. Instead, his fingers drummed against the desk, a nervous tic that didn't escape Asher's notice.

"I don't know what either of them was involved in," Oliver said at last, his voice clipped. "Morales was a shopkeeper. Diego was a student. Neither had any official connection to us."

STEALING MEXICO

"But an unofficial one?" Carlos pressed, his eyes narrowing.

Oliver let out a slow, measured breath, as if willing himself to remain calm. "You're making assumptions, Detective. And frankly, I find them offensive."

Asher exchanged a glance with Carlos, silently urging him to push further, but Carlos kept his expression neutral, unreadable.

"Look," Carlos said after a moment, softening his tone just slightly. "This isn't about politics or pointing fingers. It's about finding out who's behind two murders. If you know anything, now's the time to speak up."

For a moment, Oliver's mask cracked. His eyes darted to Asher, then back to Carlos, and Asher caught the faintest flicker of fear.

"I have nothing to say," Oliver said stiffly. "Cortez and Morales' involvement with immigration rights groups has absolutely nothing to do with the Holbrook administration or Mr. Holbrook's stance on immigration reform."

Asher's mind snagged on his last statement. He froze, his pulse quickening. "Wait. What did you just say?"

Oliver blinked, his mask of composure faltering. "I said neither of them had anything to do with the governor—"

"No, no," Asher interrupted, stepping closer. "You said something about an immigration rights group."

Carlos's gaze sharpened, his expression darkening as he took a step forward. "Funny thing is, I didn't say anything about either of them being involved in an immigration rights group."

The room grew unbearably still. Oliver's face paled, and his mouth opened as if to respond, but no words came out.

Asher crossed his arms, tilting his head as he watched the man squirm. "That's a pretty specific thing to say, don't you think?"

192

Oliver tried to recover, his hands tightening into fists on the desk. "I—You're twisting my words. I didn't mean—"

Carlos cut him off, his voice dangerously low. "You're going to tell us exactly what you know about Diego, Morales, and this immigration rights group. Or we'll make sure everyone knows you're stonewalling a murder investigation."

Oliver visibly swallowed, his polished facade crumbling. "I—I don't have to tell you anything, detective. I'm going to have to ask you to leave. I have work to do."

Carlos didn't move immediately, holding Oliver's gaze long enough to make him squirm. Finally, he nodded, stepping back toward the door.

Asher followed, but just as Carlos reached for the handle, he glanced back. "Oh, one more thing," he said casually. "The Kid sends his regards."

The color drained from Oliver's face, his composed exterior shattering. He gripped the edge of the desk, his knuckles white as his eyes went wide with alarm.

"I—I don't know what you mean," he stammered, his voice shaking.

Carlos smiled faintly. "Sure you don't."

As they stepped back into the hallway, Asher couldn't contain a grin. "That was interesting."

Carlos nodded, his expression grim. "We hit a nerve. He knows what we know now. I'm not sure if that's a good or a bad thing. We are going to have to get to whoever is behind this immigration rights group before he does."

Asher nodded, his thoughts racing. They had a lead, a slip they could exploit. But it also meant they were closer to something dangerous. Something people were willing to kill for.

His excitement faded, replaced by the weight of what they were up against.

CHAPTER 40

ASHER

Asher's eyes widened as the man approaching them came into focus. Governor Holbrook himself—calm, composed, and radiating authority—strode toward them with a polished ease that spoke of years navigating high-stakes politics. His handshake was firm, his tailored suit impeccable, and the subtle smile he wore was as practiced as it was disarming.

"Detective," Holbrook greeted Carlos with a cordial nod, before turning to Asher. "And Mr. Rhodes, from the Ledger, if I'm not mistaken? I hear you've both been quite active recently. It's always good to see proactive individuals. So rare these days."

"Governor Holbrook," Carlos replied, his tone polite but cautious. "Just following up on leads. We didn't expect to run into you here."

Holbrook's smile didn't falter, though there was a distant edge to his eyes. "Well, now you have. And I believe every meeting happens for a reason." He glanced between the two of them, his posture relaxed yet commanding. "In fact, I'd love to talk further. I'm hosting a fundraiser this Friday evening—an invitation-only gala. You're both welcome to attend. It would be a pleasant change of scenery from the usual office grind, don't you think?"

Asher blinked, caught off guard. "The... fundraiser? We're not exactly the usual guests for an event like that."

"Nonsense," Holbrook said smoothly, his gaze unwavering. "I value the insight of those who see both sides of the story. And I appreciate dedication to a cause. We've also invited Diego's family for a tribute to the young man." He tilted his head, his smile deepening. "If you'd like, my assistant can send you the details."

Asher forced a polite smile, his mind already racing. What's his angle here?

After they exchanged polite farewells, the governor walked off, leaving Carlos and Asher standing in silence. When they finally reached the lobby doors, Asher tugged at Carlos's sleeve.

"What was that? Does he know we're investigating him, or...?"

Carlos shook his head, his brow furrowed. "Either he's making a move to cover something up, or... he genuinely doesn't know we're onto him. But inviting us to a private gala?"

Asher looked back toward the elevator where the governor had disappeared, trying to process what had just happened. "Maybe it's a trap, maybe it's a distraction. Nothing's adding up, Carlos. It's like every lead we chase just gets murkier."

Carlos exhaled, crossing his arms as he stared thoughtfully ahead. "Whatever his reason, if he's willing to invite us in... we can't ignore the chance to see who else is in that room. Maybe we'll get a closer look at his connections."

Asher nodded, though unease settled in his stomach. "Then we'll go. But we need to be ready in case this is more than a social invitation."

Carlos's gaze shifted to Asher, his expression softening. "I wouldn't let anything happen to you there."

Asher felt a flicker of warmth at Carlos's reassurance, but it quickly faded as his thoughts returned to the governor. He couldn't shake the feeling that they were walking into something carefully orchestrated.

As they pushed through the building's glass doors and stepped into the brisk evening air, Asher glanced back at the towering structure.

"Carlos," he breathed, his voice tinged with a mix of dread and curiosity. "What if this gala isn't about who's in that room? What if it's about who isn't?"

Carlos frowned, turning to him, but Asher didn't elaborate. His gaze lingered on the reflection of the building's lights in the darkened sky, his chest tightening as a question clawed at the edge of his thoughts.

Who else was Holbrook trying to keep in the dark—and why?

CHAPTER 41

CARLOS

The smell of Abuela's cooking filled the house, warm and familiar, but it did little to ease the growing tension at the dining room table. Carlos sat hunched over Diego's laptop, scrolling through files with a furrowed brow, while Asher sat across from him with his own laptop open, tapping away as he searched for connections to Morales. The two of them had been at it for hours, their frustration palpable in the quiet room.

Carlos sighed, rubbing his temples. "This is like trying to solve a puzzle where half the pieces are missing. Nothing ties together cleanly, no matter how many times I go through it."

Asher didn't look up from his screen. "Tell me about it. I've been cross-referencing Morales with every lead we've got, but all I'm finding is vague mentions and a whole lot of nothing. It's like he's a ghost, just barely leaving traces."

Carlos closed Diego's laptop with a little more force than necessary, leaning back in his chair and crossing his arms. "And we still don't know what the connection is between Morales, Diego, and this immigration rights group."

Asher leaned back too, running a hand through his hair in

STEALING MEXICO

exasperation. "If there even is a connection. For all we know, we're chasing smoke."

Before Carlos could reply, Abuela appeared in the doorway, wiping her hands on a dish towel. She raised an eyebrow, her tone cutting through the room like a knife. "Why are you two sitting there looking so lost? Did either of you even check if this Morales has a police record?"

Both Carlos and Asher froze, exchanging wide-eyed looks of realization.

Carlos groaned, muttering, "Why didn't I think of that?" He pulled out his phone, dialing dispatch immediately.

Asher smirked, looking up at Abuela. "I think you just cracked the case, señora."

Abuela scoffed, waving him off. "I cracked nothing. I just have more sense than you two. Dinner's ready in ten minutes, so hurry up." She disappeared back into the kitchen, leaving the two men scrambling to catch up with her simple logic.

"Dispatch, it's Santos," Carlos said into the phone, already grabbing his notebook. "Can you send me anything you've got on a Luis Morales? Any records, past or current?"

A few minutes later, Carlos's phone buzzed with an email notification. He opened it quickly, his eyes scanning the attached report.

"Anything?" Asher asked, leaning forward, curiosity piqued.

Carlos didn't respond immediately. Locked on the screen, he scrolled to the bottom of the document, his expression darkening.

"Carlos?" Asher pressed, the hint of worry creeping into his voice.

Carlos finally looked up, his face pale. "There's a disturbance of peace complaint. Morales was hosting meetings in the back room of his shop. No details on what they were about, just vague notes about loud noise."

"Okay," Asher said slowly. "That's something. What's wrong?"

Carlos hesitated before holding the phone up, pointing at the bottom of the report. "The reporting officer…"

Asher leaned in to read it, his eyes widening. "Carlos… that's you."

"And the date? It was two days before Diego's murder," Carlos said, nodding stiffly, his mind racing.

"That's impossible," Asher whispered, staring at him. "You would've remembered filing that report."

Carlos's jaw tightened, his grip on the phone unyielding. "I didn't file it. I didn't even know the man existed. Someone's trying to make it look like I did."

The air between them grew heavy as the implications sank in. Asher broke the silence first, his voice unsteady.

"Carlos…if someone's planting your name on reports, they're not just trying to cover their tracks. They had to have wanted you to find it."

Carlos stared at the screen, his mind a storm of questions and possibilities. He didn't know who was behind this, but one thing was certain. Whoever they were, they wanted him connected to Morales. But why?

Carlos stared at the ceiling, the dim glow of moonlight filtering through the blinds casting faint patterns across the room. His mind refused to settle, leaping from one thread of thought to another. The case, the Morales report, the immigration rights group—each piece felt important, but none of it fit together. And then there was Asher, lying so close that Carlos could feel the subtle rise and fall of his chest with every breath.

STEALING MEXICO

He turned his head slightly, his eyes lingering on Asher's profile in the muted light. His lips parted slightly in a restless slumber—or not, as Asher stirred, his hand brushing against Carlos's arm before curling instinctively around it.

"I can't sleep," Asher mumbled, his voice groggy but laced with frustration.

"Me either," Carlos admitted softly.

Carlos shifted, hesitating, before running his fingers lightly over Asher's hand. The softness of his skin was grounding, a tether to keep him from drowning in the chaos swirling in his mind. For a moment, he let himself savor it, this rare, fragile moment of calm between storms.

"I keep thinking about Holbrook," Carlos said after a long pause, his voice barely above a whisper. "And Oliver Grant. Something's not right."

Asher opened his eyes, turning his head to meet Carlos's gaze. "We'll figure it out," he said, his words steady despite the exhaustion shadowing his face.

Carlos let out a quiet sigh, his hand still resting against Asher's. "Tomorrow," he began, his voice firmer now, "I need you to stay here. Look into the immigration rights group—see what you can find about their connection to Morales and Diego. Someone in that group has to know something."

Asher frowned. "You're going to the station?"

Carlos nodded. "I need to talk to Captain Davis. The Morales report—there's something going on there, and I need to know what it is."

Asher studied him for a moment before giving a small, reluctant nod. "Fine. But if anything happens, you call me. No disappearing acts."

Carlos smirked faintly, the tension in his chest easing just a little. "I'll be fine. Just... focus on digging into that group.

"Deal," Asher murmured, shifting closer. His fingers curled around Carlos's, a quiet reassurance.

Asher's eyes fluttered shut again, but Carlos stayed

awake, his thoughts still a tangled web of questions. The warmth of Asher's body next to him was both a distraction and a comfort—a reminder of what was at stake, and what he couldn't afford to lose.

As dawn crept into the room, Carlos resolved that tomorrow would bring answers. It had to. Because if they didn't start making sense of all this soon, the darkness threatening to consume them both might become impossible to escape.

CHAPTER 42

ASHER

Morning sunlight poured through the small kitchen window as Asher clicked through the web pages on his laptop. The cozy kitchen smelled of cinnamon and fresh pan dulce, Abuela's quiet humming filling the space as she moved between the stove and the counter. Asher had been scrolling through article after article about immigration rights groups in Phoenix, his focus narrowing on one name that kept cropping up: Gabby Puente.

He leaned back in his chair, sipping the café de olla Abuela had handed him earlier. Gabby was more than just a participant in these movements—she was a leader, her name tied to protests, advocacy work, and local initiatives. But even in public records, there was an air of caution surrounding her. She had a reputation for being fiercely protective of her cause and those involved in it.

"You've been very quiet, mijo," Abuela said, glancing over at him. "Is the work keeping you so busy, or are you just avoiding trouble with Carlos?"

Asher chuckled softly, closing a tab. "A little of both, maybe. He works hard enough for two people—I'm just trying to keep up."

STEALING MEXICO

Abuela smiled knowingly, setting a plate of sweet bread near him. "Carlos needs someone who understands him. Someone who stays, even when things are hard. You have been here a lot more lately... does that mean you are staying?"

The question hit him harder than he expected. Asher opened his mouth, then closed it again, unsure how to respond. Instead, he focused on the screen, his fingers tapping absently on the edge of the keyboard. "I'm just here to help with the case," he said finally, his voice quieter than usual.

Abuela's smile didn't waver, but her eyes softened as she reached out to pat his hand. "Helping is good. But don't be afraid to think about yourself, too."

Before he could overthink her words, Asher cleared his throat and turned his attention back to Gabby. The more he read, the more his conviction grew that she might hold the missing piece to Diego's investigation. She had been involved in multiple protests, including one Diego had attended a few weeks before his death. She was involved in community meetings, fundraising efforts, and grassroots organizing. If Diego had been looking into corruption connected to these groups, Gabby would have known.

He found her contact information listed on one of the group's public pages. His finger hovered over the "call" button.

"What is it?" Abuela asked, her voice breaking through his hesitation.

"I think I found someone who can help," he said, more to himself than to her. Taking a deep breath, he pressed the button.

The phone rang twice before a woman's voice answered, cautious and clipped. "This is Gabby."

"Hi, Gabby," Asher began, trying to sound calm and professional. "My name is Asher Rhodes. I'm a journalist looking into the murder of Diego Cortez. I think you might know something about what he was investigating before he died."

The line went quiet. For a moment, Asher thought she might have hung up, but then she spoke again, her tone sharper. "How did you get my number?"

"It's publicly listed on your organization's page," he blurted. "I'm not trying to bother you—I just need your help. Diego was working on something that got him killed, and I think it's connected to your group."

Gabby's hesitation was palpable. "I don't talk about my work with strangers. Especially not over the phone."

"I understand that," Asher said, leaning forward, his tone earnest. "But Diego wasn't just some random kid. He cared about what you're fighting for. He wanted to expose the truth about the people exploiting these communities. If you know anything, I need to hear it."

She sighed audibly. "What exactly are you looking for, Mr. Rhodes? Diego wasn't a member of our group, and I don't know much about him."

Asher caught the crack in her voice, a subtle indication that she knew more than she was letting on. "I'm looking for answers. You're right—I don't know exactly what Diego was investigating. But I think it's tied to corruption in the systems meant to protect immigrants. He was at one of your protests a few weeks ago. That can't be a coincidence."

There was a long pause. "Even if I wanted to help you, this isn't something you can just report on and walk away from," she said finally, her voice low and wary. "People have gotten hurt for less. Diego is proof of that."

"I know the risks," Asher replied firmly. "And I'm not walking away. Please, Gabby. You were his last lead. If you know anything, even if it seems small, it could be the break we need."

Another pause, followed by the faint sound of movement

STEALING MEXICO

on her end of the line. "There's a cafe I go to sometimes. La Paloma, on Oak Street."

Asher straightened. "Can we meet?"

"Noon," she said reluctantly. "But don't expect much. And don't bring anyone else."

"Understood," Asher said. "Thank you, Gabby."

The call ended, and Asher set his phone down, exhaling sharply. He glanced at the time: 9:15 a.m. A quick search confirmed that La Paloma Café was nearly two hours away.

"You are going to meet this person?" Abuela asked, her tone casual, but the concern in her eyes was clear.

"Yeah," Asher said, standing and grabbing his jacket. "She might have answers."

"And Carlos? Will you tell him?"

Asher hesitated, guilt tugging at him. "Not yet. He's got enough on his plate, and I don't even know if this will lead anywhere."

Abuela didn't look convinced, but she nodded. "Be careful, mijo. Carlos will worry if you do something foolish."

"I'll be fine," Asher promised, though he wasn't sure how much he believed it.

As he stepped outside into the cool morning air, Asher took a deep breath. Gabby Puente might hold the key to Diego's investigation—or she might slam the door shut entirely. Either way, he had to try. There was no turning back now.

CHAPTER 43

CARLOS

Carlos took a steadying breath, his eyes narrowing at the falsified report on his screen. His name... on a report he didn't file? This wasn't just an administrative error—it was deliberate. Someone had forged his name and badge number on an incident report he'd never responded to.

The details were chilling. The date coincided with the day before Morales, the shopkeeper, was murdered. Carlos's mind raced as he considered the implications. Whoever had killed Morales might be trying to frame him—or at the very least, drag him into the case with enough circumstantial evidence to raise questions.

His fingers drummed against the desk as he stared at the screen. He reached for his phone, ready to call Captain Davis, when a knock sounded at his office door.

"Detective Santos," a young officer called, poking her head around the corner. "I have the security footage from the shopkeeper's murder. You're going to have to see this."

Carlos stood, his heart pounding as he followed her down the hall to the AV room. The department buzzed with the usual morning activity, but Carlos felt like he was moving

STEALING MEXICO

through a fog. The falsified report and this new footage—too many pieces were falling into place at once, and none of it boded well.

The AV room was dimly lit, its air cooler than the rest of the station. A single screen hung on the wall, a small laptop wired to the display. The officer connected the video file, her face tense as she pressed play.

Carlos stepped closer, his full attention locked on the screen as the grainy footage began. The back room of Morales's shop came into view—shadowed shelves, boxes stacked along the walls, and a single table cluttered with papers and insignificant items. The space looked ordinary, but Carlos felt the weight of what was about to unfold.

At first, the scene was still. Then Morales entered from the right, clutching a worn bag. He looked over his shoulder as he moved to the table, unpacking something with hurried, almost frantic movements. His shoulders were tense, his head jerking toward the door every few seconds.

Moments later, the door to the back room swung open. A man stepped in, his face obscured by the angle. He wore a heavy jacket, the hood pulled low over a baseball cap that shadowed his features. The way he moved—calm, deliberate —sent a chill through Carlos.

The stranger approached Morales without hesitation, his posture radiating confidence. They exchanged words—too brief and tense to interpret from the lack of audio. Morales waved a hand, dismissive, and turned his back.

That's when the attack began.

The stranger lunged, pulling something from his pocket— a blade that glinted even in the low-resolution footage. Morales stumbled back, hands flying up defensively. Carlos's fists clenched as he watched the shopkeeper struggle, grabbing at shelves for leverage, anything to push his attacker away.

Morales fought hard, but the man was relentless. The

blade flashed again and again, cutting through Morales's defenses. Carlos's breath caught as Morales fell to his knees, one hand clutching his stomach while the other reached out weakly.

And then the attacker leaned in.

Carlos moved closer to the screen, watching the man crouch next to Morales. He whispered something—his lips moving briefly but deliberately. Whatever he said, it made Morales's face twist in pain or fear before his body went limp.

The killer stood, adjusting his jacket, and turned toward the camera.

Carlos's stomach dropped.

The man tilted his head slightly, a smirk playing across his face as he looked directly into the lens. The image was haunting, even in the grainy footage. It wasn't just the smirk—it was the way the man held the moment, as if he wanted someone to see him.

Carlos's chest tightened, rage bubbling just beneath the surface. This wasn't a random act—someone calculated it. The killer had known about the camera, maybe even expected that Carlos or someone else would eventually watch the footage.

The video ended abruptly, the screen going black.

Carlos exhaled sharply, his fists still clenched at his sides. "Freeze the frame," he said, his voice low but commanding.

The officer rewound the footage and froze it on the killer's smirking face. Though partially obscured by the cap and shadow, there was enough detail to work with—sharp cheekbones, a scruffy jawline, and cold, predatory eyes.

"I'll run it through facial recognition," the officer said, her voice quiet.

Carlos nodded but didn't respond. His mind was already racing ahead, piecing together what this meant. The falsified report, the footage, the deliberate nature of the attack—it all pointed to someone trying to send a message.

STEALING MEXICO

But was the message for him?

As the officer worked, Carlos stepped out of the AV room, pulling out his phone. He needed to talk to Captain Davis—and fast. Whoever this killer was, they weren't just dangerous. They were bold, and they wanted to be seen.

CHAPTER 44

CARLOS

Carlos sat across from Captain Davis in her office, the falsified Morales report sitting between them on the desk. The tension was heavy, the air thick with the weight of unanswered questions. Every fresh development seemed to push the case further into dangerous territory, and this latest discovery— the report bearing his name—was no exception.

Davis leaned back in her chair, arms crossed as she studied him. "I had IT go over this report again," she said. "Same result. No logs, no edits. It's as if it never existed, except now it's here, tied to your badge."

Carlos frowned, his fatigue clear in the lines on his face. "And you're sure no one in the department touched Morales's file recently? No updates, no leads?"

"Nothing," Davis said, shaking her head. "His case was cold until this showed up. But whoever planted this didn't make a rookie mistake. They didn't do this sloppily, and they didn't rush it. They wanted it to look legitimate, but it doesn't feel like a frame job."

Carlos leaned forward, his brow furrowed. "So, what is it?"

"It feels calculated," Davis said, gesturing to the report.

STEALING MEXICO

"Like someone's leaving you a trail. They knew this would get your attention."

Carlos's jaw tightened, the tension in his body growing. "A trail to what?"

"That's the question," Davis said, her voice sharp. "Morales? He was a small-time shopkeeper with a clean record. No priors. No obvious reason someone would care to use him as bait."

"Except now we know that's not true," Carlos countered. "Morales wasn't just some shopkeeper. He was tied to the immigration rights group Diego was investigating. Whoever planted this report knew that."

Davis tilted her head, her expression shifting to something sharper. "You're connecting this to the footage from Morales's shop, aren't you?"

Carlos nodded. The image of the grainy video burned into his memory. "The footage shows it all. The guy who killed Morales? He didn't just attack him. He knew where the camera was, knew it would capture his face—or at least a glimpse. That smirk at the end? That wasn't an accident. He wanted us to see him."

Davis narrowed her eyes. "You think it's the same person who planted the report?"

"It has to be," Carlos said, leaning back in his chair. "This isn't just about Morales. This is about connecting the dots. Diego, Morales, the immigration group—it's all tied together, and someone wants me to figure it out."

Davis tapped her pen against the desk, her expression thoughtful but wary. "If this is a breadcrumb trail, it's a dangerous one. You saw that footage, Santos. The guy who killed Morales didn't hesitate. He's not just some thug. He's calculating. And now he's dragging you into his game."

Carlos exhaled, the weight of her words pressing down on him. "If it's a game, then he's counting on me to play along."

"And are you going to?"

Carlos's smirk was faint, humorless. "Do I have a choice?"

Davis leaned forward, her tone softening. "Santos, whoever did this knows how to push buttons. They planted that report for a reason. But you can't let this get personal. We both know what happens when it does."

Carlos didn't respond immediately. His thoughts flicked to Asher, who was chasing leads of his own. He remembered the determination in Asher's voice when they'd last spoken, the fire in his eyes when he talked about Diego's case. Carlos knew how dangerous this was becoming—not just for himself, but for everyone connected to it.

"It's already personal," Carlos said finally, his voice low.

Davis sighed, rubbing her temples. "Just don't let it cloud your judgment. Whoever this is, they're playing a long game. You need to stay a step ahead."

Carlos stood, the falsified report in hand. "I'll keep my head clear. And I'll find out who's behind this."

Davis nodded, though her expression remained guarded. "Good. But Santos—don't go charging into this alone. You're a good detective, but you're not invincible."

Carlos paused at the door, glancing back at her. "I'll be careful," he said, though he didn't entirely believe it.

As he left the office, his mind churned with the implications of the report and the footage. Someone out there was pulling strings, nudging him toward a bigger picture he didn't fully understand yet.

CHAPTER 45

ASHER

Asher's heart pounded as he took a seat across from Gabby in the back corner of a dimly lit cafe. She scanned the room, her eyes flickering with a nervous intensity that instantly set him on edge. She looked exactly as he'd seen her in articles—small but fierce, with an air of determination that couldn't quite mask the worry pulling at her face.

"Thank you for meeting me," Asher said quietly, trying to put her at ease.

Gabby's gaze settled on him, her eyes sharp but wary. "I agreed to this because you said Diego's name," she said, her voice low. "But this is dangerous. More than you know."

Asher felt a chill. "You can trust me. I just need to know what he was working on. I think he was killed because of it."

She nodded slightly, then leaned in closer. "Diego was... brave. He got involved in something bigger than any of us expected." She hesitated, glancing around again before she continued, voice barely above a whisper. "At first, I thought it was about immigration. He came to our meetings, asked questions. But the more he dug, the less it made sense. He started looking into people connected to our organization—Morales included."

STEALING MEXICO

Asher's stomach twisted. "Morales, the shopkeeper?"

"Yes," Gabby replied, fingers tapping restlessly against her coffee cup. "Morales helped organize our efforts quietly, off the record. But Diego found numbers—money trails that didn't line up. I thought he was just being thorough, but now..." Her voice trailed off, and she looked away, fear flitting across her face. "Now he's dead. Morales, too."

Asher felt himself holding his breath. "You think it wasn't random? They were both targeted?"

"More than that," she said, her tone turning grave. "The records Diego found weren't just about immigration. They were coverups for something else entirely—something I hadn't even realized he'd uncovered until after he was gone. There were files, Asher. Names. Places. Financial transactions that led to offshore accounts." She drew a shaky breath. "It's a high-profile human trafficking ring."

Asher felt his stomach lurch. "Human trafficking?"

Gabby nodded, clutching her cup with white-knuckled fingers. "Diego realized that these groups—the people behind them—were using immigration rights organizations as a front. Money was moving through our groups, and on paper, it looked like donations, but it was blood money, payment for moving people across borders under horrific conditions. Morales must have found out the same thing. They didn't hesitate to kill him to keep it quiet."

Asher's mind raced. Diego had stumbled onto something massive—no wonder he'd been killed. "Do you know who's behind it? The names?"

Gabby shook her head, glancing nervously at the few other patrons in the cafe. "I don't know all of them. Just that it involves powerful people. Politicians, CEOs, government officials. People who can make records disappear and people vanish."

"Did Diego... tell you any of this?" Asher asked, trying to piece everything together. "Did he leave anything with you?"

"No. He was too careful to leave evidence with anyone. But I warned him to stop asking questions, to back off. He was fearless, though. He said he couldn't ignore it, that someone had to stand up for these people." She pressed her lips together, her voice thickening with grief. "He was such a good kid."

Asher clenched his fists, feeling a surge of anger and helplessness. This was a massive, insidious operation, and they'd killed Diego and Morales to keep it hidden. But Gabby was visibly on edge, clearly fearing for her life just by sitting here talking to him.

"Thank you for telling me this," he whispered. "Is there anything else you know? Anything that could help me connect the dots?"

Gabby paused, looking down as if weighing her words. "Just... be careful. They're everywhere, and they're watching. I think they're onto you too, after what happened to Morales. You and Carlos need to watch your backs."

The warning hung heavy in the air, and Asher forced himself to keep a calm expression, though every nerve was on high alert. "I'll be careful," he assured her. "And thank you."

She nodded, her eyes dark with worry. "Don't thank me, Asher. Just promise me you'll find justice for Diego. And if you need me... be discreet. They'll come after anyone who speaks out."

Asher gave her a grim nod, pocketing his phone and memorizing her words. As he slipped out of the cafe, he couldn't shake the feeling that someone was watching him. But one thing was clear: Diego's death was part of something far darker than he'd realized, and now, they were in even deeper than he'd imagined.

STEALING MEXICO

Asher sat in his car, nervously tapping his fingers on the steering wheel. The street outside the diner was quiet, with only a few cars parked along the curb and streetlights casting pools of dim light. He kept the entrance to the diner in clear view, his heart thumping harder than he wanted to admit. He felt this meeting was a breakthrough in the case—that he was finally going to understand what Diego had uncovered and why Morales had been killed. But as he waited, he couldn't shake the nagging doubt that he'd made a huge mistake coming here without telling Carlos.

He glanced at his phone, Carlos's number highlighted on the screen, his thumb hovering over the call button. But he lowered it. Carlos would be furious, and he'd likely demand Asher return immediately. He didn't want that. He wanted to see this through himself, to prove he could handle this part of the investigation.

The door to the diner opened, and Asher sat up straighter, his breath catching as Gabby stepped out. She moved quickly but cautiously, her eyes darting to every shadow and doorway as if expecting something—or someone—to jump out at her. Her posture was stiff, her arms wrapped tightly around herself.

Asher felt his chest tighten with unease. Something was wrong.

Then he saw the figure emerge from an alley ahead of her.

The man moved with an eerie, calculated silence, his hood pulled low over his face. Gabby didn't notice him until he was already too close.

"Gabby!" Asher yelled, throwing his car door open as the man grabbed her and yanked her into the alley.

Her startled cry echoed down the street before cutting off abruptly.

Asher bolted across the pavement, his legs driving him forward without thinking. His pulse pounded in his ears as he reached the mouth of the alley, his voice breaking as he yelled again.

"Hey! Get off her!"

The man had Gabby pinned against the wall, his hand glinting with something metallic—a knife.

"Stop!" Asher shouted, but it was too late. The blade plunged into Gabby's side, her body jerking violently as she gasped in pain.

"Gabby!" Asher screamed, lunging forward.

The attacker turned, slamming into Asher with brutal force. Asher staggered back, his head colliding with the rough brick wall. Stars exploded in his vision, and he crumpled to the ground, dazed and disoriented.

By the time he forced himself upright, blinking through the haze of pain, the attacker was gone. His retreating footsteps echoed faintly before fading into the night.

Asher's focus snapped back to Gabby. She had collapsed to the ground, slumped against the wall with one hand clutching her side. Blood seeped between her fingers, pooling beneath her.

"Gabby!" Asher choked out, crawling toward her. His hands trembled as he grabbed hers, trying to keep pressure on the wound. "Stay with me. Help is coming."

Her eyes fluttered open, unfocused and clouded with pain. Her lips moved faintly, barely forming words. Asher leaned in, desperate to hear.

"Holbrook…" she whispered, her voice barely audible. "Holbrook… he…"

Her voice faded, her head lolling to the side.

"Gabby, no! What about Holbrook?" Asher pleaded, his heart hammering. He pressed harder against her wound, panic flooding him as her breaths grew weaker.

His shaking hand fumbled for his phone, blood smearing the screen as he dialed 911.

STEALING MEXICO

"911, what's your emergency?" the operator's calm voice came through.

"Someone stabbed her!" Asher gasped, struggling to keep his voice steady. "We're in the alley behind the diner on Ninth and Cedar. Please—send help now!"

The operator asked a series of questions, but Asher barely registered them. He answered mechanically, his focus locked on Gabby as her breaths grew fainter.

"You're going to be okay," he said desperately, his voice breaking. "Help is on the way. Just hold on."

The faint wail of sirens reached his ears, growing louder with each passing second. The flashing red and blue lights illuminated the alley, and EMTs rushed toward them with their equipment.

"Sir, step back," one of them said firmly, kneeling beside Gabby.

Asher hesitated, his hands lingering on hers for a moment longer before he stumbled back, his legs unsteady. He leaned against the alley wall, his chest heaving as he watched the paramedics work.

"BP is dropping fast," one of them muttered. "We need to move her now."

They lifted Gabby onto a stretcher, securing her quickly before wheeling her toward the waiting ambulance. Asher clenched his fists, his nails biting into his palms as the ambulance doors slammed shut.

CHAPTER 46

CARLOS

Carlos stared at the text message on his phone, his stomach dropping like a stone.

> YOUR LITTLE BOYFRIEND NEEDS TO STOP POKING AROUND

His heart pounded as his thumb hovered over Asher's number. Without wasting another second, he hit call. It rang once, twice—then went to voicemail.

"Damn it," Carlos muttered, his hand tightening around the phone. He immediately redialed, but the result was the same.

Panic clawed at his chest. Asher wasn't answering.

Carlos's mind raced. If they were threatening Asher, it meant someone was watching, someone knew what Asher was doing—and where he was. Without thinking, he scrolled to Abuela's number and pressed call.

The phone barely rang before she picked up.

"Carlos?" she asked, her voice warm but curious.

"Abuela," Carlos said quickly, struggling to keep his voice calm. "Is Asher still there?"

STEALING MEXICO

There was a pause, then the distinct sound of clattering dishes. "No, mijo, he left a while ago. Something about meeting with Gabby Puente."

Carlos's grip on the phone tightened. "How long ago did he leave?"

"A few hours ago," she said. "Why? What's wrong?"

"I'll explain later," Carlos said, his voice clipped. "I have to go."

He hung up before she could ask any more questions and spun on his heel, marching straight back into Captain Davis's office. His thoughts raced with every step.

Where did he go?

He burst into the office without knocking, but Davis didn't look up. She was on the phone, her expression grim, her free hand gesturing sharply at the desk.

"Yes, I understand," she said tersely into the receiver. "We're sending a unit now. Keep me updated."

Carlos froze, dread pooling in his stomach. The moment Davis hung up the phone, she looked up, her lips pressing into a tight line.

"There's been another stabbing," she said, her tone clipped.

Carlos felt as if he'd been punched in the gut. His phone buzzed in his hand again. Another text message from the same unknown number:

TICK TOCK

"No," Carlos muttered under his breath. He clenched the phone in his hand, his mind racing with possibilities.

"What's going on, Santos?" Davis asked, her sharp gaze locking on him.

Carlos stepped forward, holding up the phone. "They're threatening Asher," he said, his voice low and deadly.

224

"Someone sent me this after." He shoved the phone forward, showing her the messages.

Davis's expression darkened, and she stood from her chair, crossing her arms. "If he's their next target, we don't have time to waste. Do you know where he is?"

Carlos shook his head, his frustration boiling over. "No. I told him to stay put, but he wouldn't listen. He went to meet with a Gabby Puente."

Davis frowned. "Get to the scene of the stabbing now! The victim was Gabby Puente..."

Carlos didn't need to hear the rest. He knew exactly how Asher thought—stubborn... determined.

"He's with her," Carlos said, already turning toward the door.

Davis stepped around her desk. "Carlos—"

"Marissa, if they hurt him!" Carlos barked, his voice sharper than he intended. He turned back, his voice softening slightly.

She hesitated, but gave a curt nod. "Be careful."

Carlos didn't respond. He bolted down the hallway, dialing Asher's number again as he pushed through the station doors and into the cool night air. It rang once, twice—voicemail.

His jaw tightened as he climbed into his car and started the engine. He punched the steering wheel in frustration.

"Pick up, dammit," he muttered under his breath.

As the tires screeched out of the parking lot, his mind raced with worst-case scenarios. Asher alone, hurt—walking straight into a trap.

His phone buzzed again, and for a split second, hope flickered in his chest. But it wasn't Asher.

It was another text from the unknown number:

> YOU SHOULD HAVE KEPT HIM ON A LEASH

STEALING MEXICO

Carlos swore under his breath, gripping the wheel so tightly his knuckles turned white. He floored the accelerator, his only focus now on finding Asher before it was too late.

CHAPTER 47

ASHER

Asher blinked against the harsh afternoon sunlight, the flashing blue and red lights from the police cars casting distorted shadows against the surrounding buildings. Officers moved purposefully around the scene, their voices low but clipped. The reality of what had just happened pressed heavily on his chest.

He glanced down at his phone vibrating in his hand. Carlos.

Asher swallowed hard, his stomach twisting. He could already imagine the anger simmering in Carlos's voice, the frustration that would come spilling out the moment Asher answered. With a steadying breath, he pressed the green button.

"Hey," he said, his voice quieter than he'd intended.

"Asher," Carlos's voice came through, tense but controlled. "Where are you? I thought we agreed you were staying at my place."

Asher winced, the weight of the day settling even heavier on him. "I... I left. I had to meet with someone."

There was a beat of silence before Carlos asked, his tone sharper, "Who?"

STEALING MEXICO

"Gabby Puente," Asher admitted, rubbing his temple. The memory of her last moments hit him like a wave. "She knew Diego. She might've been the only one left who knew what he was working on." He hesitated before forcing himself to say it. "But she's gone, Carlos. Someone attacked her right in front of me. I couldn't stop it."

Carlos didn't respond immediately, the pause on the other end of the line stretching painfully long. When he spoke again, his voice was tight, though his concern was clear. "Are you okay? Were you hurt?"

"No, I'm fine," Asher said quickly, though his hands trembled as he gripped the phone. "I tried to help her, but he was fast. He stabbed her, and then he was gone before I could stop him." His voice cracked despite his efforts to hold it together.

Carlos let out a slow exhale. "Damn it, Asher. You should've told me."

"I didn't want to waste time," Asher admitted. "She insisted it had to be today, and she was scared. I thought maybe I could help." He hesitated, then added, "She said something about Diego before she died. About a human trafficking ring."

Carlos's voice softened slightly, though the tension remained. "And now she's dead, Asher. You put yourself in danger."

"I know," Asher said, guilt heavy in his tone. "I know I messed up."

There was a long pause before Carlos spoke again, his voice more measured. "Just stay where you are. I'll come to you, alright?"

Asher nodded, though he knew Carlos couldn't see him. "Okay. I'll stay here."

"You better this time," Carlos said, and then, more quietly, "We'll figure this out. Just hang tight."

The call ended, and Asher lowered the phone, his hands still trembling.

Asher stared down at his hands. The faint, sticky residue of Gabby's blood clung to his skin, no matter how much he rubbed them together. The metallic scent lingered in his nose, mixing with the smell of asphalt and exhaust from the street.

A uniformed officer approached, a notepad in hand. "Mr. Rhodes," he said, his tone professional but impersonal. "We need to go over what happened."

Asher nodded stiffly, his voice flat as he recounted the events. He told the officer that Gabby was a friend and that they were meeting for coffee. When the attacker came, everything happened too fast to process. He avoided mentioning Gabby's connection to Diego or her last words, sticking to a sanitized version of events.

The officer jotted everything down, occasionally glancing up at him. "We might need to follow up with more questions later," he said, tucking his notepad into his pocket.

"Of course," Asher replied, his voice distant.

The officer nodded and stepped away, leaving Asher standing at the edge of the scene. He stared at the faint bloodstain on the pavement, the memory of Gabby's fear etched into his mind.

When Carlos's car pulled up, Asher felt a wave of relief and dread. He tucked his hands into his jacket pockets, hoping Carlos wouldn't notice the dried blood on his skin. Carlos stepped out of the car, his sharp eyes scanning the scene before landing on Asher.

He approached quickly, his expression unreadable but his movements tense.

"Are you alright?" Carlos asked, his voice low.

Asher nodded, though his shoulders sagged under the weight of his guilt. "I'm fine."

STEALING MEXICO

Carlos's gaze flicked to his clothes, the smudges of dirt and faint stains of blood. His jaw tightened, but he didn't comment.

"You shouldn't have done this alone," Carlos said, his tone firm but not unkind. "Asher, Gabby had a reason to be scared. She knew this was dangerous."

"I thought I could help," Asher said, his voice small. "I thought maybe I could get answers. She said Diego was onto a human trafficking ring. She said they were watching her." He hesitated, the words catching in his throat. "And now she's dead."

Carlos let out a heavy sigh, rubbing a hand over his face. "Let's get you out of here," he said finally. "You need to clean up. We'll talk more once you're back home."

Asher nodded, grateful for the reprieve. Carlos placed a hand on his shoulder, guiding him toward his car.

For now, Asher let himself follow Carlos's lead, the weight of the day pressing down on him like a suffocating fog.

CHAPTER 48

CARLOS

The sun was high, casting sharp shadows across the pavement as Carlos drove behind Asher's car. His eyes flicked between the road ahead and the rear-view mirror. The car behind him had been following them for too long—every turn, every lane change, it stayed.

Are we being followed?

Carlos's gut twisted. He couldn't tell if it was paranoia or something more. Everything about this case—Diego's files, Gabby's death, the threatening messages—felt like a noose tightening around them.

He pulled out his phone, keeping one hand on the wheel as he dialed Asher.

The call connected on the second ring.

"What's up?" Asher's voice came through, casual but tinged with weariness.

Carlos's voice was tense. "I think we're being tailed."

"What?" Asher said, his tone shifting immediately. "You sure?"

Carlos glanced at the mirror again, the car behind them matching their speed, maintaining the same distance. "Not completely, but stay sharp. Something feels off."

STEALING MEXICO

Before Asher could respond, everything unraveled in an instant.

From a side street, a box truck barreled into the intersection, running a red light and slamming into Asher's car. The sound was deafening—metal crunching, glass shattering. Asher's car spun violently, the passenger side caving in under the force of the impact.

"Asher!" Carlos shouted, his foot slamming on the brakes.

The truck didn't stop. It sped off, tires screeching, leaving Asher's car mangled in the middle of the intersection. The car behind Carlos swerved sharply around him and vanished down a side street.

Carlos threw his car into park and bolted out, adrenaline surging through him.

The midday sun glinted off the twisted metal of Asher's car. Smoke rose from the crumpled hood, and broken glass littered the asphalt. Carlos's heart pounded as he sprinted toward the wreck.

"Asher!" he called, his voice hoarse.

When he reached the driver's side, his stomach dropped. Asher slumped over the steering wheel, blood trickling down his face.

"No," Carlos muttered, yanking at the crumpled door. "No, no, no!"

The door wouldn't budge. Carlos planted a foot against the frame, pulling with all his strength until the metal groaned and gave way. Ignoring the sharp edges cutting into his palms, he leaned into the car.

"Asher! Wake up!" Carlos's voice cracked as he shook him gently. Blood streaked Asher's blond hair, and his chest rose and fell faintly.

Carlos's shaking hands fumbled with the seatbelt, unbuckling it and easing Asher out of the car as carefully as he could.

"Stay with me," Carlos whispered, lowering Asher to the

ground. His fingers found the side of Asher's neck, searching desperately for a pulse. It was there—weak, but steady.

Carlos exhaled sharply, relief washing over him in a wave. "Thank God," he murmured.

Asher's eyelids fluttered, and a faint groan escaped his lips.

"Asher, can you hear me?" Carlos asked, brushing a bloodied strand of hair from Asher's forehead.

"Carlos?" Asher's voice was faint, barely audible.

"I'm here," Carlos said firmly. "You're okay. You're going to be fine."

Asher winced, his hand twitching weakly. "What... happened?"

Carlos's jaw tightened. "Someone hit you. A truck ran a red light. But you're alive, Asher. That's all that matters."

Asher let out a soft groan, his eyes drifting shut again.

"No, no, no. Stay with me!" Carlos pleaded, shaking him gently.

The distant wail of sirens grew louder, and Carlos's shoulders sagged slightly with relief. "Help's coming," he murmured. "Just hang on a little longer."

He reached for Asher's hand, gripping it tightly. "You're not leaving me, Asher," he mumbled. "Not now. Not ever."

Asher's chest rose and fell faintly, his breathing shallow but present. Carlos held on to that small sign of life, refusing to let go.

CHAPTER 49

CARLOS

Carlos moved through the hospital halls like a man in a fog, the steady hum of fluorescent lights overhead doing little to cut through the haze. His mind refused to focus on anything beyond Asher, unconscious on the stretcher. The rhythmic beeping of medical monitors and the indistinct murmur of paramedics filled the ambulance bay, but none of it registered.

Every glance at Asher's pale face twisted into something deep in Carlos's chest. Blood matted Asher's hair. His breathing was shallow, and the image of him slumped over the steering wheel haunted Carlos.

When the paramedics arrived, they'd had to pry Carlos's hands from Asher's shoulders. He had resisted at first, but their firm insistence that they needed space finally registered. Carlos stood back, watching helplessly as they checked his vitals, their clipped words filling him with fresh dread.

"Severe head injury."

"Possible broken rib."

"Keep him stabilized."

The fragments played on a loop in his mind, each word hammering against his chest like a physical blow.

STEALING MEXICO

He barely remembered what he'd said as they wheeled Asher toward the ambulance. He only knew he would not let Asher out of his sight.

"I'm going with him," Carlos had said, his voice low and resolute.

"Sir, you can't—" one officer began, stepping in his way.

Carlos didn't hesitate. His voice hardened, sharp and unyielding. "Try to stop me."

The officer opened his mouth to argue, but a calm, authoritative voice cut through the tension.

"Let him go."

Carlos turned, relief washing over him as he saw Captain Davis approaching. Her eyes locked on him, sharp and steady, though there was a hint of understanding in her expression.

"Carlos," she said firmly, her tone leaving no room for debate. "Make sure he's okay. We'll handle the rest here. I'll have someone bring your car to the hospital."

Carlos gave her a tight nod, his throat constricting with emotion. "Thank you."

Without another word, he climbed into the ambulance, settling into a cramped seat beside Asher. The ride was bumpy and fast, the paramedics working methodically as they assessed Asher's injuries.

Carlos's gaze stayed locked on Asher's face. Every flicker of his eyelashes, every faint groan as they hit a pothole, sent Carlos's heart racing. He wanted to say something, to tell Asher it would be okay, but his throat was dry, his words trapped behind the knot of fear.

Finally, one paramedic addressed him.

"He's stable for now. He has a concussion, maybe a broken rib. We'll need scans to confirm. He'll need rest, but his vitals are holding steady."

Carlos exhaled a breath he hadn't realized he was holding. "Thank you," he murmured, his voice barely audible.

Asher stirred slightly, his head turning toward Carlos. One eye cracked open, unfocused but searching. "Carlos...?" His voice was faint, barely more than a whisper, but it was enough to flood Carlos with relief.

"I'm here," Carlos said, leaning closer. "I'm not going anywhere."

Asher's hand twitched, moving weakly toward him. Without hesitation, Carlos reached out, wrapping his hand around Asher's. His grip was gentle, but firm enough to let Asher know he wasn't alone.

"You... shouldn't... have come," Asher mumbled, his words slurred but his gaze steady.

Carlos let out a shaky laugh, the sound tinged with both relief and frustration. "You're seriously going to lecture me right now?" He squeezed Asher's hand. "You could've gotten yourself killed, and you're worried about me?"

Asher attempted a smirk, though it came out as more of a grimace. "Guess... we both have... bad habits."

Carlos's expression softened, a faint smile tugging at his lips. He reached out, brushing a stray lock of blood-matted hair from Asher's forehead. "No more near-death experiences, alright? That's not a habit I'm letting you keep."

Asher's eyes drifted shut again, his face relaxing as he slipped back into unconsciousness. But just before he fully let go, Carlos felt his hand squeeze faintly in response.

The paramedic glanced back at Carlos. "We're almost there. He's stable, but they'll need to run a full set of scans to confirm everything."

Carlos nodded, his voice steady now. "I'll be with him."

The ambulance screeched to a halt outside the hospital, and the paramedics moved quickly to wheel Asher inside. Carlos followed close behind, unwilling to let him out of sight for even a moment.

As they rushed into the ER, Carlos whispered under his

breath, a silent promise to the unconscious man on the stretcher.

"They won't get away with this."

PART FOUR

PART FOUR

CHAPTER 50

CARLOS

Carlos rubbed his eyes, the sharp artificial light of the hospital waiting room pressing down on him. His neck ached from sleeping in the rigid plastic chair, and the hum of nearby conversations blurred into the background. It had been hours, but every second had stretched, heavy with worry and helplessness.

He forced himself to stand, rolling his stiff shoulders as he approached the reception desk. A nurse with a no-nonsense demeanor typed away at her computer, barely glancing up as he leaned on the counter.

"Any updates on Asher Rhodes?" Carlos asked, his voice hoarse from exhaustion.

The nurse raised an eyebrow, finally looking at him. "Relation?"

Carlos hesitated, his heart thudding in his chest. "Partner," he said, forcing the word out.

The nurse nodded curtly, her fingers flying over the keyboard. Carlos tried to stay patient, but every second felt like an eternity. His mind cycled through the images he couldn't shake—Asher's blood-streaked face, the twisted wreckage of his car, the way his hand had gone limp in Carlos's grip for a terrifying moment.

Finally, the nurse spoke. "He's stable. In and out of consciousness earlier, but the doctor said he'll make a full recovery. Concussion, bruising to the ribs, and some superficial cuts. They're keeping him to monitor for swelling."

Carlos let out a slow breath, the tension in his chest easing slightly. Relief coursed through him so fast it left him light-headed. "Can I see him?"

The nurse sighed, clearly accustomed to such requests. She clicked her mouse a few times before nodding. "Room 312. Keep it brief—he needs rest."

"Thank you," Carlos said, his voice steadier now.

The quiet click of the hospital room door felt deafening compared to the stillness inside. Carlos stepped in, his boots barely making a sound on the linoleum floor.

Asher lay in the bed, his face pale but peaceful, the rhythmic beeping of the heart monitor filling the room. Bandages wrapped around his forehead, a dark bruise coloring his cheekbone. His breathing was slow, even, and steady.

Carlos exhaled shakily, stepping closer to the bed. He sank into the chair beside it, his eyes tracing the rise and fall of Asher's chest. The weight of everything pressed down on him as he realized how close they'd come to losing each other—how close Asher had come to being just another victim in this case.

Asher stirred, his eyelids fluttering open. It took a moment for his gaze to focus, but when it did, it landed on Carlos.

"You stayed," Asher murmured, his voice raspy but laced with gratitude.

Carlos offered a tired smile. "Of course I did. Didn't really have a choice—you looked like hell."

Asher chuckled weakly, though it ended in a wince. "Could say the same about you," he mumbled, a faint smirk tugging at his lips.

The warmth in Asher's voice made something in Carlos's chest loosen. "You scared me," Carlos admitted, the words slipping out before he could think.

Asher's smirk faded, replaced by something softer, more vulnerable. "Guess I owe you an apology, huh?" he said, his voice quiet. "I didn't mean for things to go this far."

Carlos shook his head, leaning forward. "It's not your fault. These people—whoever they are—they'll do whatever it takes to keep their secrets. But now we know what we're up against. And I'm not letting them get away with this."

A shadow passed over Asher's expression, and he turned his gaze toward the window. "Diego didn't deserve this. Neither did Gabby."

"We'll get them justice," Carlos promised, his voice firm. "And I'll make sure nothing like this happens to you again."

Asher's eyes flicked back to Carlos, something unreadable in his gaze. After a moment, he nodded, his shoulders relaxing slightly as he sank deeper into the bed.

Carlos stayed silent, watching as Asher's eyes closed again, his breathing evening out. The lines of tension in his face softened, replaced by the peaceful stillness of sleep.

Carlos sat there for what felt like hours, the hum of the heart monitor and Asher's steady breaths creating a fragile sense of

STEALING MEXICO

calm. His fingers grazed over his own hands, still raw from pulling Asher from the wreckage.

When his eyes drifted back to Asher, he couldn't stop the wave of emotions that surged through him. Everything he'd tried to keep locked away—the fear, the anger... the love— rose to the surface.

Tentatively, Carlos reached out, letting his hand hover above Asher's before finally taking it. His grip was firm but gentle, his thumb brushing over Asher's knuckles.

"I love you," he whispered, the words barely audible in the quiet room. He hadn't planned to say it, but he couldn't hold it back any longer. Even if Asher couldn't hear him, even if it didn't matter in this moment, Carlos needed to say it.

He was about to let go when he felt the faintest squeeze of Asher's hand.

Carlos's breath caught, his eyes snapping to Asher's face. He blinked, his lips parting to speak, but Asher beat him to it.

"I wasn't supposed to hear that, was I?" Asher murmured, his voice weak but tinged with amusement.

Carlos froze, heat rushing to his face. "You were supposed to be asleep," he muttered, half-embarrassed, half-relieved.

Asher's smirk widened, though his eyes were heavy-lidded. "I was supposed to be a lot of things."

Carlos shook his head, his lips quirking up in a smile despite himself. "You're impossible."

Asher's expression softened, his fingers tightening around Carlos's hand. "For what it's worth... I love you too," he breathed, the words slow but deliberate.

Carlos's chest swelled, a mix of relief and something deeper settling over him. He leaned closer, his voice low and steady. "Then you'd better stick around. No more risking your life, okay?"

"Deal," Asher murmured, his eyes drifting shut again.

Carlos stayed there, holding his hand, the weight of the

world momentarily lifting as the steady rhythm of the heart monitor filled the room.

CHAPTER 51

CARLOS

Carlos stood by Asher's bedside, the soft rhythm of the heart monitor filling the quiet room. Asher's face, bruised but peaceful, was a stark reminder of how close Carlos had come to losing him. He leaned down, his heart heavy, and kissed Asher softly on the forehead, lingering for a moment before pulling back.

"You're safe," Carlos murmured, his voice barely above a whisper.

The words tasted bitter. Asher was safe here in the hospital, but the danger lurking outside hadn't disappeared.

Carlos straightened and quietly left the room, each step feeling heavier than the last. The thought of leaving Asher alone made his stomach twist, but he needed a moment to think, to shower, to regroup. He also needed to determine his next move—because whoever had tried to kill Asher wasn't finished.

STEALING MEXICO

The hospital parking garage was dimly lit, the hum of fluorescent lights buzzing faintly overhead. Carlos walked toward his car, the sound of his footsteps echoing in the space. His thoughts were still spinning when a voice broke through the haze, smooth and cold.

"Detective Santos."

Carlos froze, his hand halfway to his car door. He spun, his instincts flaring as he spotted Oliver Grant strolling toward him. With his hands casually in his pockets, the man's confident stride and faint smirk radiated a smugness that made Carlos's blood boil.

Carlos felt his muscles tense, his jaw clenching as he watched Holbrook's assistant stop a few feet away, his gaze as cold and calculated as ever.

"I just wanted to extend the Governor's deepest sympathies about what happened to Mr. Rhodes," he said smoothly, his tone dripping with mock sincerity. "It's truly... tragic when people close to us suffer."

Carlos's fists were clenched at his sides. The thinly veiled threat beneath those words was as clear as day.

Oliver tilted his head slightly, his smirk widening. "The Governor's office is here to help in any way we can, of course. We understand how difficult it is when... curiosity leads to unintended consequences. Don't you agree, Detective?"

Carlos's chest tightened, anger simmering just beneath the surface. "Cut the crap," he said, his voice low and steady.

He feigned surprise, raising an eyebrow. "No need to be hostile. I'm just offering some friendly advice—for your sake, and for Mr. Rhodes's. Perhaps you should both consider... stepping back. Focusing on other matters. It would be best for everyone involved."

Carlos took a slow, deep breath, his hands flexing at his sides as he fought to keep his composure. "You think I'm just going to walk away because you came here with some half-baked threat? Do you have any idea how bad of a move that is?"

Oliver's smirk faltered for just a second before returning. "Detective, this isn't a threat. It's a suggestion. Nobody wants this to get any uglier than it already has."

Carlos stepped forward, closing the distance between them. His voice dropped to a dangerous growl. "Stay away from Asher. If anything happens to him—or anyone else connected to this—you'll regret it. And you can tell your boss that I don't back down. Ever."

For a fleeting moment, the assistant's confidence wavered, a flicker of unease crossing his face. But it disappeared just as quickly, replaced by his usual smug facade.

"We'll see, Detective," he retorted smoothly. "Take care. I'd hate for anyone else to... get caught in the crossfire."

With that, he turned on his heel, his footsteps echoing through the garage as he disappeared into the shadows.

Carlos stood there, his fists clenched so tightly his knuckles turned white. His chest heaved as he forced himself to breathe, his mind racing with anger and the weight of the threat. Everything about this was calculated, deliberate—a move to rattle him, to push him off balance.

But they underestimated him.

Carlos slowly unlocked his car, sliding into the driver's seat. He gripped the steering wheel, his fingers aching as he tried to calm the storm raging inside him. He couldn't afford to let his temper get the better of him, not now. To out-think them, he needed to stay focused.

They wanted him scared. They wanted him to back off.

But they'd made a mistake coming after Asher.

Carlos started the engine, the roar of the car breaking the silence of the garage. He glanced in the rear-view mirror, his jaw set, his mind already working through his next steps.

If Holbrook thought intimidation was going to stop him, he was about to learn just how wrong he was.

STEALING MEXICO

Carlos drove out of the parking garage, the sunlight cutting through the shadows as he merged onto the street. He didn't know exactly how yet, but he was going to protect Asher, unravel the truth, and bring Holbrook and his cronies to their knees.

Whatever it took.

CHAPTER 52

CARLOS

Carlos stepped into Governor Holbrook's office, his every step deliberate, his jaw tight with frustration and determination. The polished room, all mahogany and leather, reeked of power carefully curated to intimidate. Holbrook sat behind his desk, the faint afternoon light catching the silver strands in his neatly combed hair. His practiced politician's smile greeted Carlos, but it didn't reach his eyes.

"Detective Santos," Holbrook said smoothly, gesturing toward a chair. "What brings you here today?"

Carlos ignored the invitation to sit, planting his feet firmly and crossing his arms. "You and your assistant need to stay the hell away from Asher Rhodes." His voice was low, steady, and filled with quiet fury.

Holbrook's brows arched slightly, his smile twitching with amusement. "Asher? Is he alright? I heard about his... accident. Tragic, really."

He clenched his fists at his sides. The calm, almost indifferent mention of Asher's injuries made his blood boil. "Don't play dumb," Carlos growled. "I know your assistant's been trying to rattle me. The threats, the intimidation—they stop now."

STEALING MEXICO

Holbrook leaned back in his chair, crossing his hands over his chest. "Detective, I have no idea what you're talking about. My assistant has been doing nothing more than fulfilling his duties. If you're feeling... pressured, I'd suggest taking a step back. Perhaps you're too close to this situation."

"Too close?" Carlos snapped, his anger slipping through the cracks in his calm facade. He took a step closer to the desk. "You think I'm going to let you or your people threaten Asher—or anyone else—without consequences? I'm not backing off. I'm not going anywhere."

The faint amusement on Holbrook's face deepened, though his eyes turned colder. "Detective, you're making quite a few assumptions. Careful—someone might think you're becoming unhinged."

Carlos slammed his hands onto the desk, leaning in, his voice dropping to a dangerous growl. "Unhinged? You haven't seen unhinged, Holbrook. But keep pushing, and I'll show you exactly what that looks like. I've already started unraveling what you and your cronies are hiding, and I'll burn it all down before I let you hurt Asher again. Or anyone else."

Holbrook flinched ever so slightly, his mask slipping for a fraction of a second. Then he straightened, a dark edge creeping into his tone. "Detective, I'm not sure what you think you've uncovered, but let me remind you—people in your position often find their careers... cut short when they step too far out of line."

Carlos leaned even closer, his voice sharp and precise. "Is that a threat?"

"It's a fact," Holbrook replied evenly, his eyes narrowing. "You've entered dangerous territory, Detective. My advice? Walk away before you get hurt—or before you bring harm to those you claim to care about."

Carlos's chest tightened, his anger barely restrained. He stepped back, his lips curling into a stiff smile. "Let me give you some advice, Holbrook. Stay away from Asher. Because if you don't, I'll make sure you regret it."

For the first time, Holbrook's calm demeanor faltered, his jaw tightening. "You're making a mistake, Detective."

Carlos turned toward the door, his shoulders tense but his head held high. He paused just before stepping out, glancing over his shoulder. "One more thing," he said, his voice steady and unwavering. "I'll be at your gala tomorrow. Consider that your last warning."

Holbrook's smirk returned, though it looked more forced than before. "Of course, Detective. I look forward to seeing you there. Just remember... not everything is as it seems. Be careful where you place your trust."

Carlos didn't respond. He walked out of the office, letting the door close behind him with a solid click.

As he moved through the polished halls of the Governor's office, his mind churned with thoughts. Holbrook was rattled; he had seen the man trying to hide it. But the assistant's smug threats and Holbrook's veiled warnings only confirmed what Carlos already knew: they were hiding something, and they were scared of it coming to light.

Carlos's phone buzzed in his pocket. Pulling it out, he saw a message from Captain Davis: We need to talk. Call me.

His jaw set, Carlos walked faster as he headed for his car. Holbrook had made his move, but now it was Carlos's turn. He wasn't just going to protect Asher—he was going to bring everything crashing down on Holbrook's head.

Whatever it took.

CHAPTER 53

CARLOS

Carlos stormed into Captain Davis's office, the words spilling out before he even noticed the room wasn't empty. "That son of a bitch threatened me!"

The woman sitting across from Captain Davis turned her head, her smirk pulling at her lips as she leaned back in her chair. Agent Stephanie Delgado from the Arizona Bureau of Investigation—someone Carlos knew all too well. Her sharp gaze glimmered with a mix of amusement and intrigue.

"Nice to see you too, Carlos," Delgado said dryly. "As dramatic as ever."

Carlos halted mid-step, his anger faltering as he realized who was present. He straightened, forcing himself to take a deep breath and nod curtly. "Agent Delgado."

Captain Davis cleared her throat, cutting through the tension. "Carlos, take a seat. There's a lot we need to go over."

"I'd rather stand," Carlos muttered, his posture tense. "Captain, Holbrook and his damn assistant practically threatened my life. And not just me—he implied Asher's still in danger. We can't let them get away with this."

STEALING MEXICO

Delgado raised an eyebrow, crossing her arms. "And I'm guessing that's why we're all here, Detective."

Captain Davis leaned forward, her expression calm but firm. "Carlos, I understand how you feel, but there are some developments you need to know about. As of this morning, the ABI is officially taking over the lead on this case." She gestured toward Delgado. "Agent Delgado will head the operation, and we'll be coordinating with her team from here on out."

Carlos felt like the floor had dropped out from under him. "What? No way. You can't just push me out. I've been on this since the start. I know the players, I know the leads—"

Delgado interrupted, her voice calm but cutting. "And you're also emotionally compromised, Carlos. Which is why this case is shifting to a state-level operation. We're not sidelining you, but we are tightening the reins."

Carlos's jaw clenched, and he turned to Captain Davis, his voice tinged with frustration. "Captain, they already tried to kill Asher. Now Holbrook's people are trying to intimidate me. I can't just sit back and let this go."

Captain Davis's gaze softened, though her tone remained measured. "Carlos, you're not being sidelined. You're too close to this to be pulled off. But Agent Delgado has a point. This is bigger than any of us realized, and we need to approach it carefully."

Delgado leaned forward, her expression serious now. "Look, Carlos, I get it. You're angry, and you've got every reason to be. But this isn't just about you—or Asher. We're dealing with statewide corruption, high-profile players, and a whole lot of moving parts. If we don't handle this right, they'll bury us before we can prove anything."

Carlos met her gaze, his frustration bubbling just below the surface. "So what, Delgado? I'm supposed to sit on my hands and let you handle it?"

Delgado smirked faintly. "Not quite. You're staying on the case, but there are rules."

Carlos crossed his arms, his eyes narrowing. "Let me guess—no going rogue?"

"Exactly," Delgado said, her tone sharp. "First, no more solo missions. You find something, you come to me or Captain Davis. If you decide to charge into a hornet's nest without backup, I'll pull you off this so fast your head will spin."

Carlos opened his mouth to argue, but Delgado raised a hand to cut him off.

"Second," she continued, her gaze hardening, "you need to understand that this isn't just about catching Holbrook's assistant. This goes deeper than we thought. We've got whispers of human trafficking, money laundering, and political cover-ups. You can't afford to let your emotions drive your decisions here. If you want to stay on this, you play by the book."

Carlos felt his teeth grind together, the weight of her words pressing down on him. But as much as he hated it, he couldn't deny the truth. Holbrook and his people were powerful, and the stakes were higher than ever.

Finally, he exhaled, nodding tightly. "Fine. I'll play by the rules. But I'm not stepping back. Not for a second."

Delgado's expression softened just slightly. "Good. Because we're going to need your insight if we're going to take these bastards down. But remember: no impulsive stunts." She leaned forward, her voice taking on a sharper edge. "I mean it, Carlos. If you mess this up, you'll blow everything we're working for."

Carlos glanced at Captain Davis, who gave him a small nod of encouragement. He drew in a deep breath, forcing himself to tamp down his frustration. "Understood."

Delgado's smirk returned. "Glad to hear it. Now, let's get to work. We've got a hell of a case to build."

STEALING MEXICO

Captain Davis slid a folder across her desk, her tone brisk. "We've already started mapping out Holbrook's connections. Let's see if we can find a weak spot and start pulling threads."

Carlos sat down, his resolve hardening. He wasn't happy about answering to Delgado, but if it meant getting justice for Asher, Diego, and everyone else who had suffered at the hands of Holbrook's people, he'd do whatever it took.

As Delgado began laying out the plan, Carlos felt a flicker of hope amid the frustration. They had a team now, and together, they were going to bring Holbrook's empire crumbling down.

"Let's get to it," Carlos said, determination burning in his chest. "They don't get to win."

CHAPTER 54

ASHER

Asher's thumb hovered over the remote as he flipped through channels, the droning beeps of the hospital machines fading into the background. The dull ache in his ribs and the sharper sting at his temple refused to let him forget why he was there, but distractions were scarce.

When the familiar logo of a news channel caught his eye, he paused. The screen cut to a scene outside a grand building, the words Holbrook for Arizona emblazoned on a massive banner above a podium. A crowd had gathered, their voices rising in unison, carrying signs that read Justice for Diego, We Won't Be Silenced, and Season of Unity.

His chest tightened at the sight. Diego's name. Diego's cause. It wasn't just whispers anymore—it was a movement.

The camera zoomed in, panning across the protestors before landing on a familiar face at the center of the group. Asher's breath caught. Ethan Cole.

Ethan, Diego's host brother, stood tall amidst the chaos, a sign reading Justice for Diego gripped tightly in his hands. His expression was fierce, resolute, his steely gaze fixed forward.

A reporter edged toward him, microphone in hand, her

STEALING MEXICO

voice cutting through the chants. "Young man, can we get a word with you?"

Ethan hesitated, glancing back at the crowd before stepping closer. His fingers tightened around his sign as he squared his shoulders.

"Why are you here today?" the reporter asked, her tone probing but sympathetic. "Why is this cause so important to you?"

Ethan's jaw clenched, and for a moment, he seemed to wrestle with his words. When he spoke, his voice was steady but raw with emotion. "Diego Cortez was one of the best people I've ever met. He was honest, brave, and passionate about making a difference. He came here seeking opportunity, but instead, someone stole his life. And we still don't have answers."

Asher felt a surge of admiration for the boy who had once seemed so distant, so burdened by guilt. Ethan's conviction shone through now, his grief and anger fueling his determination.

The reporter pressed on. "Do you believe Governor Holbrook or anyone from his office is involved in Diego's death?"

Ethan's gaze flickered, his resolve wavering just for a second. But then he straightened, defiance sparking in his eyes. "All I know is that Diego was silenced, and powerful people have been trying to keep us quiet ever since. We're not backing down. We're going to keep pushing until we get the truth, no matter how high we have to go."

The crowd erupted in chants: Justice for Diego! Justice for Gabby! Justice for Morales!

Asher couldn't tear his eyes from the screen. Ethan's words, the strength in his stance, the voices of the crowd—it was electric. This wasn't just an investigation anymore; it was a battle cry.

When the broadcast cut back to the anchors in the studio,

Asher barely registered their words. His mind buzzed with everything he'd just seen. Ethan had stepped up, and it was changing the game.

He set the remote down and reached for his phone, ignoring the dull ache in his side as he dialed Carlos. The line rang twice before Carlos's voice came through, sounding tired but focused.

"Asher? You doing alright?"

"Yeah, mostly," Asher said, brushing off the pain. "But did you see what's happening? Ethan's leading a protest for Diego—on live TV, right outside Holbrook's press conference."

Carlos was silent for a moment, then let out a slow breath. "Ethan? Didn't think he had it in him."

"Neither did I," Asher admitted. "But he's out there, calling for justice. He said they'd push as high up as they had to for answers. It's powerful, Carlos. This isn't just about Diego anymore—it's growing into something bigger."

Although Carlos spoke measuredly, a hint of unease was apparent in his voice. "It is bigger. And it's about to get more complicated."

"What do you mean?" Asher asked, his brow furrowing.

"The ABI is stepping in," Carlos said, his frustration clear. "They're taking over parts of the investigation. Captain Davis just told me. They're planning to make an announcement soon—probably to control the narrative."

Asher's stomach twisted. "An announcement? About Diego?"

"About the case, yeah," Carlos said. "They're trying to manage public perception, especially with Holbrook in the spotlight. Could be damage control, could be something else. I don't trust them to tell the entire story."

Asher's fingers tightened around the phone. "And if they don't?"

Carlos's voice hardened. "Then we keep going. ABI or not,

STEALING MEXICO

I'm not letting this case get buried. Diego deserves better than that."

A spark of determination flared in Asher's chest. "You're right. We're not letting this go. And Ethan—he's making waves. This could be what we need to keep the pressure on Holbrook."

"Maybe," Carlos said cautiously. "But we need to be careful. This case keeps getting closer to the people pulling the strings, and they won't hesitate to protect themselves."

"I know," Asher said, his voice quieter. "Just… be careful too, Carlos. After everything that's happened, I—" He hesitated, then pushed forward. "I don't want to lose you."

Carlos's tone softened. "You won't. I promise. Get some rest, Asher. I'll keep you updated."

"Alright," Asher said reluctantly. "But don't shut me out, okay?"

"Never again," Carlos said firmly. "I'll talk to you soon."

The call ended, leaving Asher with the muted hum of the TV and the steady beep of the heart monitor. He clicked the remote, switching back to the news channel. If the ABI was making an announcement, he needed to hear every word.

Diego's fight wasn't over. And neither was his.

CHAPTER 55

CARLOS

Carlos stood just behind Agent Stephanie Delgado, the room buzzing with anticipation. Her composed demeanor and steely focus were enough to command attention, even before she spoke. The press conference, hastily commandeered by the ABI, had turned into something far larger than anyone had anticipated—including Governor Holbrook, who stood off to the side, his frustration barely masked. Carlos caught a glimpse of the thin line of his mouth, his eyes darting between the cameras and the agents flanking him.

Delgado adjusted the microphone, her voice firm and measured as it cut through the noise of the room.

"Thank you all for being here," she began, her gaze sweeping across the gathered reporters. "Effective immediately, the Arizona Bureau of Investigation, in partnership with the Phoenix Police Department, is intensifying efforts to address a string of interconnected cases involving the deaths of Diego Cortez, Luis Morales, and, most recently, Gabby Puente."

A ripple of murmurs passed through the crowd. Carlos watched the reporters' faces shift from curiosity to alarm as Delgado continued.

STEALING MEXICO

"These individuals, though from different walks of life, shared a common thread: a commitment to standing up for their communities and exposing truths that others sought to hide. With heavy hearts, we confirm that a broader, coordinated effort silenced these individuals; their deaths were not isolated incidents.

Delgado's words hung in the air, heavy with implication. The cameras zoomed in on her as she stood tall, unflinching under the weight of the announcement.

"In the course of our investigation, we have uncovered a disturbing pattern of financial transactions, offshore accounts, and shell companies—mechanisms used to obscure the truth. These transactions point to a web of corruption, cover-ups, and links to human trafficking that stretch across the state."

The room erupted in a wave of gasps and frantic scribbling. Reporters shouted questions, their voices blending into an unintelligible cacophony, but Delgado raised a hand, her sharp gaze commanding silence.

"Our team has identified several persons of interest," she continued, her voice unwavering, "but at this time, we do not have a confirmed primary suspect. However, we believe individuals with considerable resources and influence committed these crimes. Their aim is clear: to silence those who speak out."

Carlos's fists clenched at her words, his mind flashing to Asher's injuries and the near-misses that had plagued this case. Delgado wasn't just addressing the press—this was a message to the people behind the crimes.

Her tone shifted slightly, growing even more deliberate. "I must also address a critical concern. A perpetrator targeted each victim during their vulnerable, isolated moments. To the friends, family members, and community advocates connected to Diego Cortez, Luis Morales, and Gabby Puente: we strongly advise against traveling alone or staying unaccompanied. Protecting your safety is our top priority."

Carlos felt a chill run down his spine. He knew this warning wasn't just protocol—it was a reality he was already living. Delgado was putting it into words for everyone else, but for Carlos, it only reinforced the urgency that had been gnawing at him.

Delgado began fielding questions from reporters, her responses careful and calculated. But Carlos had heard what he needed to. He took a step back, the tension in the room almost suffocating. He couldn't stop thinking about Asher, alone in his hospital room, likely watching this unfold on the news.

Carlos pulled out his phone, stepping out of the press room into the quieter hallway. His fingers hesitated over the screen for only a second before he hit dial.

Asher picked up after the second ring, his voice a mix of curiosity and fatigue. "Carlos? What's going on?"

"Did you see it?" Carlos asked, his voice low but urgent.

"The press conference? Yeah, I saw it." Asher's tone sharpened. "So it's all official now. They're tying Diego's case to the others, finally admitting there's a connection."

Carlos nodded, even though Asher couldn't see him. "It's an excellent step, but it's also dangerous. Delgado's right about the pattern. They go after people when they're alone—Diego, Morales, Gabby." He paused, the weight of his next words hanging between them. "You can't let your guard down, Asher. Not for a second."

"I know," Asher said quietly. "But what about you, Carlos? You've been just as much of a target, if not more. If anything happens—"

"Nothing's going to happen," Carlos interrupted, his voice firm. "I'll be careful, but I need you to promise me the same."

There was a pause on the other end of the line, and Carlos could hear Asher's measured breaths. Finally, he spoke, his voice soft but steady. "I promise."

STEALING MEXICO

"Good," Carlos said, relief washing over him. "I'll check in with you again soon. For now, stay where you are and don't take any chances."

"I will," Asher replied. "Be careful, Carlos. This isn't over."

Carlos ended the call, slipping his phone back into his pocket. He stood in the quiet hallway for a moment, letting Delgado's words echo in his mind. The public acknowledgment of the connections between the cases was a victory, but it was also a gauntlet thrown. The people behind this would push back harder than ever, and Carlos needed to be ready.

As he stepped back into the press room, his jaw set with determination, he glimpsed Holbrook in the corner, his expression unreadable. Carlos didn't trust him, not for a second, but Delgado's announcement had forced the Governor into a corner.

Carlos's resolve hardened. The truth was out in the open now, and there was no going back. He wasn't going to let anyone else become a victim. Whatever it took, he'd see this through to the end.

CHAPTER 56

ASHER

Asher held the phone to his ear, half-listening to Carlos's steady voice as his mind drifted. The hospital room felt stifling with its sterile smell and the steady beeping of the machines. He was tired, sore, and increasingly frustrated with the layers of precautions being piled on him.

"I've been thinking," Carlos said, his voice cutting through Asher's wandering thoughts, "about your safety. I talked to Delgado, and—"

Before Carlos could finish, the door to the hospital room swung open. A tall, serious-looking man in a dark suit stepped in, his expression calm but unreadable. He gave Asher a polite nod, his movements precise and practiced.

"Mr. Rhodes," the man said, his voice even and professional. "I'm Agent Bradley, assigned by the ABI to your security detail. I'll be guarding the room. If you need anything, don't hesitate to reach out."

Asher blinked, caught off guard by the abrupt entrance. "Uh... thanks, I guess?"

Carlos, still on the phone, had clearly caught the end of the introduction. "Sounds like Bradley's doing his job," he

STEALING MEXICO

said, a hint of approval in his tone. "Good. I'll be a little less worried now."

Suppressing a sigh, Asher leaned back against the pillows. "Carlos," he said, his voice low and tinged with exasperation, "you really didn't need to go this far. I appreciate it, but it's a bit much, don't you think? I'm in a hospital, not a fortress."

Carlos's tone softened, and Asher could almost hear the smile in his voice. "I know it feels over the top, but this isn't negotiable, Ash. You're important to me, and with everything that's happened, I'm not taking any chances. Just let me do this, okay?"

Before Asher could reply, the door swung open again, this time with less precision and more authority. A petite but commanding figure swept into the room, her presence filling the space in an instant.

"Abuela?" Asher said, blinking in surprise.

Carlos's Abuela marched in, her expression a mix of worry and determination, completely ignoring Agent Bradley, who was attempting to explain the security protocol.

"What kind of hospital won't let me see mi niño?" she demanded, her voice rising as she gestured emphatically at Bradley. Her Mexican accent thickened with her indignation, and her sharp gaze fixed on him like a spotlight.

Bradley tried to regain control. "Ma'am, with all due respect—"

But Abuela wasn't having it. She waved him off dismissively, stepping past him as if he weren't even there. Her demeanor softened the moment her eyes landed on Asher.

"Oh, mijo," she murmured, hurrying to his side. She took his hand in hers, her touch warm and comforting. "What have they done to you? Look at this—so pale, so skinny. Have they even been feeding you?"

Asher couldn't help but smile despite himself. The irritation he'd been feeling moments ago melted away under her

268

care. "I'm fine, really," he said, though he didn't pull his hand away from hers.

Abuela brushed his hair back, her eyes scanning him critically. "Fine? Bah. You look like you need a proper meal and a good night's rest." She shot a glance at Bradley, who stood stiffly by the door, clearly unsure how to handle her. "And you! Are you making sure he's safe or just standing there like a statue?"

Bradley cleared his throat, his stoic expression wavering slightly. "Ma'am, I assure you, I'm here to protect Mr. Rhodes. No one will enter without approval."

Abuela gave him a long, assessing look before nodding with grudging approval. "Bueno. But let me tell you something, niño. If anything happens to him, you'll answer to me, understand?"

Asher bit back a laugh as Bradley nodded solemnly, clearly not accustomed to being scolded by fiery grandmothers.

Carlos, still on the phone, chuckled softly. "Sounds like you're in excellent hands, Ash. Between Bradley and Abuela, I'm feeling a lot better about this setup."

Asher rolled his eyes, though his smile lingered. "You do realize I'm a grown man, right? I don't need a babysitter. Or two."

Carlos's voice softened, his tone serious but affectionate. "I know you can take care of yourself. But I need to take care of you, too. Just humor me, okay?"

Asher sighed, the warmth in Carlos's words making it hard to stay annoyed. "Alright. But you owe me a break from all this once this is over."

"Deal," Carlos said, his smile audible over the line. "I'll check on you soon. Just… take it easy. For me."

Asher hung up, his irritation replaced by a quiet sense of comfort. He tucked his phone away, glancing at Abuela, who was now fussing over the arrangement of his pillows.

STEALING MEXICO

"You've got plenty of people looking out for you," she said, patting his shoulder with a firm yet gentle hand. Her gaze flicked to Bradley again, daring him to object. "But no one will do it like family. Rest, niño. You're safe here."

Asher leaned back, the ache in his side fading slightly as he let himself relax. Despite the chaos surrounding him, the warmth of her presence and the quiet reassurance in Carlos's voice left him feeling just a little more whole.

CHAPTER 57

CARLOS

Carlos stood in front of the massive whiteboard, arms folded tightly as he scanned the web of names, faces, and connections, slowly taking shape. The faces of Diego Cortez, Ignacio Morales, and Gabby Puente stared back at him from the top of the board—silent reminders of why they were doing this. Below them, a red line now linked Asher's photo to Gabby's and Carlos's, a grim acknowledgment of how close the danger had come.

Agent Delgado leaned against the table nearby, her sharp gaze flicking between the board and the scattered files her team was piecing together. On the left side of the board, thirty significant names connected to suspicious financial records loomed large—politicians, corporate executives, and high-ranking officials, each representing a potential node in the sprawling conspiracy.

"This is…" Carlos muttered, gesturing toward the board, "overwhelming."

Delgado nodded, her tone steady but grim. "And this is just what we've mapped so far. The deeper we dig, the clearer it becomes—this isn't just about trafficking. It's about power, influence, and covering tracks so well that even when

STEALING MEXICO

someone stumbles onto it, they don't live long enough to expose it."

Her words settled heavily on Carlos's chest. He clenched his jaw as he stared at the photos of Diego, Morales, and Gabby. The murders were calculated and brutal acts of violence. The connections might be tenuous for now, but Carlos could feel the truth just out of reach.

Delgado tapped on the two largest question marks on the board, positioned next to photos of Governor Holbrook and his assistant. "These two," she said, her voice tight with frustration, "are at the center of nearly every questionable transaction we've uncovered. Offshore accounts, shell companies, reallocation of public funds—it's all here. But we don't have a direct link between them and the murders. Yet."

Carlos's fists tightened at his sides. "Holbrook doesn't make a move unless he thinks he's untouchable. But there has to be something we're missing—something that connects him to Diego, Morales, and Gabby."

Delgado gave him a sidelong glance, her expression softening slightly. "We'll find it. But we need to be smart. Holbrook's a master at keeping his hands clean. Holbrook has sanitized everything we've found. If we want to bring him down, we need something solid—something undeniable."

Carlos exhaled, forcing himself to step back and focus. His eyes shifted to the Fundraiser Gala scrawled in bold letters at the bottom of the board, circled and underlined in red.

"What about the gala?" he asked, his voice sharp.

Delgado turned to face the board, gesturing at it as she spoke. "The gala is our best chance to get eyes on Holbrook's inner circle. It's a high-stakes event, with half the people we've linked to this operation expected to be in attendance. He invited you, Carlos—personally. That tells us something."

Carlos's lips pressed into a thin line as he considered her words. "He's either trying to show off or testing me to see if I'll flinch."

"Exactly," Delgado agreed. "This could be a distraction, or it could be where he feels most secure. Either way, we need to be ready. Holbrook's smart, but arrogance makes people careless. If his network operates through these events, we might catch something. But it has to be subtle. We can't afford any mistakes."

Carlos's gaze returned to Holbrook's photo in the center of the board, his eyes narrowing. "He thinks he's untouchable. That we can't bring him down."

Delgado crossed her arms, her tone firm but cautious. "Which is why we have to be methodical. You're going to the gala, but you won't be alone. We'll have undercover agents in place—discreet, no uniforms, no obvious backup. If anything happens, we'll be ready."

Carlos nodded, though his thoughts drifted to Asher. His photo, now linked to the case, was a reminder of how close the danger had come. He knew better than to voice his fears, but the thought of leaving Asher vulnerable, even for a moment, gnawed at him.

"If something happens to me..." Carlos muttered, more to himself than anyone else.

Delgado caught his tone and stepped closer, her voice firm. "It won't. That's why we're doing this as a team. You're not going in there alone, Carlos. But if you're thinking about anyone else..." she glanced meaningfully at Asher's photo, "then let this be the reason we do this right. For him. For Diego. For everyone."

Carlos drew in a slow, deep breath, forcing the tension out of his shoulders. "If this gala is where Holbrook's network operates, I'll find proof. I'll get what we need to take him down."

Delgado studied him for a moment, then nodded. "Good. Because this isn't just about bringing Holbrook down anymore. It's about sending a message to everyone involved —this ends here."

Carlos turned back to the board, his resolve hardening. The risks were high, but he couldn't afford to fail—not for Diego, not for Asher, and not for anyone else who had suffered because of Holbrook's shadowy empire.

The conference room felt unnervingly quiet after the team filtered out, leaving Carlos and Agent Delgado alone. Delgado leaned against the table, her arms crossed, her sharp gaze fixed on him like she was dissecting every thought he wasn't saying out loud.

"So," she said, her voice low but steady, "are you going to tell me what's really going on in that head of yours, or do I have to guess?"

Carlos shook his head, a weary sigh threatening to escape. "Nothing you don't already know, Delgado."

She raised an eyebrow. The look that had made rookies quake in their boots. "You've always been a terrible liar, Santos."

Carlos allowed himself the faintest twitch of a smile. Delgado had that effect on him—bringing him back to the days when he was a rookie patrol cop, watching her take down a fugitive like it was just another Tuesday. She'd been larger-than-life back then, a legend who made obstacles seem like challenges to conquer. Now, years later, her words still had a way of cutting straight through his defenses.

He rubbed the back of his neck, leaning against the table opposite her. "This case feels… different."

"Different how?" she prompted.

"Messy," he admitted. "Every lead opens up a dozen more questions. It's like trying to grab smoke. Every time I think I'm getting somewhere, it slips through my fingers."

Delgado studied him for a moment, her expression softening slightly, which was a rarity. "You always do this, you know," she said.

"Do what?"

"Try to shoulder the whole damn case by yourself." She stepped closer, her voice gentler now. "You're smart, Santos—one of the sharpest detectives I've met. But you don't have to prove it by carrying the weight of the world alone."

Carlos frowned, shifting uncomfortably. "I'm not—"

"Don't argue," she interrupted, holding up a hand. "You're methodical to a fault. You chase every lead, turn over every detail, like it's your personal responsibility to fix the world. It's why you're so good at what you do. But it's also why you burn out."

He looked down at his hands, her words hitting closer to home than he cared to admit. But it wasn't just the case weighing on him. There was something else, something he wasn't sure he could talk about.

Delgado tilted her head, watching him closely. "There's more, isn't there?"

Carlos let out a sharp breath. "I'm not sure it's... relevant."

"Does it keep you up at night?"

He hesitated. "Yeah."

"Then it's relevant."

For a long moment, he debated whether to open up. Finally, he took a leap. "It's Asher."

Delgado's eyebrows lifted slightly, but she didn't interrupt.

"I don't know what to do with him," Carlos said, his voice quieter now. "He's reckless, irritating, and he pushes my buttons like no one else."

"But?" she prompted, leaning forward slightly.

Carlos closed his eyes for a moment before admitting,

STEALING MEXICO

"But he's also brave, relentless, and he cares more than anyone I've ever met. And… I'm falling for him."

Delgado didn't look surprised, just thoughtful. "And that scares you."

Carlos nodded, his jaw tightening. "I've spent years keeping people at arm's length. It's easier that way—less chance of getting hurt. I'm good at what I do because I don't let things get personal. But with Asher… I can't keep that distance."

"You think that makes you weaker?"

He met her gaze, the vulnerability in his eyes something he rarely let anyone see. "Doesn't it?"

Delgado shook her head firmly. "No, Santos. It makes you human. Letting someone in doesn't mean you lose your edge. It means you have someone to remind you why you do this in the first place. It gives you something worth fighting for."

Carlos looked away, her words settling heavily on his chest.

"Let me guess," she continued, a small, knowing smile tugging at her lips. "You're terrified that if you let yourself fall, he'll walk away."

Carlos swallowed hard, unable to answer.

Delgado's expression softened even further, her voice almost gentle. "Here's the thing about love, Santos—it's always a risk. But from what I've seen, that man's not going anywhere. He'd follow you into a firefight if it meant helping you. Hell, he already has."

Carlos let out a short, humorless laugh. "That's part of the problem. He doesn't know how to stay out of trouble."

"Sounds like someone else I know," she quipped, earning a reluctant smirk from him.

She placed a hand on his shoulder, her grip firm and grounding. "You've got this, Santos. The case, a man who loves you, all of it. Don't let fear stop you from living—and don't let it stop you from doing what you do best."

Carlos nodded, her words settling something inside him. "Thanks, Delgado."

"Anytime," she said, stepping back toward the door. "And for the record? You're already a better detective than I ever was. Now, go close this case—and stop being so damn afraid of being happy while you're at it."

She left him standing alone in the conference room, but her words lingered long after the door swung shut.

Carlos straightened, rolling his shoulders back as he turned back to the board. He let his gaze land briefly on Asher's photo, a flicker of something unspoken passing through him. Delgado was right—he couldn't afford to let fear dictate his choices, not with the case and especially not with Asher.

CHAPTER 58

CARLOS

Carlos adjusted the lapels of his suit jacket, the tailored fabric feeling both foreign and heavy on his shoulders. He wasn't used to wearing something this polished—it wasn't exactly his usual attire for chasing leads or interrogating suspects. The polished shoes and crisp tie felt more like a costume than a second skin. But tonight, he needed to blend in.

From across the hospital room, Asher was watching him with a sly grin, propped up slightly against his pillows.

"Look at you," Asher teased, his voice still scratchy from his injuries but carrying its usual sarcasm. "If I didn't know better, I'd say you actually clean up pretty well."

Carlos rolled his eyes, but a faint smile crept onto his face. "Don't get used to it. This is the first and last time I'm ever wearing a suit."

Asher chuckled softly but winced, his hand instinctively going to his ribs. The smile disappeared from Carlos's face as quickly as it had come. His eyes darted to the heart monitor, its steady beep offering reassurance, but not enough to ease the tightness in his chest.

"I don't like this," Asher said, breaking the silence. His

STEALING MEXICO

voice carried a seriousness that wasn't typical of him. "You're walking into a nest of snakes, Carlos. Alone."

"I'm not alone," Carlos replied, his tone steady but quiet. "Delgado and her team are everywhere. They'll have my back."

"And what about your front?" Asher shot back, his brows furrowed.

Before Carlos could answer, Abuela spoke up from the corner of the room. She set down her knitting, her dark eyes sharp with concern. "He's right, mi amor. Those people you're dealing with—they're dangerous. You need to be careful."

Carlos walked over to her, crouching slightly to take her hand in his. "I will, Abuela. I promise."

She studied him, her gaze softening. "You look handsome, Carlos. Muy guapo. But sometimes I think you and Asher are both too brave for your own good."

Carlos laughed softly, squeezing her hand. "Maybe we get it from you."

He turned back to Asher, who was watching him with an intensity that made it hard to meet his eyes. "Promise me," Asher said, his voice quieter now. "Promise me you won't go after Holbrook alone, even if something happens."

Carlos hesitated for the briefest moment, then nodded. "I promise. Delgado's running the show tonight. I'm just a part of the team."

Asher didn't look entirely convinced, but before he could argue, Carlos bent down and pressed a gentle kiss to his forehead. He felt Asher's hand slip into his, the touch grounding him in a way he didn't fully understand but didn't want to question.

"Get some rest," Carlos murmured. "I'll be back before you know it."

Asher's grip lingered as Carlos straightened up, and just as he reached the door, he heard Asher's voice again.

"Carlos?"

He turned back, meeting Asher's gaze.

"Be careful."

Carlos nodded, his lips curving into a small, reassuring smile. "Always."

The gala was every bit as extravagant as Carlos had expected. The marble floors gleamed under soft, golden lighting, and chandeliers cast intricate patterns across the walls. Arizona's elite mingled in tailored suits and designer gowns, their laughter and chatter filling the cavernous space.

Carlos adjusted his tie as he stepped into the room, scanning the crowd. His earpiece crackled to life.

"Welcome to the party, Detective," Delgado's voice came through, steady. "Remember, you're just here to observe and gather intel. Don't get too close to anyone unless you have to."

"Understood," Carlos muttered, his eyes locking on Governor Holbrook across the room. A circle of admirers surrounded the man, his smile polished, his laughter easy. To the untrained eye, he looked every bit the charismatic public servant.

Carlos's jaw tightened. He knew better.

The night wore on, and Carlos weaved through the crowd, exchanging polite nods and small talk while keeping his eyes and ears open. Delgado's voice occasionally buzzed through the earpiece, alerting him to key players.

"Carlos," Delgado said, her tone shifting. "We've spotted two of Holbrook's key associates near the side corridor. We've flagged them for suspicious financial transactions.

STEALING MEXICO

Carlos shifted his focus, casually making his way toward the corridor. He took measured steps, remaining calm.

As he neared, he caught sight of two men engaged in a hushed but heated conversation. One gestured sharply with his hand, his face tight with frustration.

Carlos slowed, angling himself just close enough to catch snippets of their conversation.

"…last shipment was delayed. That's not acceptable."

"We're already under too much scrutiny. Holbrook said this needs to stay clean."

Carlos's jaw clenched as the pieces clicked. These weren't just idle complaints—this was about their operation.

Delgado's voice came through again. "What are you hearing, Santos?"

Carlos tilted his head slightly, speaking low. "They're talking about shipments and keeping things clean. They mentioned Holbrook directly."

"Stay on them," Delgado instructed. "But don't blow your cover."

The men's conversation quieted as they noticed Carlos's approach. One of them straightened, his eyes narrowing.

"Can we help you, Detective?" he asked, his tone sharp and challenging.

Carlos flashed a polite smile. "Just admiring the architecture," he said smoothly. "Beautiful venue."

The man didn't respond, his eyes hard as he stared Carlos down. After a moment, Carlos gave a small nod and moved away, his heart pounding.

"Delgado," he murmured into the earpiece, "we've got a direct link to Holbrook. They're careful, but they're slipping. We might not get another chance like this."

"Good work, Santos," Delgado replied. "Keep moving. Don't let them know you're onto them. See if you can find out what these shipments are of."

Carlos moved back toward the main ballroom, his eyes

scanning the crowd. As Holbrook stepped up to the podium, the room fell silent. Carlos listened, but his mind was already racing.

This wasn't just another gala. This was the beginning of the end for Holbrook—and Carlos was determined to make sure of it.

CHAPTER 59

CARLOS

Carlos moved through the glittering crowd of the Gala, every step deliberate, his senses on high alert. The hum of conversation and the clinking of glasses filled the grand hall, a stark contrast to the tension simmering beneath his polished exterior. He had a role to play tonight—blending in, observing, but not drawing too much attention. This was a room full of masks, and he was no different.

At a quiet corner of the bar, Carlos engaged in casual small talk with a city councilman. The conversation was light —urban development projects, the city's economy—but Carlos carefully guided it toward local incidents, hoping to tease out anything useful. The man offered vague, practiced responses, his laughter polite but empty. Another dead end.

Carlos shifted toward a group of business executives in an animated discussion about stock trends. He introduced himself with ease, weaving into the conversation with a comment about economic pressures on local projects. Their smiles were friendly but guarded, their words measured. He could sense the barriers—these were people accustomed to shielding their intentions, especially around someone like him.

STEALING MEXICO

Frustration itched at the edges of his focus. He needed something concrete, something that could connect the dots between Holbrook's network and the crimes he was investigating.

As Carlos scanned the room again, his sharp gaze landed on a young woman standing near the edge of the ballroom. She was alone, her silver gown catching the light as she swirled a glass of champagne in one hand. She didn't look uncomfortable, but there was a distance in her expression, as if her mind was far from the glittering crowd.

He recognized her immediately. Gabriela Bolucci.

He made his way over, adopting an air of casual interest. "You look like someone who doesn't want to be here," he said, his tone light but probing.

She turned to him, offering a polite smile. "Detective Santos," she said smoothly. "I've heard about you."

Carlos raised an eyebrow, matching her tone. "Good things, I hope."

Her smile flickered, a faint quirk at the corner of her lips. "That depends on your definition of good."

Carlos chuckled softly, though his instincts told him she was testing the waters. "And you're Gabriela Bolucci. I'd say it's a pleasure, but you don't seem like someone who's here for small talk."

Gabriela tilted her head slightly, studying him with an expression he couldn't quite place. "Small talk is a necessary evil," she said, her voice calm, almost bored. "Though I imagine you're here for something more... meaningful."

Carlos's eyes narrowed slightly, though he kept his tone neutral. "What makes you say that?"

Gabriela took a small sip of her champagne, her gaze drifting over the crowd. "Let's just say you don't strike me as someone who enjoys galas for the sake of it." She paused, her voice taking on a more deliberate tone. "Sometimes, though, you need a push to get things rolling. You know, a little... unexpected help to point you in the right direction."

Carlos felt his chest tighten. The casual remark hit too close to home. His mind immediately went to the Morales file —the one that had appeared out of nowhere, perfectly timed, bearing his name. His gut twisted as he replayed the moment he'd found it, the confusion that had followed.

Did she know about that?

He kept his face impassive, but his mind was racing. "Funny how things work out like that," he said carefully. "Though, sometimes, a push can lead you somewhere unexpected."

Gabriela's smile grew slightly, though it remained enigmatic. "That's the beauty of it, isn't it? Sometimes, you don't even realize you needed the push until you're already moving."

Carlos studied her, his instincts flaring. There was no way this was a coincidence. She was too deliberate, too aware. But he couldn't ask her outright—not here, not now.

Instead, he nodded, offering a faint smile of his own. "I suppose that depends on where you end up." Carlos shifted the conversation slightly. "I noticed your father isn't here tonight."

Gabriela's smile faltered for a fraction of a second before she recovered. "He's busy with... other matters," she said, her tone casual but carrying an undertone of deflection. She tilted her head slightly, her eyes flicking over the room. "Funny how events like this seem so well-orchestrated, don't you think? It seems like someone planned everything down to the last detail."

Carlos's chest tightened, the weight of her words settling heavily. He kept his tone light, but his mind raced. "Sometimes the best plans are the ones you don't see coming."

Her lips curved into a faint, enigmatic smile. "Exactly."

Before Carlos could press further, Delgado's voice

STEALING MEXICO

crackled in his ear. "Carlos, there's a silent auction. Check it out."

He straightened slightly, giving Gabriela a polite nod. "If you'll excuse me."

She returned the nod, her expression unreadable. "Don't let me keep you."

As he moved across the room, Gabriela's words echoed in his mind. Unexpected help. A push to get things rolling.

Was she involved in the Morales file? Had she—or someone connected to her—engineered that breadcrumb trail to pull him deeper into the case? And if so, why?

The questions gnawed at him as he slipped into the quieter section of the Gala, his focus shifting to the task at hand. Delgado had been right—this night was going to be more enlightening than he'd expected. But whether that enlightenment would bring answers or more danger, remained to be seen.

CHAPTER 60

CARLOS

Carlos moved through the crowd with purpose, keeping his steps measured and his face composed. The gala buzzed around him, its glamorous facade shielding dark secrets he could feel just beneath the surface. He finally spotted the silent auction tables in a secluded corner, tucked away enough that most people were too engaged in their conversations to take notice.

The items up for bid were strangely vague: exclusive experiences, unparalleled access, and special services, with absurdly high starting prices. Browsing the cards, Carlos picked up on the unsettling implication of each entry. The way the descriptions danced around specifics—it was code, a sickeningly polite veneer hiding something dark and sinister. These "items" were people.

Carlos felt the burn of anger tightening in his chest, but he forced himself to keep his face neutral as he lingered near the bidding sheets. A couple standing nearby, both clearly tipsy, began talking a little too loudly. The woman slurred something to the man beside her, mentioning "Holbrook's little side project." She giggled, not noticing Carlos's proximity.

"He always knows how to pick the best... investments,"

STEALING MEXICO

her companion replied with a smirk, the implications in his tone unmistakable. "Plenty of profit, even if the police start sniffing around."

Carlos's mind raced. Holbrook was at the heart of it. This wasn't just some tangential connection. This was deliberate, organized, and deeply entrenched. He'd finally gotten the confirmation he needed, and all he could feel was an icy resolve.

"We got it," he said into his shoulder.

As he slipped away from the table, his gaze scanned the room, looking for any sign of Delgado or her team. He caught sight of Agent Delgado entering the gala with a team of ABI agents in tow. They moved through the crowd with authority, drawing curious and wary glances from guests as they spread out around the room. Delgado's gaze met Carlos's, and she gave him a sharp nod, a signal that they were ready to make their move.

"Ladies and gentlemen!" Delgado's voice echoed through the room as she took control of the microphone on the stage. "This event is officially over. You are all being asked to remain in place until we can complete our investigation."

A ripple of shock swept through the room as guests realized what was happening. Voices rose, panic flaring in the faces of those who understood they'd been caught. Some tried to move toward the exits, but ABI agents were already blocking the doors, their expressions unyielding.

Carlos stayed near the auction tables, watching as several men and women—guests he recognized as having bid on the "items"—became agitated, whispering urgently to one another. A well-dressed man made a break for a side door, but two agents intercepted him, forcefully pulling his hands behind his back and cuffing him.

The woman who'd drunkenly mentioned Holbrook earlier looked around in wide-eyed terror, grabbing onto her date's

290

arm. "They can't do this," she stammered, her bravado quickly crumbling.

Carlos moved forward, positioning himself near Delgado as she took control of the room. As the chaos settled into a tense, quiet panic, Carlos's gaze swept the crowd, seeing the truth settle on each of their faces. This was it—the end of the line for those who had profited off others' suffering.

Delgado approached him, her expression sharp and focused. "Carlos, we've got eyes on several persons of interest, but..." she trailed off, following his line of sight. "What is it?"

"Holbrook," Carlos muttered, his voice tight. "He's gone."

Delgado's eyes narrowed, her head snapping toward the stage where Holbrook had been earlier. "Damn it. Secure the exits. No one leaves without being questioned."

Carlos didn't wait for a response. A sinking feeling settled in his stomach as he scanned the room for any trace of the Governor or his assistant. His gaze caught on a side door near the service area, slightly ajar. Without a word, he started toward it.

As he pushed through the door, he heard footsteps echoing in the empty hallway. Quickening his pace, he followed the sound, his pulse racing. The hallway opened into the kitchen, bustling with staff who looked up in surprise as Carlos passed through. He spotted a security guard standing near the back entrance, speaking into his radio.

Carlos approached him with purpose. "Which way did Governor Holbrook go?" he demanded.

The guard hesitated, shifting uncomfortably. "I—I'm not sure, sir. He—"

"Don't lie to me," Carlos snapped, his patience running thin. "You know exactly where he went. Tell me."

Before the guard could respond, a voice interrupted from behind him. "Looks like you're not getting much from him."

Carlos turned to see Gabriela Bolucci standing in the

STEALING MEXICO

kitchen doorway, her expression calm but her eyes sharp. "If you want to know where Holbrook went, I can tell you."

Carlos narrowed his eyes. "And why would you want to help me?"

She shrugged, a faint smile playing at her lips. "Let's just say I don't particularly care for Holbrook or his... endeavors. If helping you bring him down, I'm happy to oblige."

Carlos studied her for a moment, the suspicion evident in his gaze, but he couldn't afford to waste time questioning her motives. "What do you know?"

"Holbrook and his assistant left through the service doors," Gabriela said, nodding toward the back exit. "But you should hurry—they won't wait around."

Carlos didn't need any more encouragement. "Thanks," he muttered, already moving toward the exit.

"Be careful, Detective," Gabriela called after him, her voice steady. "Holbrook's not the only one who's dangerous."

Carlos pushed through the service doors, stepping into the dimly lit parking garage. The air was thick with the smell of exhaust, and the sound of an engine starting echoed through the space. He turned in time to see a sleek black SUV speeding toward the exit.

"Delgado!" Carlos shouted into his mic, sprinting toward his car. "Holbrook's on the move. I need backup now."

The SUV disappeared around a corner, and Carlos jumped into his vehicle, the engine roaring to life. As he sped out of the garage, his focus narrowed to the taillights in the distance. This was it—Holbrook was slipping away, but Carlos wasn't about to let him go without a fight. lose Holbrook—he'd been running this game for too long, and it was time to end it.

CHAPTER 61

ASHER

Asher and Abuela sat in silence, their eyes glued to the TV screen in the sterile hospital room. The news coverage of the Gala takedown was playing in real-time, flashing images of officers escorting arrested individuals from the building. But despite the chaos unfolding, there was no sign of Carlos.

Abuela sat with her hands folded tightly in her lap, her face a mixture of worry and impatience. She had been quiet, not wanting to show Asher how deeply concerned she was. But he could feel the tension radiating from her, the same way he felt the tight knot in his own stomach.

The reporter was detailing the arrests, focusing on the individuals being led out of the Gala. But Asher wasn't paying attention to any of that. His eyes never left the screen, scanning for any glimpse of Carlos.

Then, the sound of squealing tires cut through the broadcast. Asher's eyes snapped to the screen just as the camera panned toward the parking garage. The reporter froze for a moment before her voice filled the room again, now tinged with shock.

"Wait, something's happening in the parking lot..." she trailed off, and the camera shifted to the scene unfolding live.

STEALING MEXICO

A sleek black SUV sped out of the parking garage, its tires screeching as it swerved past the entrance. Asher's heart lurched. He knew instantly what it meant.

A second black car followed shortly after, trailing behind the SUV in a sharp pursuit. Asher's eyes widened. That wasn't just any car. He didn't even need to see the license plate to recognize the car. It was Carlos. He was leaving the Gala—he was doing exactly what he'd been told not to do.

Abuela's voice broke through the tension in the room. "Ay, Dios mío... That is him. What is he doing?"

Asher didn't answer, his hands gripping the edge of the hospital bed. He knew exactly what Carlos was doing. He was going after Holbrook—by himself, just as Asher had feared. His instincts had been right. The moment he'd seen Carlos walk away earlier, he knew he wasn't going to follow the rules.

The helicopter camera zoomed in, the footage now focusing on a high-speed chase down the city streets. Asher's breath caught in his throat as the black SUV tore through intersections, weaving between traffic, while the car behind it tried desperately to keep up. He could see the flashing lights of police vehicles in the distance, but they were too far behind.

Abuela was muttering prayers under her breath, her worry palpable. She knew Carlos as well as Asher did. He wasn't one to back down, no matter how dangerous the situation was. But this was different. He wasn't just chasing a criminal; he was pursuing a powerful, well-connected man. And with Carlos alone, there was no telling what could happen.

Asher felt a wave of panic rush over him. "Carlos, you're not alone," he whispered to himself. He could barely breathe as the helicopter continued to follow the cars, a constant reminder of the danger Carlos was in.

Abuela's voice trembled. "This is too much. They're all going to be in danger now."

The camera zoomed out slightly, showing the high-speed chase from above. But even in the moment's chaos, Asher couldn't tear his eyes away from the screen. His heart pounded and his thoughts scattered. He knew that if Carlos didn't get help soon, this could be the end of it.

And yet, deep down, Asher knew there was no stopping Carlos. He was a force unto himself, driven by his need to get answers, to right the wrongs that had been done.

"I have to go," Asher said suddenly, his voice filled with urgency. He pushed himself out of the bed, his body protesting with every movement. Abuela looked at him, panic flashing in her eyes.

"No, Asher," she pleaded, reaching out to him. "You need to stay here. You're not well. You cannot—"

"I'm going," he interrupted, his voice hard. There was no time to argue. Carlos was out there, and he needed Asher now more than ever. Asher couldn't sit idly by while the man he cared about was running headfirst into danger.

Before Abuela could stop him, Asher grabbed his phone from the bedside table and made a beeline for the door. He didn't care what it took, he wasn't going to let Carlos face this alone.

He had to get to him.

As Asher reached for the door handle, a sharp pain shot through his side, a reminder of the injury he'd been trying to ignore. He gasped, but quickly masked the wince, pressing his lips together as he steadied himself against the doorframe. His rib was definitely bruised, if not broken, but he couldn't afford to worry about it at that moment. Carlos was out there, and he was alone—he needed Asher, and nothing was going to stop him from getting to him.

Taking a deep breath, Asher pushed through the discom-

STEALING MEXICO

fort and opened the door. His gaze immediately locked onto the ABI agent stationed outside, a tall, broad-shouldered man who was standing with his arms crossed, guarding the hall. He was clearly not the type to let anyone slip by without notice.

Asher's first instinct was to walk right past him, act like nothing was wrong, like he wasn't in a hurry to get out of here and track down Carlos. But the agent's sharp eyes flicked up immediately as the door swung open, and he stepped forward, his expression unreadable.

"Mr. Rhodes," he said, his voice firm. "You're supposed to be in the room. You're not cleared to leave."

Asher didn't stop. He didn't slow down. "I'm fine," he said, trying to push past him. "I need to—"

"Not so fast," the agent interrupted, stepping into his path, blocking the doorway. "You're not going anywhere."

The pain in Asher's side flared up again, and for a moment, he thought he might collapse. But he quickly steadied himself, taking a deep breath. He had to keep moving, had to get out of there. He would not stay locked up in here while Carlos risked his life.

He forced a smile, trying to act casual. "I'm fine. You can't keep me in this room. I need to check on the situation. You don't have to worry about me."

The agent remained unmoved, his gaze unwavering. "Agent Delgado's orders. You're not leaving without approval."

Asher's pulse quickened, but he knew he couldn't afford to waste time arguing. His mind was already racing, calculating the best way to get past the agent. He had to make this quick.

Without warning, he shifted his weight, stepping back a little, and then lunged forward. Using the momentum, he pushed against the agent, not with force, but enough to throw him off balance. The agent stumbled back, eyes widening in surprise.

For a split second, the agent faltered—long enough for Asher to slip past him. He darted down the hall, ignoring the shout of the agent behind him. He didn't look back, didn't slow down.

The pain in his side was unbearable now, but the thought of Carlos, alone in the chaos of that chase, pushed him forward. He couldn't let him face it without him. He couldn't sit here and wait while Carlos risked everything.

Asher rounded a corner, the hospital's sterile white walls blurring in his vision as adrenaline coursed through his veins. He had no plan, no backup—just the burning need to find Carlos before it was too late.

His phone vibrated in his pocket, but he ignored it. He would not stop for anything, not now. He needed to get to Carlos.

Asher took the stairs two at a time, the pain in his side almost overwhelming, but he forced it down. He knew this wasn't the smartest move, but Carlos was more important than any of his injuries. He and Carlos were tangled in this mess, and he wouldn't leave Carlos to face the consequences alone.

By the time he reached the lobby, the sound of the helicopter camera chasing Carlos echoed through his mind. He could already see it—the high-speed pursuit, the lights flashing, the danger closing in. He had no idea how he was going to catch up to Carlos, but he knew he had to try.

As Asher pushed through the revolving doors into the night air, the cold hit him, and he could feel his body protesting every step. But the only thing that mattered right now was reaching Carlos before it was too late.

He stepped out into the cool night air. The reality of his situation hit him like a ton of bricks. He stopped in his tracks, a wave of frustration washing over him. He had no car. No way to catch up to Carlos before something bad happened.

STEALING MEXICO

He could barely focus through the pain radiating from his side, let alone think straight about how to help.

Just as his thoughts spiraled, a car screeched to a halt in front of him. Asher blinked, trying to make sense of the scene in front of him, and then the passenger window rolled down. He didn't need to see who was inside—he could already hear the voice.

"Are you just going to stand there?" Abuela called out, a mix of sass and concern in her tone.

Asher's heart skipped a beat. He knew she wouldn't just be sitting in the hospital, waiting. She'd never let him stay put.

He walked over, shaking his head in disbelief. "How are you even here?" he asked, trying to suppress the pain in his voice.

Abuela leaned out of the window, a knowing smirk tugging at the corners of her lips. "It's called a wheelchair and strong knitting arms!" she said, her words punctuated by a twinkle of mischief in her eyes. "You're in no shape to drive, and that's my grandson out there," she added, her voice hardening, concern clearly replacing her playful tone. "Let them try to stop us!"

Asher chuckled weakly, relief flooding through him. He wasn't sure how she'd gotten out of the hospital or how she was even managing this, but that she was here was all that mattered.

He pulled open the door and climbed into the passenger seat, groaning as the pain in his side flared up, but he tried to hide it from Abuela. She shot him a glance, a warning in her eyes.

"I'm fine, Abuela. We need to catch up to Carlos," he said, his voice firm despite the lingering discomfort. "Can we please just go?"

"Hold on, mijo," she replied with a smirk. "We'll catch him."

Before he could respond, the engine roared to life, and the car shot forward, tires screeching as she expertly maneuvered it onto the road.

Asher glanced over at her, still amazed by how she'd been so resourceful despite her age. He knew, without a doubt, that nothing—especially a hospital stay—could slow her down when it came to family. She'd been through too much for him to doubt her now.

The city lights blurred as they sped down the road, and for a moment, Asher felt a flicker of hope. Maybe this wouldn't be such a disaster after all. His injuries and poor shape couldn't stop him from fighting for Carlos, especially with Abuela there, so close to stopping whatever was coming.

The chase was far from over.

CHAPTER 62

CARLOS

Carlos's heart pounded in sync with the beat of the helicopter blades cutting through the night sky above. Its spotlight followed them, illuminating patches of the road as they weaved through traffic at breakneck speed. Holbrook's black SUV loomed ahead, dipping in and out of lanes before veering sharply off the freeway, skidding into an exit that led toward an old industrial district.

Carlos was right on their tail, his hands gripping the wheel as they sped past rows of dark, abandoned warehouses looming like silent sentinels. They finally screeched to a stop at a cluster of run-down buildings, their cracked windows and graffiti-covered walls stark in the flashing white and blue lights emitting from his car.

Carlos barely had time to react before the SUV's driver's door flung open. Oliver Grant jumped out, a gleam of metal in his hand catching Carlos's attention. A handgun.

Without missing a beat, he bolted toward the nearest warehouse, his silhouette swallowed by the shadows of the towering structure.

Carlos swore under his breath, his mind racing. He jumped out of his own car and sprinted to the SUV, throwing open the doors and checking inside, hoping to find Holbrook. But the vehicle was empty.

Carlos's stomach dropped. Holbrook wasn't here.

"Dammit!" he hissed, his jaw clenching as he looked around the area. The assistant was making a run for it, and Holbrook was still out there, slipping further away every second Carlos stood still.

Carlos pivoted, his instincts kicking into high gear. He couldn't let this guy get away, not with whatever he knew about Holbrook's operations. Gritting his teeth, he pulled his weapon, double-checked his surroundings, and raced toward the warehouse, following Grant's shadowed figure.

As he neared the entrance, the man disappeared inside. Carlos slowed his steps, pressing himself against the building's wall, eyes scanning for movement as he steadied his breath. He knew backup was on the way, that ABI agents would be here soon enough. But he also knew that the lack of time was a problem—his escape now could mean burying everything they'd uncovered.

Carlos took a calming breath and stepped into the darkness of the warehouse, his senses on high alert. He didn't know what waited for him inside, but one thing was clear: this man was armed and dangerous.

Carlos moved silently through the shadows of the dimly lit warehouse, his steps deliberate and controlled. The smell of rust and stale air filled his nostrils as he advanced, his gun raised and eyes locked on the faint flicker of motion ahead. Oliver Grant was fleeing deeper into the labyrinth of rusted machinery and crumbling storage containers. His footsteps clanged against the metal flooring, the echoes masking his exact location.

Carlos clenched his jaw, adrenaline sharpening his every sense. He'd tracked criminals through places like this before, but this was different. Holbrook's operation was a network of power, money, and influence—dangerous enough on its own. And now, cornered and desperate, Carlos knew that desperate people are the most dangerous.

He edged closer to a stack of crates, peeking around the corner just in time to see Grant's silhouette dart past a flickering fluorescent light. Carlos moved quickly but carefully, keeping to the shadows, his finger steady on the trigger.

"Grant!" Carlos called out, his voice low but carrying through the empty warehouse. "There's nowhere left to run. Make this easy on yourself."

The reply was the sound of hurried footsteps scrambling over debris. Grant wasn't listening. Carlos swore under his breath and pressed forward, his boots silent against the gritty floor.

Suddenly, the clang of a metal door slamming reverberated through the space, followed by the unmistakable sound of a bolt sliding into place. Carlos rounded the corner and spotted the door, his instincts kicking in. Holbrook's right-hand man was trying to barricade himself in one of the back offices.

Carlos didn't hesitate. He braced himself and slammed his shoulder into the door, the rusty hinges groaning under the impact. With a second hit, the door burst open, slamming against the wall with a deafening crack.

Inside, Oliver Grant stood frozen for a split second, his chest heaving as he backed against a desk. His expensive suit rumpled, his tie hung loose, and fear contorted his normally composed expression.

"You don't want to do this, Grant," Carlos said, his voice steady as he raised his gun. "Hands where I can see them."

STEALING MEXICO

Grant's gaze darted to the gun holstered at his waist, then to the window behind him. Carlos saw the calculation in his eyes, the desperation of a man cornered.

"You're not walking out of here," Carlos said, taking a step closer. "But you can still make this easier on yourself. Tell me where Holbrook is."

For a moment, it seemed like Grant might comply. His hands twitched, hovering near his sides as his chest rose and fell in rapid breaths. But then his expression hardened, and he lunged for the window.

Carlos reacted instinctively, kicking the desk into Grant's path. The younger man stumbled, cursing as he hit the edge of the desk. He swung a wild punch, which Carlos easily ducked, countering with a sharp elbow to Grant's ribs.

The two crashed into a metal cabinet, the sound reverberating through the room. Grant's hand shot toward his holster, but Carlos grabbed his wrist, twisting it sharply and forcing the gun to clatter to the floor.

"Where is he?" Carlos demanded, pinning Grant against the cabinet, his voice low and dangerous.

Grant groaned, struggling against Carlos's grip. "He's gone," he spat, his voice laced with defiance. "You're too late."

Carlos slammed him against the cabinet again, the impact drawing a pained grunt. "Where did he go?"

Grant's lips twisted in a grimace, but the fight was draining out of him. "The airstrip," he muttered, his voice barely above a whisper. "Private hangar, off Route 77. There's a plane waiting for him."

Carlos tightened his grip on Grant's arm, forcing him to meet his gaze. "You better not be lying to me."

Grant let out a bitter laugh, his face twisted in resignation. "Why would I lie? He's leaving, and you're not going to catch him."

Carlos didn't reply. Instead, he yanked Grant away from

the cabinet and shoved him toward the door, his gun trained on him. "You're coming with me."

They scampered through the warehouse, Carlos keeping a firm grip on Grant's arm. The sound of distant helicopter blades echoed outside, mingling with the faint hum of the city. Carlos's mind raced, piecing together the fragments of the chase. Holbrook was running, but he would not get away. Not this time.

Outside, the night air was cool and sharp, the warehouse district eerily quiet. Carlos shoved Grant toward his car, opening the passenger door and forcing him inside.

"Give me directions," Carlos demanded as he slid into the driver's seat, the engine roaring to life.

Grant hesitated, but a pointed glare from Carlos made him comply. "Straight for a mile, then left onto the access road. It's about fifteen minutes from here."

Carlos didn't waste time. The car shot forward, tires screeching as they sped toward the highway. He weaved through traffic with precision, his focus unshakable. Every second counted, and he would not let Holbrook slip through his fingers.

Grant shifted nervously in his seat, glancing at Carlos. "You don't know what you're dealing with," he said, his voice quiet but tense. "Holbrook has people—powerful people. You think catching him will stop this?"

Carlos's grip tightened on the steering wheel, his jaw clenched. "It'll be a damn good start."

Grant fell silent, his expression uneasy. Carlos could feel the weight of his words, the truth of the power they were up against. But he didn't let it deter him. He'd come too far to back down now.

The road ahead stretched out into darkness, the faint glow of lights from the city fading behind them. Carlos pushed the car faster, his thoughts a whirlwind of determination and resolve.

STEALING MEXICO

"Hold on," he muttered, his voice a quiet promise. "We're getting him."

As they neared the turnoff for Route 77, Carlos's adrenaline surged. Holbrook thought he could run, thought his wealth and power would shield him from justice. But Carlos wasn't about to let him escape.

Not tonight.

CHAPTER 63

CARLOS

Carlos skidded to a stop just outside the gate of the small airfield. The lights from the hangar cast long shadows across the tarmac, and there, parked beside a sleek private jet, was Governor Holbrook. Grant, now silent and visibly shaken, had guided him here, but Carlos knew there was no turning back now. Holbrook wasn't getting away this time.

He stepped out of the car, the chilly night air biting at his skin as he stared across the runway. Holbrook was just approaching the plane, his briefcase clutched tightly in his hand. The man's back was turned, and he didn't notice Carlos at first.

"Holbrook!" Carlos shouted, his voice cutting through the air. Holbrook froze, his shoulders tense before he slowly turned around.

Carlos moved quickly, leading with his gun raised, every muscle in his body taut as they approached the plane. Holbrook reached the top of the stairs, a briefcase in one hand, the other gripping the rail as he glanced back. His expression was a mixture of irritation and contempt when he spotted them.

"You're persistent, Detective," Holbrook called, his voice

STEALING MEXICO

carrying over the hum of the plane's engines. "But you're too late."

Carlos didn't slow. "Step away from the plane, Holbrook. This is over!"

Holbrook smirked, a condescending tilt to his head. "You really think you can stop this? You have no idea what you're dealing with. Arrest me, kill me—it won't matter. You'll just be cutting off one head of the Hydra."

Carlos clenched his jaw, his voice cold. "I'll take my chances. Now get off those stairs."

Holbrook turned as if to continue boarding, ignoring the command. Without hesitation, Carlos aimed and fired. The shot rang out, shattering the stillness, and the hydraulic support of the boarding stairs buckled under the impact. The stairs screeched as they collapsed onto the tarmac, leaving Holbrook clinging to the railing.

The Governor steadied himself and dropped back to the ground, his polished veneer cracking as frustration contorted his face. "You've just made a big mistake, Santos."

Carlos stepped closer, his gun unwavering. "I'm not the one making mistakes, Governor. You're done."

Holbrook scoffed, glancing at the jet as if it were still his escape. "You think this is about me running? You've missed the point entirely. All of this—Diego, the others—this is just the cost of something much bigger. You wouldn't understand."

Carlos narrowed his eyes, sensing the lie in Holbrook's words. "Cut the crap, Holbrook. You killed them. Diego and those others. And you've been covering it up from the start."

Holbrook shook his head, the facade of the untouchable politician slipping for just a second. "You think I did it? You're wrong, Detective. I didn't kill them. I just... enabled it." His voice softened, as if the weight of the truth were just too much to bear. "You don't know how deep it goes. You have no idea who's really behind all of this."

Carlos took a step forward. "Who then? Who's pulling the strings?"

Holbrook's eyes darkened. "You really want to know? You think I'm the mastermind here?" He laughed bitterly, then glanced at the assistant, standing nervously behind Carlos. "It's all bigger than me. It always was. The real puppet master? It's him."

Carlos's heart dropped as he realized who Holbrook was talking about. But before Carlos could advance further, he felt it—a shift in the air, a presence behind him. His instincts flared too late.

"Drop the gun," Oliver Grant's voice came, cold and commanding.

Carlos didn't turn immediately, his jaw clenching as the pieces clicked together. He spoke without looking, his voice razor sharp. "So it's you."

"Obviously," Grant sneered. "Took you long enough."

Carlos pivoted, his gun still raised, now trained on Grant. The man stood a few feet away, his hands empty but his posture predatory, the shadows of the tarmac casting eerie angles across his face.

"You've been orchestrating this from the start," Carlos growled. "Diego, Morales, Gabby—you killed them."

Grant tilted his head, the smirk on his lips widening. "That's right, Detective. And I'll admit, Diego was a little... stubborn. He just had to dig too deep. Morales? He wouldn't shut up, wouldn't take the hints. And Gabby?" Grant chuckled, his tone chilling. "Well, she was just collateral damage. You can thank your little journalist boyfriend for that. But you... you've been a pain in my ass from the start."

Carlos felt a surge of anger so fierce it almost overwhelmed him. "You're going to pay for what you've done."

Grant's smirk didn't falter. "Am I?"

Without warning, Grant lunged. Carlos fired, but Grant was faster, knocking the gun from Carlos's hands with a

STEALING MEXICO

sharp upward blow. The weapon clattered across the asphalt, skidding into the shadows.

Carlos barely had time to react before Grant was on him. The first punch landed hard, sending Carlos stumbling back. The second came quickly, aimed at his ribs, but Carlos twisted away just in time.

The two men clashed like opposing storms, their movements brutal and desperate. Carlos blocked Grant's next blow and retaliated with a punch to the jaw, the impact snapping Grant's head to the side.

"You're not walking away from this," Carlos growled, driving a knee into Grant's midsection.

Grant grunted, stumbling back, but his recovery was immediate. He charged forward, his shoulder slamming into Carlos's chest, sending both men crashing to the ground. They grappled, rolling across the tarmac, their breaths coming in harsh gasps.

Carlos reached for his gun, but Grant saw the movement and slammed his elbow into Carlos's face. Pain exploded in Carlos's vision, but he refused to let go, twisting his body to break free from Grant's hold.

"You're just like Diego," Grant hissed, grabbing Carlos by the collar and yanking him close. You think you can stop me, but you are alone and it's too late. Perpetual tardiness is your issue.

Carlos landed a solid punch, freeing himself and scrambling to his feet. But Grant was already there, pulling a knife from his belt. The blade gleamed under the harsh floodlights, and Carlos felt his pulse spike.

Grant smirked, advancing with the knife held steady. "You're going to die here, Santos. Just like the others did."

Carlos ducked as Grant slashed, the blade slicing through the air inches from his chest. Grant attacked again, his movements calculated and vicious. Carlos dodged and countered, landing a kick to Grant's knee that sent him staggering.

But Grant was relentless, recovering quickly and pressing the attack. His knife flashed dangerously close, forcing Carlos to stay on the defensive. Every move was a fight for survival, every second a desperate attempt to stay alive.

Carlos spotted his gun lying a few feet away, half-hidden under a stack of pallets. He feinted to the left, drawing Grant's attention, before diving for the weapon.

Grant lunged after him, his knife raised high. Carlos gritted his teeth, grabbing the gun just as Grant brought the blade down.

A shot rang out.

Grant cried out in pain, stumbling back as blood seeped from his shoulder. His knife clattered to the ground, and he clutched the wound, his face twisted in rage and agony.

Carlos rose to his feet, his gun trained on Grant, his chest heaving. "It's over," he said, his voice steady despite the adrenaline coursing through him.

But Grant's fury didn't wane. He staggered back, his movements erratic but deliberate. "It's never over," he spat, his eyes wild.

Before Carlos could react, Holbrook bolted from the plane, his briefcase forgotten on the stairs. The Governor sprinted across the parking lot, his suit flapping in the wind.

Carlos cursed under his breath, glancing at Grant before taking off after Holbrook.

Carlos closed the gap between him and Holbrook, his gun raised. "Stop!" he shouted.

Holbrook didn't listen, his strides frantic as he neared a line of parked cars.

The roar of an engine cut through the chaos.

Carlos turned, his heart leaping into his throat. A car sped into the parking lot, its tires screeching as it swerved toward them.

Grant was running, knife in hand, his face a mask of rage

STEALING MEXICO

as he barreled after Carlos and Holbrook. He didn't see the car until it was too late.

The vehicle slammed into Grant with bone-shattering force, sending him flying onto the hood. His body rolled off the side and hit the ground with a sickening thud, motionless.

Carlos turned, his gun still raised, as the car screeched to a halt.

The car door opened, and Carlos' eyes widened.

CHAPTER 64

CARLOS

Carlos stood frozen, his mind unable to process the sight before him. The car door swung open, and out stepped Abuela, her tiny frame somehow towering with authority, her gaze fixed straight ahead. She didn't hesitate for a moment, striding toward Governor Holbrook with a resolve that made Carlos blink in disbelief.

"Abuela?" he stammered, the word barely forming as he watched her march toward the man who had caused so much devastation. "What... how...?"

Holbrook looked equally stunned, his usually composed expression faltering as this fierce, elderly woman bore down on him like a storm. Before anyone could react, Abuela raised her hand and slapped him hard across the face. The sharp crack of the impact echoed in the night air, silencing what little noise remained.

"¡Maldito desgraciado!" she spat, her voice trembling with anger. "You put my Carlos and his Asher through hell! You think you can just ruin lives and walk away? ¡Estás loco! You are nothing but a coward!"

Holbrook stumbled, his hand instinctively going to his

STEALING MEXICO

cheek as his baffled gaze darted between Abuela and Carlos. For once, he was utterly speechless.

"Abuela—" Carlos tried again, his voice cracking, but she didn't even glance at him. Her attention was fully on Holbrook, her feet tapping the ground with every furious step she took back toward him, as if daring him to speak.

Carlos shifted his gaze toward Abuela's car, his heart dropping further at the sight of Asher. He stood just outside the passenger door, gripping it tightly for support, his other arm clutching his side. Asher's paleness and pain were clear, yet his determined blue eyes remained fixed on Carlos, causing Carlos's chest to ache.

The wail of sirens growing louder shattered the silence, followed by a swarm of flashing red and blue lights. The scene turned chaotic in an instant as police cruisers, ambulances, and ABI vehicles filled the parking lot. Carlos barely registered the flood of activity—the agents, the shouting, the flashing lights. Everything felt like a blur.

Captain Davis was the first to approach, her expression a mix of frustration and relief. She wasted no time, her voice cutting through the noise. "Santos! What the hell were you thinking? I told you not to go rogue! Do you have any idea how much danger you put yourself in?"

Carlos opened his mouth, but no words came out. He could only nod mutely as she continued, her sharp tone drilling into his already overwhelmed mind.

Agent Delgado joined her, shaking her head as she folded her arms. "You've got some nerve, Carlos. But I guess that's your style, isn't it? Ignoring orders, charging headfirst into chaos..."

Carlos barely heard them. His focus drifted back to Asher, who was standing near the car, his breaths shallow but even. The ache in Carlos's chest deepened as he saw the vulnerability etched across Asher's face. He shouldn't have been here

—not in his condition, not in the middle of this—but Carlos couldn't imagine him being anywhere else.

EMTs were lifting Oliver Grant onto a stretcher, his face pale and contorted in pain as he groaned weakly. Holbrook, meanwhile, was being pulled to his feet by two ABI agents. One read him his Miranda rights as Holbrook sneered, his gaze snapping to Carlos.

As they dragged him past, Holbrook spoke venomously. "This isn't over, Santos. You've made yourself a target now. They'll come for you. And for him." He tilted his head toward Asher, a cruel smirk tugging at his lips.

Carlos barely spared him a glance. Holbrook's words meant nothing to him—not when Asher was standing there, looking at him with those bright blue eyes filled with quiet strength. Without thinking, Carlos pushed past the agents and the noise, moving straight to Asher.

Asher's gaze followed him, his lips parting as if to speak, but Carlos didn't wait. He cupped Asher's face gently, his hands cradling his jaw, and pressed his forehead against Asher's. The world around them disappeared—the flashing lights, the chaotic voices, the sirens. Nothing existed but the two of them.

"Carlos," Asher whispered, his voice barely audible over Carlos' heavy heartbeat.

Carlos pulled back just enough to meet Asher's gaze. The words came before he could stop them, raw and unfiltered. "I love you, Asher Rhodes."

Asher's breath hitched, but before he could respond, Carlos leaned in, capturing his lips in a kiss that made everything else fade away. Asher's lips moved against his, soft and warm, and for a moment, Carlos felt a completeness he hadn't known he was missing. This—this was what he'd been fighting for.

The moment ended too soon. A firm hand on Carlos's

STEALING MEXICO

shoulder brought the world crashing back into focus. He pulled away reluctantly, turning to see Agent Delgado standing behind him, her expression a mix of understanding and urgency.

"Carlos," she said, her tone softer now. "We've got this from here. Go. Take Asher back to the hospital. You both need a break."

Captain Davis nodded, her earlier frustration replaced with a trace of approval. "You did good tonight, Santos. But Delgado's right. Let us handle the cleanup."

Carlos hesitated, his instincts screaming at him to stay, to see everything through to the end. But as he looked back at Asher—pale, exhausted, but still managing a small, tender smile—he knew what he had to do.

"Alright," he said finally, his voice steady. He gently wrapped an arm around Asher's waist, supporting him as they moved toward Abuela, who was already waiting by the car, her expression a mix of relief and triumph.

Carlos gently guided Asher toward his car, his arm wrapped securely around his waist. He could feel how much Asher leaned into him, his strength waning but his determination still shining through. Carlos opened the passenger door and helped him ease into the seat, careful not to jostle him too much. Asher hissed softly, his face tight with pain, but he managed a small smile.

"I'm fine," Asher said, though his voice was barely above a whisper.

Carlos lingered for a moment, brushing a stray lock of hair from Asher's forehead. "You're not fine," he murmured. "But we're going to fix that."

Asher chuckled weakly, the sound strained but real.

Carlos stepped back and closed the door, turning toward the driver's side. As he walked around the front of the car, he paused. His eyes drifted over the chaotic scene—the flashing lights, the officers still swarming the area, and the distant silhouettes of Holbrook and Grant being loaded into separate vehicles. The weight of the night pressed down on him, heavier now that the adrenaline was wearing off.

He closed his eyes and inhaled deeply, letting the chilly night air fill his lungs. It wasn't over. Holbrook's parting words echoed in his mind, a grim reminder of the target now painted on his back. On Asher's back. But Carlos pushed it aside, focusing instead on the moment.

When he opened his eyes, he glanced at Asher through the windshield. Asher was watching him, his blue eyes tired but still full of that unshakable spark. Carlos felt a surge of something deeper than determination—something stronger.

He had a duty to Asher, to Diego, to every life that the corruption they'd uncovered had torn apart. He couldn't let himself falter now.

Carlos turned back toward the scene one last time, his fists clenching and relaxing at his sides. He thought about the hospital, about Delgado's words, about the rest they both desperately needed.

But first, there was something they had to do.

Carlos straightened and walked around to the driver's side, sliding into his seat. He started the engine, the familiar hum grounding him. Asher glanced at him, a flicker of curiosity crossing his face.

"We're not going straight to the hospital, are we?" Asher asked, his voice soft but knowing.

Carlos shook his head, his jaw set. "Not yet. There's something we need to do first."

Asher tilted his head slightly, watching Carlos with a mix of exhaustion and intrigue. He didn't ask what—it wasn't necessary. He trusted Carlos completely.

Carlos shifted the car into gear and pulled out of the parking lot, the flashing lights of the scene fading into the distance behind them.

STEALING MEXICO

"Just hang on," Carlos said, glancing at Asher. "We'll make this right. All of it."

Asher nodded, leaning back in his seat, his eyes fluttering closed as the car picked up speed. Carlos kept his gaze forward, his grip firm on the wheel.

Whatever came next, they'd face it together. But tonight wasn't over yet.

CHAPTER 65

CARLOS

Carlos stood outside the weathered motel door, the muted glow of the neon sign above casting long shadows over him and Asher. The chilly night air seemed heavier than usual, as if weighed down by the burden he carried with him. His hand hovered near the door, hesitating for a moment before he glanced at Asher.

"You ready for this?" Carlos asked, his voice low, almost hesitant.

Asher gave a small nod, his expression calm but serious. "They deserve to hear it from you. From us."

Carlos exhaled slowly, then knocked. The sound echoed in the stillness, each second of silence that followed feeling heavier than the last.

The door creaked open, revealing Diego's father. His face was gaunt, sunken from weeks of grief and exhaustion, his eyes dull as they moved from Carlos to Asher and back again. For a moment, he didn't speak, but then he nodded, stepping aside silently to let them in.

Carlos entered the small room first, the air thick with sorrow. Diego's mother and sister sat side by side on the edge of the bed, their faces pale and drawn. A muted television

STEALING MEXICO

flickered in the corner, casting faint shadows on the worn walls.

Carlos stopped a few steps in, his hands at his sides, unsure how to begin.

"Señor and Señora Cortez," he said, his voice soft, steady. "You know me. I'm Detective Santos. This is Asher Rhodes." He gestured toward Asher, who stood just behind him, his expression gentle as he gave a small nod in greeting.

Diego's mother tightened her grip on the rosary she held, her lips pressing together. His sister looked up, her tear-streaked face illuminated by the faint light from the TV.

Carlos took a deep breath and stepped closer. "I wanted to tell you in person. We've arrested the man responsible for what happened to Diego."

Diego's mother inhaled sharply, her fingers frozen on the rosary beads. Diego's sister covered her mouth with her hand, her eyes wide with disbelief.

Carlos continued, his voice tightening with emotion. "Your son... what he did, the risks he took—they made all the difference. He was brave, stronger than most people I've ever met. He uncovered something that set everything into motion. Because of him, we've taken down a powerful and corrupt group of people. His sacrifice... it saved countless lives."

Asher stepped forward, his voice gentle as he added, "What Diego did wasn't in vain. He stood up for what was right, even when it meant putting himself in danger. And because of him, so many others won't have to suffer."

Diego's mother's lip quivered, and tears spilled silently down her cheeks. She clutched the rosary tightly, her voice barely above a whisper. "Mi hijo... They took him from us. These people, they take everything. They steal from us, from Mexico, from our families. All for their greed."

Her words broke something in Carlos. He clenched his jaw, forcing himself to remain steady.

Diego's sister's voice was soft but resolute, breaking the silence. "Diego wouldn't want us to stop fighting. He believed in standing up for those who couldn't stand up for themselves."

Carlos felt his chest tighten. He nodded, her words hitting something deep within him. "You're right. No one has to stop fighting."

He moved toward the small bedside table, grabbing a notepad and pen. Scribbling down a name and a number, he tore the page free and handed it to Diego's sister.

"Ethan Cole," he said, his voice firm but kind. "He was Diego's friend, and he's continuing the fight. Call him. Connect with him. Nobody has to stop fighting for what's right—ever."

Diego's sister took the paper with trembling hands, her eyes filling with determination as she looked at it.

Diego's father finally spoke, his voice rough. "Thank you," he said, his words slow and deliberate. "Thank you for telling us. For not forgetting him."

Carlos met his gaze, his own eyes heavy with the weight of everything they'd lost. "We'll never forget him," he said. "Diego's bravery changed everything. And I promise you, the world will know what he did."

Diego's mother nodded, her tears falling silently as she whispered, "Gracias, Detective. For bringing us this. For not letting his memory fade."

Carlos swallowed hard and gave them a small nod. "We'll leave you to rest," he whispered.

Asher placed a hand on Carlos's arm as they turned to leave. Carlos glanced back one last time, taking in the quiet strength of Diego's family, the grief and resolve mingling in their expressions.

As they stepped out into the chilly night, Carlos took a deep breath, his chest heavy but his resolve stronger than ever.

STEALING MEXICO

"You okay?" Asher asked, his voice breaking the silence.

Carlos nodded, his gaze fixed on the horizon. "Yeah," he said, his voice steady. "Diego deserved that. And they deserved to know."

Asher gave him a small smile. "He'd be proud of you, Carlos."

Carlos didn't reply, but the weight of Asher's words settled over him like a balm. Together, they walked toward the car, the quiet night stretching around them. Diego's fight wasn't over—and neither was theirs.

CHAPTER 66

ASHER

Asher leaned his head against the passenger-side window, the cool glass soothing against the dull ache radiating through his body. The city rolled past in blurred streaks of orange streetlights and glowing storefront signs. The car's engine hummed steadily, the sound filling the quiet that hung between him and Carlos.

They'd just left Diego's parents' motel room—a cramped, dimly lit space filled with grief and hope in equal measure. Telling them about the arrest, about the man behind Diego's murder, hadn't been easy. Asher could still feel the raw emotion in the room, could still see the tears streaking down Mrs. Cortez's face as she clutched her daughter close.

Diego's sister had said something before they left, something that had stayed with Asher: Diego wouldn't want us to stop fighting. The words looped in his mind like a mantra, persistent, as the world outside the car blurred by.

Asher glanced over at Carlos, taking in the way he sat with his gaze fixed ahead, jaw set, but the slightest hint of relief softening his eyes. Carlos looked exhausted, worn down in a way that went beyond the events of the night. Now, however, Asher deeply understood the unbreakable gravity

STEALING MEXICO

and strength that had always attracted him to Carlos. Carlos had given everything he had to the truth, to justice—and despite everything, he was still here, still fighting.

A soft exhale escaped Asher, and he looked back at the cityscape. He'd never thought he'd fall for a cop, least of all one as intense and guarded as Carlos. But he'd been wrong. He loved him. Every single part of him. The stubborn strength, the unwavering sense of duty, the flashes of vulnerability Carlos tried to bury behind a wall. Even the jagged edges—the ones Carlos kept carefully hidden—felt like they belonged to him now.

Carlos must have felt his gaze because he looked over, one eyebrow raised. "What?" he asked, a hint of that guardedness creeping back in.

Asher shook his head, smiling softly. "Nothing," he murmured. But he knew it wasn't nothing. They'd been through hell together, and there was no denying what was between them now. He just wasn't ready to say it—not here, not yet. Instead, he settled for a quiet smile, one that hinted at everything he wasn't saying out loud.

As they neared the hospital, Asher felt a pang of regret that this moment, this strange cocoon they were in, would soon come to an end. They'd have to face the questions, the aftermath, and the unknown path that stretched out before them. But for now, he took a breath, savoring the calm before it all started up again.

Carlos's hand reached over, resting on Asher's for a brief second—a grounding touch that held a thousand unspoken words. Asher closed his eyes, letting the warmth of that touch settle deep in his chest.

Whatever came next, he was ready.

EPILOGUE

ASHER

Two months later, Asher sat in a corner booth at a small diner, the hum of light conversation and the clinking of dishes filling the background. His fingers flew across the keyboard, each tap deliberate as he added the final edits to what he knew was the most important piece he'd ever written.

But it wasn't just his story.

This was for Diego. For Morales. For Gabby. For every life torn apart by the corruption they'd exposed.

He paused, rereading the last line: A brighter future begins with the courage to face the shadows—and the unwavering promise to honor those who brought the truth to light.

Asher exhaled deeply, his finger hovering over the "send" button. He felt the weight of everything he was about to release, not just the facts but the heart of it all, the humanity behind every statistic, every crime.

The soft chime of the diner door broke his focus, and he glanced up. Carlos walked in, his presence commanding but warm, as always. He wore a rare, serene smile Asher had grown to cherish.

"You ready?" Carlos asked as he slid into the seat across from him, his dark eyes locking on Asher with a steady gaze.

STEALING MEXICO

Asher leaned back in the booth, feigning a thoughtful look. "A whole week at a tropical resort? Hmm, sounds like overkill."

Carlos shook his head, chuckling softly. "You're forgetting the best part."

Asher tilted his head, playing along. "Oh yeah? What's that?"

Carlos leaned forward, his voice dropping to a murmur. "An entire week at a tropical resort... with your incredibly handsome boyfriend."

Asher laughed, the sound light and unrestrained, as he finally clicked "send," dispatching the article to his editor. He closed the laptop with a satisfied sigh, the weight he'd been carrying for months lifting at last.

Reaching across the table, Asher caught Carlos's hand, their fingers intertwining. "I've never been more ready for anything," he said, his voice soft but sure.

Carlos squeezed his hand gently, his smile widening. "Good, because there's nothing I want more than to have you all to myself with no distractions."

They stood together, Carlos grabbing Asher's laptop bag and slinging it over his shoulder as they made their way toward the door. Asher's heart felt lighter than it had in months, his steps matching Carlos's stride as they moved in sync.

Just as they reached the exit, the low hum of the TV behind the counter caught their attention. Asher glanced back, his eyes narrowing as the flashing "Breaking News" banner scrolled across the screen.

The news anchor's voice filled the diner: "Alejandro Bolucci, prominent local tech mogul, has been reported missing. Sources say he was last seen at his Paradise Valley estate yesterday afternoon. Authorities have not released further details at this time."

Carlos stopped, his grip on Asher's hand tightening

slightly. They exchanged a glance, the warmth of their moment shifting into something sharper, more focused.

"You think it's connected?" Asher asked, his voice low.

Carlos's brow furrowed, his lips pressing into a thin line. "If it's Bolucci..." He trailed off, his mind already racing.

Asher exhaled, tilting his head slightly. "And here I thought we were finally going to get an actual break."

Carlos turned to him, the corner of his mouth lifting in a small, knowing smirk. "One day," he said, his voice calm but resolute. "But I don't think that's going to be today."

They stepped outside, the cool evening air brushing against their faces as they stood on the sidewalk. The city stretched out before them, alive and unpredictable, full of mysteries they knew wouldn't wait.

Asher leaned into Carlos, their shoulders brushing as they started toward the car. Whatever came next, they'd face it together. That much, at least, was certain.

COMING NEXT

Carlos and Asher thought the hardest battles were behind them. They had exposed the corruption, brought powerful men to their knees, and begun to heal the scars left by the storm. But shadows don't vanish with the light—they grow longer, deeper, and darker.

A haunting new case pulls them back into a web of lies and danger. As whispers of a re-surging conspiracy emerge and ghosts from their past refuse to rest, Carlos and Asher must navigate a treacherous path where trust is fragile and betrayal is deadly.

With each step forward, the lines between justice and survival blur, and the stakes become painfully personal. As secrets unravel and new enemies close in, one truth be- comes clear: some shadows are born not to be chased, but to consume everything in their path.

The fight isn't over—it's only just begun.

Their story continues in
CHASING SHADOWS

MAKE A DIFFERENCE

Human trafficking is a hidden crime affecting millions of people worldwide, exploiting individuals for forced labor, sexual exploitation, and other forms of abuse. It thrives in secrecy, often in plain sight, within our communities. It's time to raise awareness and take action.

What is Human Trafficking?

Human trafficking involves the use of force, fraud, or coercion to exploit individuals against their will. Victims can be anyone, regardless of age, gender, or background, and traffickers often prey on vulnerability—financial struggles, lack of support, or personal trauma.

Recognize the Signs

Understanding the indicators can save lives. Some common signs include:

- **Isolation:** Victims may be physically or socially isolated, unable to speak freely.

MAKE A DIFFERENCE

- **Lack of Control:** They may not have access to identification, finances, or personal belongings.
- **Unusual Behavior:** Fearful, anxious, or submissive demeanor, avoiding eye contact.
- **Work Conditions:** Long hours under poor conditions, with little to no pay.

What You Can Do

Educate Yourself: Learn the facts about human trafficking to better recognize it.
Spread Awareness: Share information with your community to amplify the message
Report Suspicious Activity: Call the National Human Trafficking Hotline at 1-888-373-7888 or text "HELP" to 233733. Your call can remain anonymous.
Support Victims: Donate to organizations that provide support to survivors of trafficking.

Together, We Can Make a Difference

Human trafficking is a complex problem, but every step taken against it makes an impact. By raising awareness, supporting survivors, and working together, we can build a world where no one falls victim to exploitation.

Learn more and take action. Visit polarisproject.org or contact local organizations in your area. Let's be the voice for those who cannot speak.

ABOUT THE AUTHOR

Matti Martinez is a passionate storyteller and advocate for the unheard. A Southeast Iowa native, Matti channels a love for true crime podcasts (Crime Junkie, Morbid, That's Spooky), documentaries, and the depths of unexplained mystery iceberg videos on YouTube into thrilling and heartfelt fiction. When not writing, Matti enjoys casual gaming and exploring narratives that delve into the complexities of humanity and justice.

With Stealing Mexico, Matti masterfully combines a love for romance and thrillers, creating a story that raises awareness about the impact of human trafficking and its far-reaching effects on society. A member and proud advocate for LGBTQ+ and minority communities, Matti writes with a mission to illuminate voices that often go unheard.

Connect with Matti:
Email: msmartinez.author@gmail.com
Instagram:

www.ingramcontent.com/pod-product-compliance
Lightning Source LLC
LaVergne TN
LVHW090502100225
803145LV00001B/1